CW00538640

Hold Back the Night

Jessica Moor studied English at Cambridge before completing a Creative Writing MA at Manchester University. Moor was selected as one of the *Observer*'s debut novelists of 2020, and her first novel, *Keeper*, was chosen by the *Sunday Times*, *Independent* and *Cosmopolitan* as one of their top debuts of the year. *Keeper* was nominated for the Desmond Elliott Prize and an Edgar Award. Her second novel, *Young Women*, was first published in 2022 to great acclaim. *Hold Back the Night* is her third novel.

Hold Back the Night

Jessica Moor

MANILLA
PRESS

First published in the UK in 2024 by
MANILLA PRESS
An imprint of Zaffre Publishing Group
A Bonnier Books UK Company
4th Floor, Victoria House, Bloomsbury Square, London, England, WC1B 4DA
Owned by Bonnier Books
Sveavägen 56, Stockholm, Sweden

Copyright © Jessica Moor, 2024

All rights reserved.
No part of this publication may be reproduced,
stored or transmitted in any form by any means, electronic,
mechanical, photocopying or otherwise, without the
prior written permission of the publisher.

The right of Jessica Moor to be identified as Author of this
work has been asserted by her in accordance with the
Copyright, Designs and Patents Act, 1988.

This is a work of fiction. Names, places, events and
incidents are either the products of the author's
imagination or used fictitiously. Any resemblance to
actual persons, living or dead, or actual
events is purely coincidental.

A CIP catalogue record for this book is
available from the British Library.

Hardback ISBN: 978-1-80418 137 9
Export ISBN: 978-1-80418-869-9

Also available as an ebook and an audiobook

'The Normal Heart' from *The Normal Heart*, Larry Kramer, reproduced by
permission of Nick Hern Books.
Line from 'The Love Song of J. Alfred Prufrock' from *The Complete Poems and
Plays*, T.S. Eliot, reproduced by permission of Faber & Faber Limited.

1 3 5 7 9 10 8 6 4 2

Typeset by Palimpsest Book Production Ltd, Falkirk, Stirlingshire
Printed and bound in Great Britain by Clays Ltd, Elcograf S.p.A.

Manilla Press is an imprint of Zaffre Publishing Group
A Bonnier Books UK company
www.bonnierbooks.co.uk

To all the ghosts we failed to see

I mind how once we lay such a transparent
summer morning,

How you settled your head athwart my hips and
gently turn'd over upon me,

And parted the shirt from my bosom-bone, and
plunged your tongue to my bare-stript heart.
Walt Whitman, *Song of Myself*

There's always a plague. Of one kind or another.
Larry Kramer

Prologue

THERE WAS NEVER A time – at least, none that Annie can remember – when she did not know herself to be a nurse. When they were very little, Eddie, her younger brother, could occasionally be convinced to lie down while she alternately instructed, cajoled and prodded him into being still, 'like a proper patient'. In those very early days she undertook ambitious surgeries, sawing off legs, reattaching heads, delivering Eddie of the football that she'd stuffed into the shirt of his pyjamas.

Or so Annie's mother always told her; Annie herself could remember those images only partially, as if they'd been blotted out by great ink stains.

When she was three or four, Annie had been sitting in the garden on a very cloudy day. Vera Lynn was singing on the wireless – 'There'll Always Be an England'. Annie was looking at the worms, telling herself that if she was brave enough to touch one then nothing very bad would happen, when the sky exploded. She didn't remember screaming or putting her hands over her head. Only going very still, and understanding, in that gap where sound and movement were supposed to be, that everything was over.

It turned out that a bomber had been shot down just over their back garden. There had been a direct hit on the fuel tank and the whole thing blew up mid-air. A sudden downpour of wreckage all over their street. That afternoon, Annie found a man's hand in the middle of their vegetable patch. It had a ring on the middle finger.

She remembered walking around the hand, inspecting it from all angles, staring for a long time at the end where the arm was supposed to be, where the flesh just stopped. It was a hot, muggy summer afternoon; she remembered thinking that the blood made the poppies in the paving-stone cracks look faded. She crouched down and started to reach towards the hand. Slowly. She wanted only to brush it with her fingertips; she supposed it would feel like a hand – like any other.

Her whole body jerked as she was pulled away. Annie's mother pulled her up into the air, and in a high, frightened voice told Annie that she needed to go back into the house. Inside, Annie stood for a long time looking at the white-washed wall. Vera Lynn had been singing on the wireless. Even though she knew the music was still playing, she could hear nothing.

April, 2020

THIS MORNING, JUST AFTER I'd finished reading the paper, as I was putting on my coat, the landline rang. It was Paul. He was ringing to let me know that Rita had died.

He said she'd gone at nine minutes past four in the morning. He said that bit over and over, as if it was the only information that really mattered. Nine minutes past four.

'They wouldn't let me in with her,' he said, and I could hear his voice start to crack. I thought he might cry – men do, these days. 'I was sitting outside. In the car.'

He was worried, he said, that at the end she might have been frightened.

I told him, in a voice that I haven't needed to use for a long time, that Rita wouldn't have had much of an idea of what was going on while she was in hospital. She was probably doolally on morphine. I didn't know if it was true, but the dead are gone and you can't do them any more harm. It makes sense to take care of the living.

'She didn't have her mobile with her. She never does – I'm always telling her. I should have checked, when the ambulance took her. If she'd had it I could have rung. You know. Talked to her. Done the thing where she can see my face.'

He gave a little gasp and started to weep. Then there was a rustle and an interruption. Lizzie, their daughter, had taken the phone.

'Annie?'

In truth, I'd have preferred her to call me Mrs Reynolds, but I've always liked Lizzie.

A fall, Lizzie said, then a broken hip. Pneumonia. All happened very quickly.

'I'm here with Dad now. He's in shock. But he's all right.'

I said nothing. She read something into my silence that wasn't there. 'I double-checked all the government guidelines. It's legal now, obviously. Because Dad's on his own.' A pause, then she added, 'I'm wearing gloves and everything.'

Never would have expected a daughter of Rita's to be a stickler. I wondered why Paul had been alone and what on earth Alec was doing with himself. Maybe he'd got stuck somewhere. Always the jet setter, Alec. But I wasn't sure how much Lizzie and Alec had to do with each other, so I just said, 'Oh, of course, dear. You must look after him now.'

'Yes, Annie, I know.'

That made me wince. It only ever takes a second, just a dip in concentration, to slip into a thoughtlessness that veers very close to cruelty. As if she needed me to point out how much he'd be relying on her.

4

Time was that I had a lot of these sorts of conversations. Now I'm getting older I'm doing it all over again. I know the script well. When she didn't say 'we'll be in touch about the funeral' the absence yawned wide between us.

'I expect we'll speak soon,' Lizzie said finally. I told her I was thinking of her, and rang off. She's a nice girl. I say girl, though I suppose she'll be sixty this year.

After we'd said goodbye I stood for a while in front of the bay window. My kitchen's on the ground floor, which offers me a good view of the street. It used to bother me a bit that people could see in, but nowadays I'm hungry for the sight of faces.

There was a tall young woman – puffs of blonde hair – walking down the street. Heels and lipstick, which you don't see much these days. A determined look, a sense of having somewhere to be. You don't see that, either.

It was Rita who taught me about watching people. We used to do it for hours on our days off, getting the bus from the Hall and sitting in the upstairs room of that little tea shop in Fairlie, peering down through the layer of condensation on the windows to the little street below. There can't have been that many passers-by – it was only a little village. But I seem to remember seeing all sorts of people. And Rita would make things up about them. She'd point at some prim-looking old widow and say, 'She's got three husbands buried in the back garden.' Or some dignified old boy in his tweeds – 'A communist spy.' I always thought she was being a bit daft, but I'd smile along. She'd

5

look at me eagerly – she used to get a kick out of making me laugh.

I don't think about the bad bits at the Hall as much anymore. These days I just remember Rita, and me, and the way we were together.

I watched the young woman disappear around the corner. The sound of her heels faded and the silence reinstated itself, so complete that it was hard to believe it had ever been broken. Rita is dead, I said quietly to myself. Rita is dead.

I ended up going out for my walk. When you're not sure how to take a loss, I've always found it's best to stick to whatever plan you had to begin with. The loss will settle, in its own time. Meanwhile, you need to metabolise the shock. The best way to do that: eat, sleep, move.

I put the mobile in my pocket. I never forget it, or let the charge run down. Then I set out, the same route I take every day. Spring's seeped into Pimlico; it seems that overnight the trees have conjured up their blossom – now it flares bright against the black-and-white livery of the stucco-fronted houses. No cars along the road and just a few people in the street. Everything feels hollowed-out, trapped in a moment of crystalline shock.

I've timed my walk to an hour. I'm not really sure that's actually a rule. Rosie tells me that people have got hold of all sorts of ideas – she sees it on the internet. They read the guidelines and fill in the blanks. They decide you can't buy daffodils from the supermarket because they don't count as an essential. That you can't nip out for a pint of milk, you've got to wait for your weekly shop. And if anyone should so much as smile at you then you must turn your face away. Head down, don't let anyone catch you enjoying the sunshine. Exercise like the whole world is your prison yard.

We've been living like this for just a month. It's funny how quickly novelty turns into habit, and then habit turns into law.

Across the bridge I go. Pace as brisk as I can manage, showing the world that I'm not malingering. I don't do badly for my age, but these days I'm starting to sense which parts of me might be liable to crack. I don't weigh much at all anymore and today I feel light and wispy, less surefooted than usual.

I take a good look at every face. It's the usual joggers. The day is clear and bright enough to see the city's distant glass spikes as they scrape against the hard blue sky. I've always thought they were eyesores, those buildings, but now I quite like them. Or perhaps I'm just pleased to be reminded that they're still there.

Even the river isn't its usual flat brown. It sparkles in the morning light, as if to tempt you in for a plunge. I often worry, crossing that bridge, that one of the kids on bikes – or perhaps a runner, absorbed in their telephone – will crash straight into me, pitch me over the edge and into those depths. If the fall doesn't kill me then the shock of the cold surely will.

Then I'll be dead. Like Rita.

Part of me isn't at all surprised that she's the first of us to go. Eighty's not considered as old as it once was, but I've known for a while that she's been on the decline.

I saw her last at Christmas. It feels like a long time ago. Anything before this lockdown feels like a long time ago. We always called on each other around Christmas time – sometimes that was the only time we'd see each other for the whole year. She was letting Paul do a lot for her, sitting too much, using the arms of chairs to pull herself up.

'Paul likes to fuss over me,' she'd said. She blinked those great blue eyes, which had never faded or gone rheumy. 'So I let him.'

And Paul gave her a little pat on the shoulder.

'He's a fusspot,' she'd said, looking up at him. 'Wants everything done exactly his way.'

She's tough, in her own fashion, but it's never been about discipline for her. She likes to take things as they come, doesn't always recognise when it's time to fight. 'You'll lose your core strength,' I told her. 'That's how you end up falling.'

She just laughed. 'Got to die of something, Annie.'

I thought she was talking rubbish, and I told her so. I keep myself in as good shape as I can manage. It isn't vanity. I used to dash up three flights of stairs every hour and think nothing of it, then you start to realise how difficult it all feels, how you're running out of breath.

I've been doing this walk for so long that my boots seem to know the incline of the road as it slides down into the park. They take me away from the wide path laced with children on scooters, teenagers on pushbikes. They know the dip and rise of this piece of earth, the firm press of ground hardened by spring warmth. They understand each clod of this hill, anticipating exactly where the roots might trip me up, where they seem designed like a set of steps to propel me upward. I know that the bench at the top is waiting for me, and that when I get there, I will need a certain amount of rest. The length of time seems to get longer every day, but that might just be the way time is stretched out at the moment – like a piece of elastic that's lost its shape.

Most people probably wouldn't call my little spot a hill, but let me tell you, it's a hill when you're eighty. My regular bench is in memory of John (1930–2014) and Mary (1935–2014) Eldridge. *In celebration of their love story*, the little plaque says.

They say we ought not to sit down when we go out for our exercise. They also say that we must make sure we stay well, mustn't add to the pressure on the health service. Mostly they say again and again that we must use our common sense, as if no one ever went wrong that way.

On the path below me I can see an old man walking. He wears a beautiful three-piece suit and carries a gold-topped cane, a Panama hat pulled over a dark, weathered face.

Ghost, I say to myself. But the voice in my head is Rita's.

Rita taught me to see these people. The people who are separate and strange, who don't quite fit. She told me that she thought of them as ghosts and at first I didn't know what she meant. But after a while I understood that she meant people who seemed to have somehow got dislodged in time, who washed up in the wrong place.

When she pointed them out I started to see them everywhere. The women with victory rolls and red lipstick. The Edwardian gentlemen in boater hats and striped jackets, appearing in a sea of ordinary suits and mackintoshes. A flapper – waistless, droplegged, unsmiling – amid the cardigans of the church social. She always said that the only difference between her and me was that she could spot the ghosts, and I couldn't. Not back then, anyhow.

Sam used to call us the twins, which was his idea of a joke because we looked so different. I was small, she too tall for a girl. She was fair where I was dark, buxom where I was slight. Our uniforms only exaggerated the differences between us. I was better-looking by most people's reckoning, but men always seemed to prefer her.

I suppose we were outsiders together. There weren't many girls of twenty who shared our peculiar choice of employment. Though choosing a job wasn't really such a big decision back then, just a question of how one might usefully spend a few years before one was – hopefully – married. Though we parted suddenly, we must have stayed in touch because I was there at Rita's wedding to Paul, and later she was at mine to George. But, even in the Eighties, when we saw a lot of each other, we were never quite as close as those months at Fairlie Hall.

Rita was the sort of girl who would dance to any radio, no matter where she was or who was watching. I could see why some people might make fun of her, but she wasn't daft, Rita.

I take my phone out to glance at the time, though I've got nowhere much to be.

It's ten fifteen in the morning. No missed call from Paul, to let me know that it's all a mistake, that the hospital was mixed up. That Rita's perfectly all right. No calls or texts at all. I wonder whether I ought to ring Jim, to let him know. Not because he and Rita were ever very close, but because he's always been the custodian of these sorts of moments, the chief rememberer.

But I'll speak to him later, after the call with Rosie.

Rosie rings every day, but not till four o'clock, after they've released the day's numbers. Late enough for the day to be drained of any purpose, but still too early for wine, dinner and telly. When she calls I'm often in the garden, urging my plants to bud and flower. They're coming along perfectly in this weather, but for some reason I want them to hurry.

I always go inside before I answer the phone. I don't want Rosie to feel that she might be interrupting something. We talk for an hour or so – mostly it's her doing the talking, trying to disguise her own voiced fears as reassurances. She goes over the numbers as if she's planning some sort of strategy; my job is to make the right noises. Sometimes she asks if I've got enough food in, and urges me to give up doing my own shopping.

11

'Those nice guys next door offered to drop it off for you, didn't they? You can just give them a list, Mum, and then they can leave everything in the porch. Yes, just give them a list. It's so much safer.' She says it like the matter's settled, and I make a noise as if I'm going to consider it. But we both know I won't. I'm sure she thinks I'm just terribly set in my ways, but the truth is that at my age, if you stop doing something, there's no guarantee that you'll ever start again.

'I don't think you quite understand the reality of the situation,' she keeps saying. That's when I get a bit sharp with her and remind her that I'm a trained nurse, thank you very much. I did my Introduction to Pathology course. I understand it better than she might think – the pathogens and the viruses. The immune system – how it holds the line, where it fails. The white cells in the blood-red. She goes quiet at that point, and then she says, 'It's the uncertainty. There's nothing worse than uncertainty, is there?'

Then she starts her list of 'it's justs'. It's just that I'd love to go for a big walk on the Downs. That can't hurt anyone, can it? But you're not supposed to. It's just that I'd kill for a proper flat white. It's just that we were supposed to be going to Seville in May, and I've been looking forward to it so much.

'It's silly to complain, really. I know I'm lucky.' She always rounds off with that part, says it quickly.

Yet I feel it myself. The shock that, as it turns out, every part of my life – big or small – is dispensable. It's just that I can't bear the colour of my own walls anymore. It's just that I miss people's voices, voices that aren't distorted by a phone line. It's just that I wish I could hold a hand, any hand.

It's just that Rita's dead and now she won't have a proper funeral.

So I say I know love, it isn't fair. Then we talk about what we're having for our tea and we say goodbye. By the time I've stepped back into the garden it's too cool to sit out anymore. These warm days can trick you into feeling like it's summer. That's when I pour myself a gin and tonic. Sometimes I call Jim, and we complain about the evening's telly.

The park bench is starting to feel chilly through my old jeans. I close my eyes to the morning sun and notice how, for a second, the skyline remains imprinted in the dark. Silence in the city sounds like birdsong now. There's a soft rustle of the wind as it runs through freshly unfurled leaves.

For a moment I feel as if there's a presence beside me. Close as skin, but not touching.

I've recovered my breath now. It's time to be getting on. If I stay any longer then I really will be malingering. But as I get up I feel myself sway slightly, on the very edge of losing my balance. I clutch at the back of the bench for support and breathe slow and deep. Beneath my feet the grass is green and smooth as water, so regular that it's a surprise when it falls away and slopes into the dark trees below.

I don't want to turn back to the bench. I can see her so clearly now, sitting there with her eyes narrowed against the sun. As always, a little uncomfortable in her starched uniform, the bands of the red cape crisscrossing her chest, her white cap almost disappearing in that mop of blonde curls.

'Rita,' I say out loud.

And then here we are again. Sixty years slip away into the empty sky. It's Rita and me, side by side, our hearts beating hard and loud beneath our stiff new uniforms. We're afraid to look at each other, afraid to give our nerve away as the green of the park grows lurid around us.

And there it is again, below. Fairlie Hall, crouched in the dip between its two hills, dark brickwork pulling in all the light, chimneys like thin fingers reaching for something beyond their grasp.

'Come on Annie, keep up,' I hear Rita say beside me. And together we make our way down.

October, 1959

RITA IS NOTHING MORE than a voice when Annie first meets her. A voice that rings bell-like through the cramped space of the little flat.

'Hull-oh!'

Annie draws her red hands out of the water as if suddenly burned. She stands still, listening. There's so much steam that she can barely see the sink. All around her the world presses close – fresh, billowing, white.

'I'm here!'

The golden head appears between the two wet sheets that Annie has hung on either side of the kitchen door. Through the veil of steam, Annie can see blue eyes, a broad bow of lipstick, blonde curls deflating in the sudden heat.

'Good evening,' Annie says.

She had been intending to use her nurse's voice, the cool, calm voice she's been working on. But she knows that she waited a second too long to speak, and now she's feeling stupid and out of place. Her hands are full of sopping pillowcases, and the steam from the warm kitchen is spilling hastily out of the door and into the chilly hall. The estate manager told her that the stone cottage, of which she and another trainee nurse are due to occupy the top half, is over four hundred years old. As old as the Hall itself, he says. Even on a warm day like this Annie has noticed lingering spots of cold, in the corners and the passages.

'Cleaning already?' The blue eyes flit around the tiny kitchen, pausing momentarily on the sink, on the kettle, on Annie herself. The last of the steam drains away and the room seems to come into focus under that restless gaze.

'I smelled damp when I came in,' Annie says, seeing the glance at the hanging sheets. 'I couldn't . . .'

'Very clever of you to take care of things,' the girl interrupts.

Annie feels a little surge of warmth. 'It was nothing.'

'Rita, by the way.' Rita sticks her arm through the sheets. It is bare to the shoulder. Annie too is dressed for summer – though it's October, day after day there persists a static, lifeless heat. Annie seizes a threadbare towel, dries off and takes the hand. The grip is soft, warm, capacious.

'Annie,' she says.

'I just arrived,' Rita continues. She steps fully into the cramped kitchen and flings open the window, almost knocking over the milk jug in the process. 'Stifling in here. Dad dropped me off, which was good of him, wasn't it? Especially considering he'd rather I weren't here at all. Are your parents like that? Did you get the bus here? You poor thing – it's inhumane in this heat,

16

isn't it? Why *is* it so hot, I wonder? I expect everything to be turning golden at this time of year, don't you? But it's just all brown, brown and brittle and dry. I can't stand it. Though the paper said it's forecast to rain tonight. Thank heavens, eh?'

'Thank heavens,' Annie echoes. And she really does feel thankful. Looking out of the window at the blanket of bruised cloud, she imagines the whole thing bursting. Pictures herself – with Rita – running out into the lane, barefoot and whooping, savouring cool drops on bare skin.

'Glorious little hovel, isn't it?' Now Rita's leaning out of the window, lighting a cigarette. Annie remembers the dry thatch, and wonders if the whole cottage might catch fire.

'I've put my things in the back bedroom,' Annie says. 'Is that all right?'

'Why shouldn't it be?' Rita straightens back into the room. From this new angle Annie can see for the first time just how much of Rita there is. She has the fashion-ably generous hips and bosom, her waist too is rather thick. Or, Annie thinks, that might just be the effect of a pair of rather badly-cut navy slacks. She's also wearing a sleeveless white blouse, fastened a little too tightly across the bust by a row of little pearl buttons. Annie can see a dampness under the arms.

'I'm so glad we'll be here together,' Rita carries on. She smiles, and Annie finds herself smiling back. 'You know, I had the horrors about living "in" – it sounded

17

like being back at school, or in the dormitories at the university. I'm no good at institutional life. But this is a snug little place . . . I suppose that for once it's a perk, being a girl. All the live-in nurses are men. Not nurses, I mean. What do they call them?'

'Attendants.' Annie does the customary little eye roll that she's seen mental nurses exchange at the mention of attendants. But Rita doesn't seem to notice this. She carries on talking – about the work day, the lectures, her own – in her words – 'appalling laziness'. Annie doesn't mind listening. It gives her a chance to look at Rita properly.

In the time that it takes Rita to make a pot of tea, she volleys a dozen or more questions at Annie. Where did she train? Why did she decide to become a nurse? Why this *sort* of nurse?

'You must be an unusual sort,' Rita says, showing all her white teeth as she smiles at Annie. 'Most people are so frightened of mental illness.'

'I'm not frightened,' Annie says. It's not entirely true, but it feels difficult to explain that there are so many other things that frighten her more than the mad.

'Of course you're not.' That radiant smile again. 'You seem like the quietly fearless type. A born nurse.'

'I started a course in general nursing, actually.' Annie feels her cheeks growing warm. 'It turned out not to suit me. But what about you?'

'Did you really? How funny, I was just the same. I've always liked science and that sort of thing. I thought nursing, that'll do for me. Then I went onto all the different wards and it became obvious that I'm no Florence Nightingale.' She gestures down at herself, though Annie is not sure what she's supposed to be seeing. 'I can't find a vein to save my life. When I try to patch people up I always seem to make something worse.' She laughs. 'But then I did a rotation on a mental ward. Of course I was scared at first – you're always scared at first, aren't you? People tell you about the nuthouse and you believe them, of course. You don't know any better.'

'I suppose.'

'But then, do you know?' Rita leans forwards, close and confidential. 'On my first day on the ward I met this older chap. Schizophrenia, I think it must have been, though they never tell you, do they? He was in a terrible state. But I could chat to him. Do you know, it was easier to talk to him than other people. Normally I don't know what to say and I just rabbit on. You probably think I'm rabbiting on now.' Annie shakes her head. 'But with this sweet old boy it didn't matter a bit. He was interested in talking to me, I was interested in talking to him. And considering that he thought I was a KGB spy, he was terribly polite and kind.

'So I switched to mental nursing. I was terrified to make the switch, but I just did it and it felt marvellous. Not that anyone understood. It's so nice to be with someone who understands.'

Annie is feeling that she understands very little, but there is something refreshing about Rita's frankness. She wants to understand whatever it is that Rita thinks she does.

'My dad was horrified that I wanted to be a nurse at all, let alone this sort of nurse. I suppose he thinks girls oughtn't to work at all if they can possibly help it, and if they can't help it then they should have the decency to be secretaries. Teachers if they're pushing it.' She sighs and lights a cigarette. 'He thinks nursing's for wartime, I suppose. What did your parents make of it?'

'I don't think my mother minds.'

Cares, Annie thinks. That's the proper word.

'People have all sorts of reasons for doing a job like this,' Rita carries on. 'I have a feeling that we must be rather a funny bunch. But you – weren't you tempted by the typing pool? You're awfully glamorous-looking – you'd have made a splendid secretary.'

Annie looks down at her blouse and skirt. They're ordinary enough, though the colours are rather good. She makes her own clothes and she has a knack for copying good patterns, but she's never been described as glamorous before, not by anyone.

'Thanks,' she says.

'Anyway, that's me rabbiting again. Why nursing? Why mental nursing?'

'I want to make people better.' Annie's answer is automatic. 'It's always been that way for me.' That was what you were supposed to say at nursing college. That it was a vocation. The vocation was the source of infinite patience, of compassion, of the ability to deal with dreadful things without flinching. There was nothing particular to be admired in those qualities – they were all part of the vocation and therefore in limitless supply. One could not take credit for them.

And it's true, for Annie, that the motivation – she can't quite call it a calling – has lived inside her, small and strong, for so long that she's never questioned it. It's an urge to smooth things out – to make clean what is dirty and to sew up what gapes open.

She realises that Rita is still looking at her intently. 'I'm a practical sort of person too,' she adds. 'I'd get bored to death in a typing pool, I think.'

Rita starts talking about how she's always been told off for fidgeting and chatting. It's a while before the conversation has any slack at all. After a while Rita produces a bottle of brandy and they slip some into their teacups, which Annie has never done before. They relish the warmth in their stomachs as they tuck their feet together beneath a crocheted blanket. Rita changes out of her slacks and blouse and into a lilac flannel dressing gown. Annie puts on her nightie, her cotton dressing gown. Both are old – she made them for herself when she turned fifteen and developed a meagre bosom. The neat little waist still fits perfectly.

After a long while, in which they've talked about their favourite films and Rita has recommended half a dozen records that Annie has never heard of, Rita says she's tired. The sheets are still wet. Rita insists that sleeping on a bare mattress doesn't bother her. She wraps her soft dressing gown more tightly around her shoulders; her golden curls have collapsed in the warm, damp air and drift softly about her neck, framing flushed pink cheeks.

Annie stays in the kitchen for a good while longer, her dressing gown close about her, feet drawn up. October seems to have arrived at last through the open window.

At two o'clock in the morning she makes up her bed. Her limbs cramp up in the cold of the sheet, which is dry in some patches and still soaking in others. Eventually she takes a scratchy towel from the basin and lies down on it, curled up very small. The towel is stiff and smells of soap. Annie closes her eyes. The walls of the little flat are so thin that she can hear, in the next room, the soft sound of Rita's breathing.

April, 2020

THE FEELING HITS ME in the chest on the steps outside my house. How can a sensation be so familiar, and yet still new? At first, I don't understand this noise – its guttural force – I know only that it comes from me: a low, baying sound, the cry of an animal in mortal pain. I lean my forehead against the front door. My whole body has stiffened and curled in on itself.

Part of me welcomes it. The pain. I knew it had to come, and now here it is. Proof of what she was to me, what we were to each other.

Part of me is mortified. Why couldn't I hold it together until I got indoors? Just a few more steps?

Then I hear her. *Breathe, Annie*, she tells me. Not in the soft, airy tones from her dippy yoga phase, but the voice of the twenty-year-old girl on the ward. *Breathe into it.*

I obey. I breathe. My stony body softens. I breathe until I can unfurl myself. Just cramped fingertips at first, then hands – I realise that my keys have been biting into my clenched palm.

I hear hurried footsteps behind me; someone is walking away. A passer-by, I suppose, who stopped at the sight of me. Who is relieved to be spared the task of helping me.

I unlock the front door and carefully lie face down on the hall carpet. I push the door shut with my foot. Then I cry – silently this time. I am alone; there's no one to protect from my tears, no one whose greater loss I must defer to. I cry until my tears soak into the carpet. I cry until I'm exhausted, and until the exhaustion brings with it a strange calm.

Then I get up – carefully, again – and make coffee. I ring Jim, give him the news. He was the one who kept a lot of stuff from that time. Photos, diaries, medical records. The quilt that Davey made. Letters, of course, but also restaurant bills and invoices from florists. Stuff that most people wouldn't have bothered holding on to.

'I'll have a look through for you,' he promises.

'Only if it's no bother.'

'Of course it's a bother, trawling through all that rubbish. But what else would I be doing?'

Jim's funny about the lockdown. He says it's a relief, not having to pretend to want to go for coffee or dinner or hear about people's holiday plans. He says he's reading a lot, but he's fed up with the galleries being closed. I think that's his way of saying that he misses me.

I thank him. I don't have many photos of me and Rita. There've been plenty taken – I remember a good few at Fairlie Hall. Then of course there were none for a while – there was that long stretch when we only saw each other in passing. I suppose that was when she was angry with me, even if we never talked about it.

The photographs from Jim start pinging through on my iPad. Just one at first, a snap of me and Rita at the kitchen table in this house. Up to our elbows in clay. Davey's sitting between us, already very thin but smiling widely. Then they start to come through faster and faster. Dozens of them. Rita in the garden, wearing a purple boiler suit. Rita carrying a birthday cake over to Mackie. I count the candles. Twenty-four. Rita after Mackie's funeral, flanked by a pair of drag queens, all toasting the camera.

I rifle around in a few drawers to find the postcards. I'm not great at photos, but I tend to hold on to papers and correspondence. Rita and Paul travelled a lot around the time that Lizzie was at university, going to all sorts of places. That was before Rita and I were back in touch, before Alec, before this house.

I did a few big trips in the late Nineties, when the boys were gone. Rosie was well grown up by then and there was no call for me to look after anyone. I told myself that I was striking out on my own, but really I was just following the trail that Rita had left me twenty years earlier. Porto. Marrakesh. Goa.

The postcards were all I heard from her for a long time. We were in and out of touch before George died. When we found each other again I wasn't the same person as the girl who'd worked at Fairlie Hall. But when the crisis came, I understood that the nursing part of me still needed Rita.

I don't remember deciding to ring her up and ask for help. At that time everything was so chaotic that I don't really remember making any decisions. They're the hardest thing to properly remember, those crossroads moments. Try as you might, you can never get back that feeling of the future forking out in front of you. It always feels like it could never have ended up any other way, that all was inevitable.

Another ping on my iPad. Jim again. It's a photo of me, and him, and Rosie, and Robbie. I don't remember who snapped it, but I remember the picnic. Rosie's fourteenth birthday. Jim with his dark curly hair, the moustache he had back then, a shirt of deep sea blue. Robbie smiling, striking a silly pose, all limbs and teeth. Rosie cuddled between them.

Jim adds a message underneath. *Remember this.* It's not a question, of course I remember. It's a reminder of the task the two of us share, the final part of our work. Remember this.

October 1983

IT WAS LATE AT night by the time Annie left the hospital.

Rosie'd had a hard time settling, saying that her stitches itched and that she didn't like the hospital bed, didn't like the hospital smell. She was thirteen, but something about the fever had made her slip into a much smaller self. It was as if the bravado, the watchfulness that she'd acquired lately had all melted away under the harsh lights of the hospital, and there was Annie's baby girl again: tiny, pale, overheated. When the fever reached its peak she had wailed that she was cold and Annie held her close. When she laid Rosie back on the bed, it was as though the shape of the small body was burned onto hers.

Then the fever had broken. The brow became sweaty but temperate. Annie had sat for a long time with her hand on her daughter's forehead, periodically switching so that the palm touching Rosie would always be cool.

Now she was asleep. The night was so much colder than the children's ward; it felt like such a long time since Annie had been able to breathe easily. She took in great lungfuls of air as she walked along Westminster Bridge Road, scarcely aware of her direction.

The sudden terror of Rosie's illness had come like a crack of thunder, breaking through the long, thick haze that had hung over Annie since George died. Here was the threat: a tiny, living bomb, hiding inside her daughter's body. And here was the solution: the surgeon, the scalpel. Everything stitched back together: the work of an evening.

Annie pulled the collar of her mackintosh closer around her neck, taking long, slow sips of night air. Once the initial scare had passed and the diagnosis had been given, she had understood quickly that such a routine procedure hardly called for much alarm. That did nothing to dissolve the fear, of course. She had sat clenched in her chair in one of the inner chambers of Casualty while they took her daughter away. They told her that Rosie would be transferred to a ward after the operation, in an hour or two, that then all would be well.

Then there was nothing for it but to sit tight. She calmed herself by explaining to George, in her mind, what an ordinary ailment this was. If she squeezed her eyes shut she could see him nodding, his faith in her complete.

'Let me get you some tea, Mrs Reynolds,' the nurse said. The tea had been in steady supply, cup after cup. The sky grew darker, the lights of Central London roared into life, and still it kept coming, in a proper cup with a saucer. You don't see that so much these days, Annie thought distantly.

There had only been one other person in the waiting room, and at first it would have been easy to mistake him for a bundle of coats, perhaps left behind in someone's flurry of panic. But when Annie's breathing had eased slightly and her vision widened out she understood that the bundle of coats was a man. A young man – a boy, even. The thin face and sunken eyes couldn't conceal the fluffiness of a moustache that he clearly wasn't quite able to grow. His thin body, his face, they reminded Annie of pictures that she'd seen and only fractionally understood in the papers when she was very small, just after the war ended.

The boy caught her looking at him and managed a smile. She began to notice that when the nurse brought her the cups of tea she did not walk straight to or from the nurses' station, but rather in a peculiar arc, giving the boy in the corner a wide berth. Perhaps he was smelly, Annie thought, though she couldn't smell anything. He looked like he might be a tramp. But then, wouldn't anyone look like a tramp when they were swathed in oversized clothes, all fleshless bones?

On Annie's third cup of tea the boy asked the nurse, in a quiet voice, whether he might have a cup too. He was ever so chilly, he said. The nurse stopped in her tracks and, without turning to look at the boy, said, 'I'll have to go and ask the doctor.'

She disappeared for a while. The boy hunched deeper into his coat, looking down at his lap. Annie wished that she'd returned his smile when he'd offered it; now he looked at no one. He was singing something under his breath – she couldn't hear what the song was, and could get no sense of the melody. But every so often she caught a phrase as it came through his dry, cracked lips. *Hold back the night.* He sang slowly, a soft murmur that Annie could barely differentiate from the ambient sounds of the hospital.

Eventually, a figure entered the room. From the walk, Annie realised that it was the nurse, but she wouldn't have recognised her, for she was now wearing a plastic gown, a mask which covered her face, thick rubber gloves. Annie tried to remember if she'd ever worn gloves like that when she was a nurse. The teacup was plastic too. Annie could see the tag of the teabag hanging over the side. Matron would have had a fit if she saw that, Annie thought.

When the boy reached out an arm – so thin that it scarcely resembled one – to take the cup, the nurse withdrew her hand so quickly that some of the liquid slopped over the rim and onto the boy's papery skin. His eyes widened in shock and pain, but he said only 'thanks'. He didn't sing anymore after that and Annie realised that his soft voice had been sparing her an awful, yawning silence. She wanted to give him an encouraging smile, but he was staring at the floor, his shoulders hunched.

The swinging doors opened and the surgeon entered. Annie leapt to her feet, then sagged with relief at the sight of his brisk smile.

'Oh, Doctor,' she said. She realised that all the time that she'd been sitting there she'd imagined George sitting beside her, drawing reassurance from her calm. She gave a little gasp, felt a tear slide down her cheek.

30

'Not a thing to worry about, Mrs Reynolds,' the surgeon said. She had nodded. Nothing to worry about. The hospital seemed to blur then, so that the only fixed points in her swimming vision were the city lights through the windows.

Rosie was so still at first. Annie had clenched her fists in her lap, needing to touch her daughter – to stir or even slap her into life. But then her eyes were twitching and Annie was laughing with relief as Rosie stirred and said, 'Mummy', then something nonsensical about dogs. Then she'd rolled over, both palms pressed together under her cheek, the way she'd slept ever since she was a baby.

Annie stayed utterly still, still gazing at her daughter. After a moment she carefully laid her forehead on the bed, next to Rosie's shoulder.

She had no idea how long she'd been sleeping for when the hand woke her, only that the sleep had been a deep one. For a moment she knew neither where she was nor the time – it was the latter that disoriented her more. Blinking rapidly, she sat upright, shoving her chair back.

A nurse stood beside her. No – not just a nurse. Annie's eyes flicked over the uniform. A Ward Sister. She was smiling the sort of smile that is more intended to conceal irritation than show kindness. Rosie slept on.

'Time for you to be getting off,' the Ward Sister said. Then she added, as an afterthought, 'You're exhausted.'

'I'd rather stay with my daughter.' Annie heard the tremor in her own voice, and was surprised by it.

'That goes against our policy, I'm afraid.'

'I thought I could stay as long as I wanted.'

'That used to be the policy, yes.' The Ward Sister's lips tightened. 'But some people abused it, you see.'

Annie stood slowly, and gathered up her handbag.

'Thank you,' she said. Not because she meant it, but because there were too many other things threatening to burst from her lips. She took one last look at Rosie and said, 'I'll be back first thing, love.'

Rosie did not stir. Annie's hands were shaking as she left the ward.

Annie walked on, past Westminster Bridge. She looked across the river to where Parliament speared into the smeary yellow night. The river made a soft sound below her, a ream of black silk. She crossed at Waterloo Bridge, thinking of the old song by the Kinks. George had hummed it every time they crossed the bridge together, right from when they first moved to London. He had been very old-fashioned in most respects, never ordinarily letting her take his arm in public. But whenever they'd crossed the bridge he'd insist they stop, look out at the city. And he'd always put his arm around Annie there.

She quickened her pace. She wanted to glance over her shoulder, but she knew that it would do her no good to see the outline of the hospital where her daughter might or might not be sleeping. She was bone tired, the nursing muscles of her body cramped from reactivating after so long. It occurred to her that this would be her first night

32

alone in the Pimlico house, without Rosie's presence to wrap herself around, anchoring her in this new, fuzzy world where there was no George.

It was only when the music swelled closer that she realised she'd been fitting her steps into its beat for some time. In the dark of the night the music seemed to have a colour of its own, seeping out of a doorway beneath the railway bridge.

A group of men were standing outside the doorway, smoking. Annie had never seen men dressed quite like that before – T-shirts slashed to show brown, lithe stomachs. Eyes rimmed with kohl. Leather waistcoats over bare skin. Annie quickened her pace again, breaking with the rhythm of the dance music. She didn't want them to see her looking, to wonder what such a dowdy, shapeless woman was doing in a place like this.

The beat of the club, the distant synths, they reminded her of the boy in the waiting room. She wondered what it was that he was singing.

'Robbie!'

Someone said the name so loudly that she stopped in her tracks, as if it was her own name that had been called. Then she recovered her pace, hoping that none of the men had noticed. They could all just pretend not to see each other.

'Robbie!' The name again, in a voice that made her listen more carefully even as she kept walking. Whoever was speaking didn't sound drunk. Annie looked down at the ground and did the tiniest of double-takes, as if she'd just noticed that one of her shoelaces was undone. She bent down, turning her head as she did so to look at the group of men.

A dark-haired, slightly round-bellied man in his late thirties was propping up the rangy, lolling figure of a boy. He must have been drunk, Annie thought; he could barely keep himself upright.

'Here's one,' one of the other men said, the one wearing a leather waistcoat without anything underneath. 'Light's on, just get him in—'

'Where am I taking him to?' The round-bellied man looked frazzled. 'I told you, his landlord's chucked him out.'

'You can take him to yours again, can't you?'

The other man didn't answer. The taxi had driven on without pausing, its light still ablaze.

'Little bastard,' the man in the leather waistcoat said, spitting after the taxi. He was from Manchester, Annie could tell. When he swore, he sounded just like her brother.

'There'll be another,' the other man said. He had dark curls and a dark moustache. His face appeared very pale, though that might have been the light. He kept his voice level, as if any instability in his tone might dislodge the boy leaning on his shoulder.

Annie looked more closely at the boy. Despite his obvious fragility he was a big chap, broad-shouldered and square-jawed, high cheekbones. He looked, Annie thought, as though the flesh had recently evaporated from his frame; he was wearing a sequinned vest that flapped baggily at the armholes. He was slumped forwards, with the sweep of his blond hair covering his eyes. He said, 'I'm all right', in a way that didn't sound drunk to Annie.

'He's as bad as Glenn was the other week,' the man with the dark curls said. 'He's got to go to hospital. If the taxi won't stop then we'll just have to ring an ambulance.'

'Jim, they won't let you go in the ambulance with him.'

'They might.'

'They didn't with Glenn.' The man in the leather waistcoat folded his arms. 'You know no one's been allowed in to see him?'

'We'll make sure they take him somewhere else then. It's that bloody hospital. We'll get them to take him somewhere more sensible, and they're bound to let us in.' The man called Jim ground his cigarette butt decisively beneath the ball of his foot. Robbie's head flopped on his shoulder.

'They're not bound to do anything, darling.'

'Well, what do you want me to do? He's been on my sofa this last week. And he can have the bed, I don't mind, but I've got work first thing. I can't keep an eye on him.'

'He doesn't need keeping an eye on, Jim. Look, I'm sure he's just overdone it a bit. He's healthy as a horse, our Robbie. You saw him knocking back the vodka and cokes. He's done a bit too much dancing, probably. He'll be all right in the morning.'

'He's lost a stone in a week, Russ.' Jim's knees were buckling slightly. Though the boy was little more than skin and bone, his great height must have made him heavy.

'We could call Gay Switchboard. I've heard they've been pretty good.'

'Why Gay Switchboard? You're not saying ...'

'I'm not saying he's got it,' Jim said hurriedly. 'I mean the landlord thing. They can help him find a new landlord.'

Russ seemed to relax slightly. 'Fine, we'll call in the morning. But what about tonight?'

'Look, I'll take him to St Thomas's. They might be all right there.'

'They're not.'

Annie only realised a moment after all the men had turned to look at her – even Robbie – that she'd spoken aloud. Her own voice sounded ridiculous compared to their low tones, which were honeyed and smoothed with a little drink. Shrill, splintery, uncertain. She cleared her throat and stood straight, trying again.

'They're no good at all.' She nodded at Robbie. 'I've just come from over there and there was a man – you know, a man like him – sat in Casualty.'

'What're you trying to say, a man like him?' Russ stepped forwards, scowling.

'Leave off her, Russ,' Jim said as Annie shrank back. He nodded at her. 'Carry on.'

'They weren't looking after him properly,' Annie said, all in a rush. 'Not like he needed.'

Russ looked at her for a moment, then nodded curtly. 'OK love, ta.' He turned back to Jim. 'Well, all the more reason to take him home. If he's not better in a couple of days we can always ring the doctor.'

'A couple of days?' Jim gave a little laugh, as if in disbelief. He was clearly breathless from holding Robbie up. 'I'm not sleeping. I'm waking up every hour to check on him.' Annie could see the darkness under his eyes. 'Why the hell did you let him come out tonight, anyway?'

'Let him? Didn't realise I was his mother. He said he was feeling better.'

'And you believed him?'

'Why wouldn't I? He's an adult.'

Jim said nothing, but looked pointedly at the boy lolling on his shoulder. Then he sighed. 'Either way, I can't keep going like this.'

'So you're just going to ditch him in a hospital?' Russ folded his arms. 'You've seen all those signs – biohazard and all that shit. What if they won't let him out again?'

'Of course they'll let him out – what's that supposed to even mean? I can't talk to you when you're being dramatic.'

'You know damned well that even if they do let him out, they certainly won't let us in.'

Annie looked at Robbie again. His eyes were open, she realised, just slightly. Dark irises seemed to catch on her for a second. And then she just said it.

'I'll take him.'

Jim and Russ were both staring. Even Robbie seemed to have a sharp intake of breath. Annie felt herself faltering.

'I'll take him,' she said again.

'He's not a stray dog,' said Jim.

37

'You said his landlord had chucked him out, didn't you?' Annie was thinking very fast. 'Well, I'm looking for a lodger.'

Russ laughed and made a show of turning back to Jim. 'Lodger. All right. That reminds me, Jim – do you know if he's got his dole sorted out? No point in calling Gay Switchboard about finding a flat if he can't pay his rent now he's been sacked.'

'I need a lodger,' Annie repeated firmly. 'He's entitled to housing benefit, isn't he? Why shouldn't he stay with me?'

Annie realised why she'd hesitated. She felt like she ought to ask George first. But George was gone. It was down to her to get some income now, not just for herself but for Rosie.

Russ opened his mouth to reply, but Jim interrupted. 'Hold him for a second, will you? He's murder on my back and you're loads stronger than me.'

Relieved of Robbie's frame he stood up straight, shifting anxiously from foot to foot and looking alternately at Annie and Robbie.

'Look, it's very kind of you,' he said after a moment. 'But you can obviously see that he's not well.'

'Yes,' Annie said. 'I can see that.'

'And I'm happy to pop in on him wherever I can, but I don't know.' He looked at the bundle of emaciated limbs, which seemed to be held together only by the scquinned vest. 'I'm worried that he'll get even worse.'

'I'm a nurse,' Annie said. She hadn't said it in such a long time. 'I've looked after people in a worse state than him.'

It was true. Robbie didn't look so different from those patients on the ward at Fairlie Hall with tertiary-stage syphilis. But the big difference was that those had been old men, emaciated frames weathered by the years. This boy's body could have belonged to any of them, yet the eyes were still round and childlike.

'If you say so.' Jim didn't look convinced, but Annie could see that he was longing to accept some help. 'Look, if he could stay at yours for a night or two – just while we find him the right care. Maybe there's a hospital.'

'Maybe,' she said. She wasn't a big one for the news, but she'd seen a TV programme the previous year about the homosexuals in America. George had switched it off, but not before muttering, 'Poor devils.' It was an immune thing, Annie had gleaned that much. A slow coming-apart.

'Look, I've seen it,' she said. 'It's not a question of whether or not they'll take him. They'll take him all right. They'll hide him away. You won't have to ever think about him again.'

'Never think about him again . . .' It wasn't clear whether it was from Annie's words or Robbie's weight, but Russ's voice had become a low hiss, as if all the air was being let out of him. He straightened, readjusting his grip on Robbie's waist. 'How . . .'

'Well, look, it's up to you,' Annie interrupted. 'I'm just saying. If you put him in hospital then he doesn't have to be your problem anymore.' She looked at Jim steadily. 'But I'm not sure that's what you want.'

Russ and Jim exchanged looks. Robbie gave a little moan and seemed to sag still further.

'Look, here's another taxi.' Annie glanced to her left and saw the orange light. 'I'm getting in either way – I've had a long enough day.'

She stepped out into the road, raising her right arm while tucking her handbag more securely under her left. The cab stopped and she opened the door.

'Where to, darling?'

Annie sat there silently, looking steadily at Jim, who in turn looked at Russ.

'I'll go with him,' said Jim quietly. 'I don't mind.'

Perhaps it was just because Russ could no longer hold Robbie's weight, but he nodded.

'Pimlico, please,' Annie said, as Russ pushed Robbie onto the back seat and Jim climbed in after him. Annie moved to the backward-facing seat so that Robbie could lie down. 'All three of us.'

October 1959

ANNIE WAKES JUST AFTER five. Her neck is stiff and when she lifts her head, she feels a pinch at the base of her skull. She slips from the nest of rough warmth and into the cold air, her dressing gown crossed tightly around her. She pauses for a moment outside Rita's door, listening for any movement. She can hear breathing clearly. Rita is still asleep. She can almost see it, the mussed golden head on the pillow

She hurries to the little kitchen, striking a match to light the gas ring and setting the kettle over the flame. Her hands are steady as she spoons tea into the pot.

She's pretty sure that she knows what to expect from the coming day; she's seen mental wards before. She reminds herself that this was what she wanted – or rather, that this was what she chose. There's a sort of prestige attached to Fairlie Hall – of a type that only those in the mental profession recognise. And of the options that have come her way, it is still the mental profession that fills her least with dread.

After finding the hand in the vegetable patch, blood had started to bother Annie. Yet her desire to become a nurse had only grown. Her little brother was enlisted again. For hours, it seemed, he would wriggle and complain, insisting that she was hurting him with the slightest touch. But finally Eddie would 'settle', an old tablecloth tucked around him, and then a great sense of wellbeing would wash over Annie, as if some unbearably restless impulse had been wrung out of her.

By the time she was eight Eddie had started to propose gory alternatives to her suggestion that he was simply 'poorly' ('Look, that Jerry bomb got my leg off!'). Annie said no, and then eventually they'd reached an age where he preferred to run around with the other boys in the street and climb on the rubble, picking up real cuts and bruises. By that point, Annie had started to notice how much help their mother needed, and imaginary nursing had to take a back seat.

Beginning menstruation had been very hard on Annie. The first jammy stains in her knickers were followed by the sordid terror of the sanitary belt. The only relief came in the form of douches and perfumes. Annie could almost convince herself, every month, that the awful thing was banished forever. Yet nurse training, what with the white uniform, had brought the fear back into the foreground. For the past year she has not left the Ladies without checking the back of her skirt.

On one of Annie's first days on the ward she'd seen an amputated foot. Diabetes. The idea of amputation itself didn't distress her; she understood the mechanics of the thing. Scalpel, bone saw, cauterisation. But somehow the blood had not occurred to her. The foot in the kidney bowl looked like a plucked bird – swollen and pallid, sitting in a nest of bloody gauze. Annie had stood there for a long time with her hand pressed over her mouth, staring at the blank wall above the sink. It wasn't so much fear that she was experiencing, but rather a terrible, dizzying emptiness – a sense that she would soon fall and never be able to right herself.

You'll get over it, she told herself sharply. But although there was no particular emotion that she could identify, the sight of the blood seemed to strip away her age and vocation. Her hands would start to shake, and she became childish and dumb.

Eventually it became clear to Annie that general nursing was simply not going to work. In hospitals there were industrial qualities of the dreadful stuff, passed to her in sluice buckets, spattered recklessly across uniforms, smeared over tiled floors. And it was supposed to be her trick to make it disappear. Yet mopping only seemed to spread the blood further, to press it into the cracks and grouting from where it might never truly be banished. Surgical nursing, therefore, was out of the question. So was anything to do with the recovery of wounds. People would often suggest obstetrics, as if there were something innately soft and gentle about that. Annie would press her knees together and shake her head silently.

Then someone had given her a pamphlet about mental nursing. All those pictures of clean, white coats; it occurred to Annie that the mind was far safer than the body. Not many people wanted to be mental nurses, but stigma had never bothered her. Growing up around her mother, she

43

had established to her own satisfaction that madness was not catching.

There was still some amount of blood in mental nursing, but it was a quantity that Annie felt she could manage. The syllabus had hinted at perhaps the occasional wound – a bite, the pinprick of an injection, a patient seizing the opportunity to dash their head against the wall. To prepare for this, Annie had trained herself to look at the blood set aside for transfusions, in its many rows of square, regular packets. Stacked on a shelf, the pouches didn't look so very different to a large quantity of anything else. The liquid was dark enough that if she narrowed her eyes she could tell herself that it was black.

She goes to a great effort to arrange her dark hair in the correct little row of curls in front of her cap. She struggles for a while with the starched apron, looking critically at herself in the mirror. She wonders if they'll be able to see it, the patients. The way that, despite her care, there's still something of the schoolgirl about her.

'Ready?'

Rita is standing in the doorway of Annie's little bedroom. She'd only emerged at twenty-five to six; Annie is trying not to be irritated. Rita's apron is pinned over her great chest, her eyes crinkled with childlike excitement. It's as if the two of them are off dancing. 'Come on!'

She holds a hand out towards Annie, who pauses for a moment. Then, with a smile, she hurries across the room to take it. Her laced shoes strike loudly on the floorboards, and the whole cottage creaks.

Outside, the air in the lane seems to sparkle with rain. The two girls huddle under their umbrella.

'Told you it was going to rain,' Rita says. 'Aren't you glad? That drought was starting to unnerve me.'

But she looks a little worried. It's a ten-minute walk through the grounds to Fairlie Hall itself.

'We could just walk a little faster,' Annie says doubtfully, glancing at her watch. 'Get out of the worst of it as quickly as we can.'

Either they hurry, she thinks, and risk spattering their snowy uniforms with mud, or they go slowly and carefully under the umbrella, letting the rain wilt the starch. Arriving late.

'If we're to be reprimanded either way,' Rita says, peering down the puddle-strewn lane, 'then we may as well get out of it as quickly as possible. Anyhow, isn't Dr Lewin supposed to be rather alternative? Maybe they won't be so silly about the little things.' Annie can tell that Rita doesn't really believe this. She looks at her watch. 'Come on.'

So they run. Their laced shoes splash in the puddles; the rain sings against the black umbrella. Despite the puck of worry in her stomach, Annie can't help but be entranced by the emerald of the trees, the shimmer of the downpour, the infusion of sunlight breaking over the distant hills. It's as if she can taste the green, hear the light, smell the rain. They run until they come into sight of Fairlie Hall, and then they both stop.

45

It's a grand house, ivy-clad. More beautiful than any that Annie has seen before. Yet looking at Fairlie Hall somehow gives her the sensation of falling. She grinds her heels into the wet earth, so as not to slip on the green, smooth, downward-sloping lawns.

The main front of the building is wide and graceful. But a Tudor wing, which Annie supposes must be the original building, sticks oddly out on one side. The darker brick and angular lines of the old wing's gables give the building a grim-faced look, as if some spectre is lurking just at its shoulder. There is no sign of any person, and every door that Annie can see is shut so firmly that it might have been shut forever. There is a sense of amplified gravity in this place, so strong that Annie is unsure whether she'll be able to uproot her feet from the wet grass. She feels something brush lightly against her arm and jumps. But it's only Rita's hand.

'Ramshackle sort of place, isn't it?' Rita narrows her eyes against the early morning light. 'I rather like it, don't you?'

Annie gives a little laugh, which she hopes will serve just as well as 'yes' and 'no'.

'I wonder if the mad appreciate it,' Rita continues. She smiles, and Annie smiles back. But looking at Fairlie Hall, she cannot understand how anyone could say that they liked it. There's something in the way that it crouches, with its back to the horizon, that unsettles Annie, makes the nylon of her stockings itch and the seams of her uniform chafe.

'We'll be late if we don't get on,' Annie says. Rita shrugs, as if she doesn't much care. She's looking at the Hall in a way that Annie doesn't understand. She remembers how little the two of them know each other. But then Rita turns back to Annie, and her wide smile is restored. 'Ready?'

Annie nods. Rita sets off down the slope of the lawn. For a moment she seems on the verge of slipping – teetering for a second, then righting herself. Then she turns, and calls over her shoulder, 'Keep up, Annie!'

October 1983

ANNIE COULD SEE WHAT Jim was thinking, when the taxi pulled up in Cumberland Street. Funny sort of place. Everyone thought that the first time they came into the Grid. Houses that ought to be beautiful, only many of them were grey rather than white and had a haggard look to them. What sort of eccentric, he was probably thinking, was this woman who'd offered refuge to Robbie? She could see him glancing at her dress, perhaps wondering if she was just doing a good job of disguising some secret wealth.

Even people who knew London well never came to Pimlico – it wasn't on the way to anywhere. Annie had never been here herself, until just before she bought the house.

She and Rosie had gone together to the lawyers' office in Victoria, to talk about the payout from George's company after his death. Annie had felt awkward, unsure if she ought to smile when she accepted condolences, sheafs of paper for signature, cup after cup of tea. How exactly should a widow be, she had wondered? But no one seemed very interested in her demeanour. She'd been a mourner before, when her mother died. There hadn't really been pain then, only a strange and shapeless numbness that was equal parts freedom and loss. Eddie had stood at her side and he'd been a stranger, but that hadn't mattered, because in the pew beside her, his grip firm on her arm, had been George.

And now he was gone. The world was full of so many things – solicitor's letters and settlements and insurances and apologetic smiles – so many things, so many people, and none of them were him.

The awkwardness of the whole situation had given Annie a kind of physical cramp, and she'd suggested to Rosie that, since it was such a nice day – perhaps the last day of summer – they might as well walk home. It was what George would have suggested, and Annie could tell from the way that her daughter agreed that Rosie knew that too.

They found themselves in a strange little grid of streets, crisscrossing each other like the hedges of a maze, with the facades of the houses warmed by blood-red geraniums in window boxes.

'It's like the houses in *Mary Poppins*,' Rosie had said, and Annie had agreed. She thought of the blonde, pretty, silly mother in the film, all full of righteousness at her cause, without having the least idea of what was going on with her own children. And then she thought of Julie Andrews, with those enormous blue eyes.

Buying the house was the first time in her life that Annie had ever made a large decision all by herself. It had been George who had decided that they would get married – he'd proposed, she'd agreed. And, despite what Rita had long been saying about the pill, Annie had never thought of herself as making a decision when it came to having a baby. Rosie just happened; Annie no more chose to have her than she chose, from moment to moment, for her own heart to beat.

And then of course, there was George's death, which made the whole idea of choices feel irrelevant, almost ridiculous.

She had been cleaning the kitchen floor when it happened. She'd realised that later, when they gave her enough information to work out the time of death. There had been an instant, as the dirt was washed away from the tiles, when every atom in her world had been jolted out of place, never to be restored again, and she'd had no idea.

There was the call from his office, his boss's shaking voice. Annie had known immediately, though she had no memory of hearing the words. She had poured the dirty water from the bucket and put the mop away before setting off for the hospital. She did not remember how she got there. She'd signed all the papers, the legal admissions of her husband's death, and walked home alone. She'd been trembling with a new, shapeless shame. How could she have missed her cue so catastrophically? How, when she'd seen George off that morning, had she not said a proper goodbye?

He'd been killed instantly, a falling iron beam. A bolt from the blue, the site manager said, as he handed over George's wallet, his wedding ring, his house keys. Would she feel any less shattered, Annie wondered, if he'd faded away over the course of a few hours? If she'd held his hand in the hospital? There was no way to know. But to her, in those moments, anything seemed better than a departure without a farewell. At home she'd sat at the kitchen table, at a loss. She wasn't the type to miss anything, not a loose button. How could she have missed this?

Then the front door was opening. Rosie was clattering about, making instant coffee – a new affectation – and toast, putting the telly on. It was only then that she called out to Annie. Annie had gone and stood in the doorway, watching her daughter absorbed in *Grange Hill*, a smear of jam on her cheek already.

Just wait, Annie told herself. Wait until the end of the episode.

One programme became two, and before Annie knew it she was cooking dinner for the both of them. It wasn't unusual for George to work late, so Rosie saw nothing alarming in the two glasses, two plates, two sets of cutlery that Annie set out. Getting through dinner wasn't so difficult – she just asked Rosie about her day and nodded as her daughter raged on about her chemistry teacher. Rosie wasn't the type to question it when her mother produced Sara Lee from the freezer. Then it was tea and *Coronation Street*. It was odd, watching it without George doing his Deirdre Barlow impression.

It was July. A long summer's day. I'll tell her when the sun goes down, Annie told herself.

Did it help, giving Rosie those last few hours of normality before sitting on the edge of her bed and telling her there'd been an accident? No, Annie wasn't sure that it had helped, at least not in the long term. But she couldn't quite believe that it had done any harm. She did not remember saying the words to Rosie, just sitting on the end of her bed and not knowing if or how to hold her.

It didn't feel possible to carry on living in that house. She could not begin to think about the house as her own when for so long it had been theirs. When the lawyers told Annie about the payout, it all fitted together. The house in Pimlico cost twice as much as the terraced place in Battersea. But Annie could afford it. She didn't have a husband anymore, but she could have this, this black and white house that seemed to fit her like a second skin. And, she reasoned, she could let out all the spare rooms. Make a nice little income to support herself and Rosie, to supplement George's life insurance.

And now here was Robbie.

Jim had a struggle, getting him up the couple of steps and through the door. He had paused in the hallway, red-faced, Robbie's arm braced over his shoulders. Annie thought that she ought to help, but she was unsure whether it would be wise to touch this boy. There was Rosie to consider, after all.

She beckoned Jim through into the living room, where Robbie fell limply onto the sofa. His enormous feet stuck out over the arm of the sofa.

'Tea.' Annie hurried through into the kitchen and slapped the kettle into life. She filled the teapot – she mostly used bags herself, having little call to make tea for company. But she could well remember the German Ward

Sister on her first rotation of general nursing college. Sister Schneider had embraced certain aspects of English life wholeheartedly; she'd sooner have died than allow anything but proper loose-leaf tea on her ward.

'Oh,' mumbled Jim, when she pressed the cup into his hands. Now that Annie could see him properly in the lamplight, it was obvious that he'd had his fair share to drink that evening. Relieved of Robbie's weight, a fuzziness seemed to be overtaking him.

'You need your strength,' said Annie. A kindly firmness was coming to her, or rather coming back. It felt so different without Matron breathing down her neck. Easier to think clearly. She poured out three cups into her nice pink and white china, and added milk. 'Does he take sugar?'

'Sugar?' Jim looked blank. 'No idea. Don't think I've ever seen him drink anything weaker than . . . Robbie?'

The boy was shifting, a slight noise emerging from his mouth, like wind through an old, ill-fitting windowpane. He was still very pale, though Annie wondered if there wasn't a little colour coming back into his cheeks.

'Four sugars,' Robbie mumbled.

'Not on your life.' Annie added a teaspoon of sugar to the cup and stirred, placing it gently in its saucer on the coffee table. 'You'll ruin your teeth.'

For the first time the boy smiled, and Annie saw behind the parched lips there was indeed a row of beautiful white teeth. A movie-star smile, she thought, strange in the face of this boy. This boy who looked like he was every age, from baby to old man.

'Knew it,' she murmured, taking the cup from the table and placing it gently in his hand. 'You're a heartbreaker.'

She heard a slight noise, and looked around. Jim was holding very tightly to the back of one of her armchairs.

'Let's get you into some pyjamas,' she said. She could see that the edges of the sequinned vest had made a row of purple impressions along Robbie's skin all around the armholes, like the bite of dozens of little teeth. His skin would be fragile, and there were infections to think of.

She found a pair of George's old pyjamas in the chest of drawers in her bedroom. She'd been so quick to get rid of all his things in the wardrobe – the overcoats, the suits, the shirts, the mackintosh. But somehow the drawers had been overlooked, and when it came to moving she'd just packed them up along with everything else. These pyjamas were old – he'd had them for years. But he looked after things well and he'd never had the chance to go to fat. Nonetheless, Annie was sure that she could have fitted two of Robbie inside the trousers.

'Pop those on him, why don't you?' She tossed the pyjamas the two or three feet to where Jim stood. He seemed to catch them on reflex, then stayed still, looking blankly down at his lapful of cotton. After a moment he nodded and went over to the sofa.

'Come on Robbie, give me a hand, will you?'

Robbie did not respond, but there was a sliver of brightness between the thick dark lines of his eyelashes, so Annie thought that he was probably awake.

'He'll be much more comfortable once he's changed,' she said firmly. 'Go on.'

Jim took hold of Robbie's wrist and made to pull him into a sitting position. Robbie made a little groaning sound, and Jim stepped back, looking terrified, and a little frustrated.

'What do I do? Just stuff him into them?' His voice hardened slightly. 'He needs to just let me sort him out. Robbie . . .'

Annie remembered those first days on the ward, when she'd had to do the same with all those emaciated old men.

'Just be gentle,' she said.

October, 1959

TILES, CRACKED BUT POLISHED. A pair of feet on the floor. The shoes are solid, ugly and unyielding, but buffed to such a bright shine that they possess a kind of grotesque beauty. The ankles stick out from the heavy shoes, skinny as a little girl's. They do not curve into calf before being swallowed up by a great expanse of starched skirt.

'New trainees,' Matron says coolly. 'Good morning.'

Annie leaves it to Rita to introduce them both. She forces herself to take her eyes off the floor and look at the Matron's face. When she does, she's struck by the thought that it resembles a single long, white bone. Not a skull, like the one they were briefly permitted to handle in the first term of nursing college. Something more featureless. A tibia, perhaps. Matron has eyes like chips of black ice, features that might be beautiful if they weren't so colourless. A mouth, surprisingly soft-looking, round and shell-pink.

There is a stretched-out moment of silence as the cold black eyes drop to the floor. It seems to take forever for them to inch up Annie's body, inspecting shoes, stockings, apron, flicking up to the cap before finally resting on her face. Matron does not exactly make eye contact, but rather seems to look straight through Annie as though she were a ghost.

'Nurse Graie,' she says. Annie is surprised. She hasn't told Matron her surname, and wasn't expecting her to pronounce it correctly. Like the colour, she always told people. Most got it wrong at first. 'I cannot fathom ...' Here Matron leaves a pause, sucking in a breath. Then she begins again. 'I cannot *conceive* how you could possibly consider it appropriate to report for your first day on my ward covered in mud.'

Annie looks down to her ankles, and sees three drops of dark, muddied water, standing stark against the beige sheen of her nylon stocking.

Annie glances over at Rita's shoes and stockings. By some miracle – it certainly wasn't care – they look no different to when the two of them set off this morning. The patent leather is slightly cracked where the feet spill wide, but nonetheless they are polished to a decent shine.

'I'm very sorry, Matron.' Annie is aiming for a tone that sounds at once humble and professional, and suspects that she has achieved neither. But Matron does not seem interested in hearing her. She turns on her own polished heel and sets off at a swift pace, her footsteps ringing and her voice carrying over her shoulder.

'A place like this can rapidly descend into chaos, you know.'

'Yes, Matron,' Rita replies. Annie realises that she has missed her cue, and moves her lips soundlessly in the affirmative. Rita gives Annie a side look, pulling a little face.

'Chaos is the enemy of hygiene,' Matron continues. Her words bounce off the stone walls.

'Yes, Matron,' Rita says again. There's something in her voice that Annie is sure is not intended – just the edge of a smile. Annie does not dare to look at Rita, nor does she ask herself what will happen next, where she is expecting Matron to lead them. But whatever she's expecting, it isn't to go through a heavy door and into a stone courtyard. It's surrounded by sheer windowless walls that scale up into a distant square of grey sky.

'One of the airing courts,' Matron says over her shoulder. 'For the patients.'

Annie does her best not to shiver, even though the day is hardly cold. The rain has stopped falling, yet the air feels waterlogged. Matron marches to the centre of the little court and glares at Annie, as if expecting her to know what she is supposed to do next. Annie takes a single, confident step forwards, hoping that the action in itself will offer her some kind of clarity. Growing up with her mother has meant that Annie is usually rather good at understanding the unsaid, but that intuition has deserted her now. She stands there foolishly, waiting for instructions.

'Well?'

It sounds like a question, but Annie instinctively knows better. She looks around the courtyard. On all sides the walls lurch close, to every appearance upright and yet giving Annie a terrible, inexplicable sense that they might collapse inward, burying the three of them alive.

Yet, through some steely will that she did not truly know she possessed, she manages to focus. She sees that on one crumbling, dark brick wall there is an iron tap, heavy-looking and braced with rust. Matron's eyes are fixed on it, and finally Annie understands. She must wash her stocking. Yes, she sees now.

She hurries across the courtyard, hoping that her brisk movement suggests more assurance than she feels. She glances back at Matron, hoping for some affirmation. But the pale face remains impassive. Annie tries to turn the tap with her right hand, but the thing clearly hasn't been used in a long time and remains very stiff. The metal seems so much chillier than the mild day.

Annie tries again to turn the head. Her whole wrist seizes up, a sharp protest that shoots up her arm. She enlists her left hand. The cold metal bites and resists – but then at last, with a violent shove, the tap turns. Chill water spurts out. It floods over and into Annie's shoes. She holds her dirty foot under the icy cascade for as long as she can bear. Then, with a jerking motion, she shuts off the tap. With trembling hands she bends to sluice the worst of the water off.

The nod of the white face is almost imperceptible. It's only by the way that Matron turns and starts back towards the door that Annie understands that the ordeal is over. That she has, in some way, passed. Still, she does not look at Rita.

April, 2020

'I JUST CAN'T SWITCH off from it,' Rosie says. I hold the phone to my ear with one hand while using the other to ease the weeds from the earth. I nod, even though she can't see me. 'I can't stop reading the news, can you? I lie awake at night in this weird fugue state. It's like if I can just focus on it long enough then I'll come up with a solution and everything will go back to normal.'

I don't know what she's expecting me to say. All I know is what's on the news. They say it came from a wet market in a place called Wuhan. I've never heard of Wuhan, but apparently it's a city of more than eleven million. Geography was never my strong suit. They also say maybe something more sinister is going on. I can see why people like that idea. Who can trust the Chinese government? In the Eighties, some of my boys were convinced that it was the CIA that made them ill.

'Necropolitics,' Jim says on the phone, later on. 'Every government makes decisions about who it's all right to kill. Who's disposable.'

'I don't know that they sit down in a meeting and make a list,' I say. Not that I'm keen on this bunch of clowns. But still.

'They don't need to make a list. You remember what it was like. You know what it's still like. Just because it's not here doesn't mean people aren't still dying. More and more every year. South Africa. Nigeria. They've just decided to let it happen.'

I could tell him that he sounds paranoid. It might even make me feel better. But he isn't wrong.

I used to ring Jim about once a week. It was never for long chats – just to arrange a meetup. We've never been very creative about it – we meet at the Tate Britain for a look at the Henry Moores and the Turners and the Rothkos, then we have a cup of tea in the Members' Room. It sounds repetitive. It is. But we like it.

Since all this started Jim and I have talked nearly every day. He sends me a text message to let me know it's time to make myself a gin and tonic, then we settle down for a chat. Rosie keeps telling me we should do video calls instead. I tell her that after thirty-six years I know what Jim looks like. We talk on the phone, sometimes staying on to watch the News at Ten together.

He rang me as soon as we had the first cases here, wanting to know if there was anything in particular he ought to be doing. I think he only asked me out of habit. I didn't have a clue. But we're good at not knowing things together, Jim and me.

'It's the same bloody thing again,' I say at one point, when the despair hits.

'It's never quite the same thing twice,' Jim reminds me. That was what I'd said to him, only the night before. We used to say it a lot when someone got their diagnosis. *It's never quite the same thing twice.* You never know for sure how it's going to turn out. After all, we know more every day, we'd say. And there's surely a vaccine coming just around the corner.

We used to tell each other: tomorrow might offer what today failed to bring. You can live for years that way. Even when you reckon the writing is on the wall. We'd say, maybe it won't be as bad as all that.

Maybe he'll live.

Or maybe he'll go peacefully.

It feels like cruelty, that sort of hope. Cruelty to ourselves, but mostly cruelty to the suffering person. We can't quite bring ourselves to suffer alongside them.

'Oh, I'm not talking about the dying,' Jim says. His voice is light. 'They didn't care about that then. They don't care about it now. You don't matter, get to the back of the queue.'

'We're elderly, Jim. I reckon when the cure comes along, we'll be the first to get it.'

'You might be elderly, Aunty Nan, but I'm bloody not.' Jim's voice has its old steel. 'And if they're only bothered about me because I'm old then well, that just proves my point, doesn't it? We'll get round to sorting you out. You brought this on yourself. Know your place. All that old rubbish.'

I look out of the window. Someone's getting their shopping delivered. Each item is removed from the delivery crate by a woman wearing winter gloves. She douses it in kitchen cleaner before passing it to her husband. At the bottom of the porch steps stands a delivery driver in a high-vis vest, who looks unhappy.

'Do you remember how they used to say it was caused by poppers?'

Jim laughs. That little surprised laugh when you open a drawer in your mind and find a memory there, untouched by the decades.

'God, yeah. That wasn't even the worst of it, was it? They basically said it was just too much sex. That we'd just sort of overdone it, that the body shuts down from all that fucking.'

'We knew nothing then. Less than nothing.'

'Knew who to blame, didn't they? Then the haemo-philiac kids started getting ill. Everyone decided it was a problem after all.'

'I always think about their mothers,' I say.

'What about them?'

'Well, they were the ones administering the infusions to their kids, weren't they?' The big medical innovation. You could treat the child at home, no need for doctors. 'They thought they were doing the right thing. And then their children died.'

'Lots of people died, Nan.' Jim pauses. 'I'm not saying it wasn't sad though. About the kids.'

'I know you're not.' I don't really know what I'm getting at. 'I'm just saying. I think about those mothers all the time.'

Jim doesn't reply to this. I don't think he's keen on this line of thought, but I carry on regardless. 'Easiest thing in the world, isn't it? Blaming mothers.'

At Fairlie Hall they said homosexuality was caused by overattentive mothers. Or mothers who weren't attentive enough. Mothers who stifled, mothers who sucked the life from their sons, mothers who might as well have been made of stone.

I look across the road. The woman is still disinfecting her shopping. The delivery driver now looks furious, but she meets his eyes and I can see the defiance.

October, 1959

THERE'S NO ONE ON the ward. At least, no one that Annie can see. No one crying, no one screaming, no one running around, loose from their straitjacket. No people at all.

Instead, stretching away and blurring into the distant ebony panelling, is row after row of skeletal iron bedsteads. For a second, in the gloom, Annie's eyes fall out of focus; the rows seem to tilt sharply to one side. But then she blinks. The world rights itself. She's following Matron down the aisle between the bedsteads, Rita's footsteps reassuring behind her.

Now, in motion, she can perceive small movements emerging here and there.

Grey-white faces – slowly, like cogs in an abandoned machine – turning to look at her. Dry mouths, opening to release soft groans. Spiderling hands, grasping covers, clawing at blankets, as if longing to rip them into ribbons.

'This is the geriatric ward,' Matron says. Her voice is the same volume as before. There is no concession to the faces on the pillows, still slack with sleep. Yet the sound here is muffled. Perhaps it's all the bedding, or the enormous tapestry that runs the length of one wall.

The unstirred air. Something seems to absorb the sound of her voice. 'This will be your first rotation.'

Annie distantly hears a cheery noise of assent from Rita.

'Fifty male patients,' Matron is saying. 'You'll need to get them washed, dressed and shaved.'

'All of them?' Annie thought she had just whispered the words to herself. But Matron hears.

'Of course, all of them.' Matron's eyes sweep the floor, linger over the walls, travel up the length of the heavy curtains. 'The ward requires cleaning. You won't be able to do that until they've all had breakfast and gone to occupational therapy. Ah . . .' Annie hears light footsteps coming up the ward. 'Anthony will be able to assist you.'

Annie, feeling that she has composed herself, turns to look at Anthony. She gives a quick, directionless smile and looks away. She has seen blacks before, in Manchester, but never this close. The darkness of Anthony's face and eyes make her feel ghostly, as if she barely exists.

Matron demonstrates, on a patient who is still mostly asleep – how to do the shaving. The steam unfurls from the basin, the shaving soap feather-soft as she spreads it across his face. He seems to respond to her lightest touch, turning his face this way and that.

'Just be gentle,' Matron says. Her voice is different. But when she turns back to Annie and Rita and gives a nod, her movements are restored to their jerky manner. Then she leaves.

Anthony leads Annie and Rita down the ward. He speaks softly and continuously, gesturing lightly towards the rows of beds on either side. He seems to know each indistinguishable face by name, and greets them as they slip or jerk into wakefulness. Annie doesn't understand most of what he's saying, and she doesn't look at the occupants of the beds. Instead she focuses above them, at the heavy panelling which seems to absorb all sound. Something in the stifled quality of the air feels almost familiar, reminds her of home.

The idea that it is Anthony who is assisting Annie and Rita proves ridiculous. There was nothing in any of their training for this, Annie thinks, standing dumbly by as Anthony summons basin and razor from some unseen place and seems to shave an old man's papery face with three swift strokes. His careful movements make the touch of the blade look tender.

'There.' Now that Annie has had chance to absorb the cadences of his speech for a few minutes, his words are beginning to take shape through the accent. 'Now you are a smart man again.'

The patient nods, and Annie sees that Anthony is right. Much of the grey that had cast his expression into shadow is gone. There is a flush to his cheeks from the razor, and the water adds shine and dimension to the dull face. His eyes seem brighter too – although perhaps that's simply because the sun has started to peer through the window and illuminate the ward.

Anthony tries to get Annie and Rita to shave some of the patients. 'There's no secret,' he says. Rita takes to it with some success – her touch is confident and friendly, her chatter continuous. But Annie nicks half a dozen

67

cheeks. Some of the patients scream with fury when she cuts them. She shrinks back, razor still in hand. The blood of old men, she sees, is no different to any other sort of blood. Just as red.

'Bitch,' one of them says, before she's even laid the razor against his cheek – a cheek more purple than pink. 'Bitch bitch bitch.' He smiles and looks her straight in the eye. 'Slut.'

The razor hangs in the air, then Anthony steps forwards to take it from Annie. 'Come on, Ronnie. Don't be silly.' Ronnie, who is a big man, looks down at the hand holding the blade. Then he turns his face away with a look of radioactive contempt.

'Don't worry too much about Ronnie,' Anthony mutters as they move down the ward. 'None of us do.'

It takes two and a half hours.

'You will get quicker.' Anthony seems to mostly be addressing Rita. 'You will learn. You'll see. No need to worry.'

As the patients file out of the ward, Anthony shepherding them towards the breakfast hall, one turns his face to Annie. His eyes seem to focus.

'Oh, now you turn up, do you?' His voice is loud, the note of accusation giving it strength. 'Now you decide to visit your own father?'

Anthony steps in. 'Now Billy, that's the new nurse. That isn't your daughter.' He pauses, then adds, 'I believe your daughter is planning to visit soon. Next month.'

The old man looks blankly from face to face. 'Next month?' This doesn't seem to be of any use to him. His gaze settles on Rita. 'Well, I suppose she won't be any less of a pain in the arse in a month, will she?'

Rita laughs. The laugh seems to break through the stifling air of the ward. It rings off the floors, the windows, the walls. The patient shuffles away. After a few moments, Annie cannot tell which grey-shirted back belongs to him.

October, 1983

ANNIE HEARD JIM'S TREAD on the stairs and knew that Robbie must be asleep.

She was standing by the sink with the carbolic soap in her hand. She looked over to the coffee table where Robbie's untouched, sugar-laced cup of tea sat cold, and tried to remember if she had a fresh pair of Marigolds under the sink. Somehow the thought of checking was beyond her.

When Jim came in she jumped slightly. She wasn't used to having a man around, not in this house. She could see the apologetic look on his face, as if he'd abruptly remembered that they were strangers.

'Tea?' She made the offer before Jim could open his mouth.

He paused for a second. 'Don't have anything stronger, do you?'

Annie looked over to the Welsh dresser, where George's whisky stood. He hadn't been a big drinker, but there'd been evenings when he'd come through the door and given her a certain exhausted smile, and there had been a little glow inside her from the thought that she knew exactly what he needed. She'd brought the decanter over from the old house and filled it from the bottle. No sense in wasting it, she'd told herself.

'I don't think it's anything fancy,' she said, finding one of the old cut-crystal tumblers at the back of a cabinet. She paused, then placed the tumbler by the decanter, gesturing that he was to help himself.

'I'm nothing fancy,' Jim replied, pouring out a measure. Annie suspected that this wasn't quite true – there was something rather cultured about Jim. She realised that he was holding the tumbler out to her. His grip was loose and careless, and she feared that if she didn't take the thing it might crash and splinter on the floor. She took it. Jim unhooked a mug from the dresser. He poured whisky into it – Annie could not see how much, but from the glugging sound it seemed like a fair amount.

Annie looked down at the tumbler, thinking of George's fingers clasped around it.

'How long's he been poorly?' She spoke in an undertone, though she knew no sound would carry in this house. Jim shrugged.

'I don't know really.' He sighed. 'He had this funny bug a few months ago – temperature, really weak, couldn't do much at all – but then he bounced back. Obviously. He's twenty-three. It's what they do.'

Annie nodded. She knew that there were half a dozen or so questions that it would make sense to ask. 'And you said he'd lost weight.'

Jim hesitated. 'You said you were a nurse, didn't you?'

Annie paused, then shrugged. 'I am. In a manner of speaking.'

'But you've seen all sorts of sickness?'

'I have.'

'Right.' He unfolded his arms, and spoke to the floor. 'So what I've been wondering is . . . well, we can't ask the GP, he's a homophobic old sod – he doesn't have a clue – but . . . but I don't think it can be the thing they've got in America, do you?'

'I couldn't really say.'

'They say it's like a cancer, don't they? This is much more of a stomach thing, so I don't think it can be that – do you?'

'Cancer can look like all sorts of things,' Annie said, reaching back through twenty-five years to rifle through her oncology notes from general nursing. They'd only spent two weeks on it. 'I wouldn't like to say.'

'I'm pretty sure. I mean, I've checked him all over, and there's no . . .' Jim paused, his lips tightening. 'Well, he's got no fat on him. I know he's really thin now but he's always been thin. Little swine.' He forced a laugh. 'If there was a lump or anything I would have found it.'

'Yes.'

'So . . .' He was looking at her expectantly. She had no idea what it was that he wanted her to say. So she just said again what she hoped he already knew.

'He can stay here.'

Jim nodded and drank some of his whisky. Then he walked over to the back door and looked out into the garden. Annie's garden, though she hadn't been able to bring herself to tackle it yet – that had been George's department. There wasn't much there but a tangle of rose bushes, which had been neglected for so long by the previous owner that they stretched up into the sky. In the darkness the moonlight reflected off the last white petals.

'What do you think I should do?' Jim asked.

Annie looked down at the cake of carbolic soap, still held loosely in one hand.

'I think whatever you do, you'd be best off deciding in the morning,' she said at last. She tightened her hand on the soap, only to have it slide from her grasp and onto the floor. Jim bent to pick it up, and held it out to her.

'You're sure he can stay?' His eyes were dark, all shine. Annie nodded.

'It makes no sense, just me and my daughter, rattling around in this place. I really do need a lodger.'

She decided to let Jim stay too, just for one night, until Robbie was settled. She felt that she'd done a respectable enough job of implying that the sofa was comfortable. But if it was all as bad as Jim said then she didn't want to be worrying about it through the night. She'd need to be up and strong for Rosie, who'd be coming home in a day or two. Besides, it wasn't as if either of them were in any shape to get up to anything under her roof.

And perhaps, she thought as she finally settled down to sleep on her side of the bed, it wasn't actually like that. Robbie was a good deal younger than Jim, after all. Perhaps he was just looking out for the younger man. As anyone decent would.

October 1959

AFTER A DAY OR so, Annie starts to wonder if she's ended up working in an old people's home by mistake. Many of the patients are so elderly that it's impossible to tell whether they ever had their marbles.

Each day begins in the same manner as the first. Annie had assumed that the getting the patients dressed and undressed, the shaving and the shepherding, was just the first stage. That there would at some point be work that felt like *nursing*. But eventually she realises that the preparation is itself the task. In fact, shaving and dressing the patients is almost her sole interaction with them. First everyone must be set into order. Then, once the patients have been readied for the day, they are dispatched to the airing courts. Then the real work, of cleaning the ward, can begin.

The ward is always cold. This is partly because Matron believes in ventilation, though it somehow does little to help the odd, clinging quality of the air. Nor does it dispel the smell of aged flesh. Mainly, Annie discovers, the ward is cold because the windows do not fasten. Because of this, things are often blown over by sudden winds, or dampened and warped by blasts of rain. When Annie and Rita push the curtains open in the mornings the cold air breaks over them and the sunshine follows, slicking in like yellow fat and illuminating the dust particles in the greasy air.

Each patient has a bedside table, upon which he is allowed to place his possessions. A single framed photograph is permitted, so long as the glass has been removed. There are pictures of mothers with longing eyes, fathers with expressions like closed doors, sisters and wives. Most of all there are pictures of little boys in Victorian dresses – boys with long curls and milkswelled cheeks. The patients themselves – before they became what they are now.

There is scant space to clamber between the beds, although this is relatively little trouble for Annie, with her lithe figure. Rita, however, seems barely in control of her own extremities; she's forever knocking into bedsteads, causing them to clang into each other. She often treads on bed linen – usually dirty, but sometimes clean, meaning that it must be sent down to the laundry all over again. Jugs of flowers seem especially placed for Rita to knock over, with water and blossoms spilling across the ward floor and collapsing into a multicoloured slurry. When all these things happen, Rita is prone to whispered bouts of swearing. Yet it is Annie who somehow seems to always get caught at the wrong moments, who comes up lacking whenever Matron materialises on the ward.

It happens on the second day. A single white feather drifts across the buffed floor, pushed along by the icy breeze from the open window. Matron walks with slow, deliberate steps to the centre of the ward and picks up the feather, holding it delicately between thumb and forefinger.

'Do you know what this is, Nurse Graie?'

Her tone is so mild that Annie is caught off-guard. Can this be a real question?

'It's a feather.'

'I can see that. Where did it come from?'

The only response that Annie's brain offers is 'a goose'. She knows she cannot say this.

'I expect it's from one of the pillows, Matron.' It's Rita, interjecting from further up the ward. Matron turns slowly to Rita with a quelling look.

'It's a contaminant,' Matron says, speaking very softly. She turns back to Annie and holds the feather up to the light, softly tracing the fine fringe of down with one slender white finger. 'Do you know how much bacteria a single feather can hold?'

Annie nods. She once saw a feather under a microscope. Saw how the soft strands became gaunt and skeletal under the lens's exacting gaze. She thinks of sinister, undefinable masses of pathogens drifting there: the filth from living birds, smut from contaminated air, debris of human skin.

'See that it is taken care of.' Matron holds the feather out, and Annie allows it to drift into her own palm.

When Matron is gone, Rita squeezes Annie's arm and says, 'Don't let her worry you. It's all an act, I'm certain of it.'

77

Annie begins to see feathers everywhere. Under beds, caught in the piping below sinks, drifting out of reach at the tops of window frames. The more she sees, the more the feathers disgust her. She thinks of the geese themselves – squalling, cawing, covered in shit and dirty water. Do they have to kill the geese, she wonders, to get all those feathers? They must do. How could you make a business out of it otherwise?

On their third morning at Fairlie Hall, Annie and Rita are called away from the ward by Matron, just after they've finished getting the patients out of bed. Annie can feel ease starting to enter her movements. Indifference, too. Dressing, shaving, wiping, it's all beginning to feel the same to her. The patients have shuffled off to the mess hall for breakfast. Now, for a few hours, there is no drool to swab away, no unyielding limbs to lift, no blank stares to meet with a mechanical smile.

There is only the endless expanse of the ward floor: a great sheet of blue vinyl, beneath which one can feel the creak of ancient floorboards. Every morning, this vinyl floor must be swept, mopped, buffed to a bright shine.

'Nurse Blythe.'

There is a clatter as Rita fumbles her mop and it falls to the floor. The sound bounces the length of the ward.

'I'm so sorry, Matron . . .' she says. 'Yes, Matron?'

'Come with me.' Annie goes very still. Were Rita's trans- gressions seen after all? Is Matron taking her aside for

78

some particular unusual punishment? Then Matron adds, 'Nurse Graie, perhaps you'd better come along too.'

She leads them out of the ward and down a corridor, up one of the vertiginous staircases of the Tudor wing through a dusty attic. Annie walks gingerly, worried that the greasy dust might smear across her apron. They move down a thickset staircase, and into a part of the building that Annie has not seen before. A part that, looking from the outside, you wouldn't have even known existed. It's a small, densely-knotted jumble of modern rooms, all fluorescent lighting and asbestos boards. The rooms look as though they might have been put up temporarily in some moment of crisis – then no one ever thought to replace them.

Annie looks at Rita. Even that lovely complexion looks sallow in this light. Or is she simply tired? She sleeps no more than Annie does, after all, and Annie has never been so tired in her life.

Matron opens a small, grey-white door, which seems slightly sticky on its hinges. She indicates that Annie and Rita are supposed to enter.

'Do as you're instructed,' she says. Annie and Rita follow her gesture through the door, and she closes it behind them. The hinges give a faint cry. The door is thin, yet once it's shut any sound from the rest of the building is blocked out. They cannot hear Matron's footsteps as she walks away.

In the tiny room are several people standing around a gurney. A tall, broad-shouldered young doctor, swathed in the anonymity of his white coat. He's holding a set of notes, his back half-turned to the rest. On the other side of the gurney, facing Annie and Rita, is an enormous bald man – six foot four at least and very wide – wearing the uniform of an attendant. His face is clean and pink, a bruise on the colourless room. He gives Annie and Rita a smile; Annie smiles back, but from the corner of her eye she can see that Rita has turned away. Another attendant – a ferrety-looking young man – stands at the foot of the gurney, looking bored. And between them, lying on the gurney, is a patient.

It's a young woman, perhaps a little older than Annie, wearing a nightdress made of the same shapeless stuff as the old men's pyjamas. The patient is thin and very pale. She might resemble a corpse if her dark eyes weren't moving so quickly around the room. Annie wonders if she is having some sort of fit.

'Hello,' Rita says. It isn't clear whether she's expecting the doctor or the attendants to reply, but when Annie turns to look, she sees that Rita is addressing the patient. 'What's your name?'

'Never mind that.' The doctor appears to have come to the end of whatever notes he's reviewing, and glances up sharply. His eyes are black; they seem to lack the shine that brings most eyes to life.

'Hold her hand,' he says to Annie. It takes Annie a moment to understand, but then she steps forwards smartly and reaches out to take the woman's hand in her own. It's cool and slippery.

'No, no.' The doctor does not hide his irritation. 'Hold her hand. Hold it down, like this.' He pulls the patient's

80

hand from Annie's; it slips away. He adjusts the hand so the patient's arm is straight, and places his own palm flat on the patient's wrist, his other hand braced against her shoulder.

'Otherwise she'll flail,' he says. 'Go on.'

Annie waits for him to step back, then replaces his grip with her own. The patient's wrist feels fragile, as if it might crack under her weight. But then she feels the ligaments; they are as taut as steel.

The doctor, meanwhile, turns to Rita. He seems to examine her figure and find something to approve of in it. 'Now you – when she bucks you'll need to throw all your weight across her hips. Don't be deceived.' He glances carelessly down at the figure on the gurney. 'I know she looks pretty much wasted away, but there's plenty of fight in there. So – all your weight, you understand?'

Rita says nothing, but looks down at the patient. Not at the hips, where she has been instructed to direct her attention. At the face.

The doctor has wheeled a small trolley forwards from a corner and positioned it at the top of the gurney, behind the patient's head. The big attendant seems to respond to some unspoken cue, and swabs at the patient's temples with some foul-smelling stuff from a bottle. Something is slipped into the patient's mouth; she bites down. Annie can't tell whether this is a show of rage or just the reflex of an animal constrained. The smell of the swabbing stuff seems to engulf all Annie's other senses. She hears the metal plates being fastened to the patient's head. The big attendant is holding the head firmly between the two paddles in his hands, staring straight ahead.

The doctor says, 'Ready?'

For the first time he looks Annie properly in the eye. She nods. Rita is still staring down at the gurney; the doctor and the attendants operating on some shared, silent understanding.

'And . . .'

The single syllable hangs in the air, full of anticipation. Annie remembers her school choir master, the way he used to cue them in for a rendition of 'All Things Bright and Beautiful'. That moment of silence, braced for the force of sound.

Then the doctor presses a switch on the trolley.

The wrist beneath Annie's hand jerks demonically. Annie recoils, then remembers her task. She presses down – all her weight. She has realised that the doctor is right. Despite appearances, this fragment of a woman possesses a terrible, secret strength. If Annie fails in her task, if she does not continue to hold this patient down, hold her with every bit of mettle, some nameless, savage thing will be unleashed.

She only distantly hears Rita moving beside her.

Then the sound stops. All is still again, even lethargic. The figure on the bed is restored to her painful fragility. The only difference is that now her eyes have stopped moving. They are half-open, as if she's just come around from a long stupor. Annie knows that the whole thing only lasted a few seconds. How much could really have been achieved, for good or for harm, in just a few seconds?

She thinks of the exploding bomber plane. The moment of strange silence afterwards, as wreckage fell from the sky like snowflakes.

'How do you feel?'

For a second Annie is wrongfooted. Then she realises that the doctor is talking to the patient. She had assumed that there was no reason to speak to the creature on the gurney. That she was mute, or perhaps incapable of understanding speech.

But the patient sighs. 'Oh . . .' She pauses, the sound fading into nothing. She turns her head very slowly to one side. Then, after a long while, 'I'm all right, I suppose.' Her throat sounds dry. Annie looks around. No water. The patient's voice is much softer and more refined-sounding than Annie would have expected. There's a dreg in that voice of something that might once have been vivacity, honey-warmth. It's a voice that you'd expect from a teacher, or a lady on the radio.

'Excellent.' The young doctor's voice is hearty. He pats the patient on the shoulder. 'A few more rounds of treatment and I expect that we'll have made some good progress.' He glances at the big attendant. 'You can take her back now.'

October, 1983

FOR THAT FIRST WEEKEND she made soup, a big batch for when Rosie got home. When she was about to go out to the hospital to fetch her, Jim came downstairs, looking worried. He asked if he could use the washing machine. She came home that evening to find the kitchen decked out with drying bedsheets, white as clouds, draped over the chairs, the table, the dresser. For a moment she half expected to hear that first 'Hull-oh!', to see Rita's hand appearing through the sheets to grasp hers.

She brought Rosie back in a taxi. Learning to drive was one of those things that she'd always meant to get around to, but really there had been no need. George liked taking them around, shuttling her to tea with friends and Rosie to hockey on Saturdays. Before Rosie was born, and then when she was a baby, they'd gone on drives just for the sake of it, out to Box Hill or deep into Kent, to Whitstable and the sea.

She'd need to learn, she thought, sitting in the back of the taxi with all of Rosie's warm weight on her. Everything had changed – Rosie's illness made her see that. Getting her act together with the lodgers was just the beginning.

'We've got a lodger,' she told her daughter. She wasn't sure whether she heard – she just shifted against her shoulder. Perhaps she was asleep.

'It's good. Bit of extra money.'

Rosie had been the compromise that Annie had made, with George and with herself. She was sure that he would have been happy to have a house filled with children, but Annie couldn't face the idea of so much chaos. Childbirth had been hard on her, and she'd spent her pregnancy swollen with dread. All that blood.

Getting herself on the pill was as easy as falling asleep. It was funny, she always thought, how she had no memory of the pill coming into being. You never did, with these miracle drugs. They came into the world and shifted its every cell, yet no one really noticed. And of course, she couldn't have gone on it when it first came out anyway, because she wasn't married in those days.

And now they lived, Rosie and she, in this house with all these rooms, rooms that served no purpose. She'd got as far as buying bedsteads and mattresses, but no further. Before Rosie got home she'd asked Jim, as nicely as she could manage, if he could move Robbie up to the top floor. If he minded, he didn't say anything about it.

She'd made up Rosie's bed with sheets new from the packet, and scrubbed the bathroom until her hands were raw.

And even though Jim was back at work that week it was all easy enough. Soup for Rosie, soup for Robbie. Everything scrubbed. She told Jim that Robbie needed fresh air, that he ought to leave the room with the windows open. It was only on the Thursday of that first week, when she was chopping carrots for yet more soup, that she looked up to see Robbie standing in the doorway of the kitchen, carrying a pile of dirty plates and cups.

'Hullo,' he said, and she jumped.

It was partly that she hadn't been expecting to see him out of bed, and partly the way he greeted her, grinning like a favoured nephew.

'You all right?' Annie heard herself. She sounded snappish, she knew.

'Think I'm over the worst of it,' Robbie said. He was very pale, and looked a little unsteady on his feet. 'Nasty one, but I've thrown worse things off.' He laughed, a big laugh. 'Funny way to get myself a new landlady.'

He looked at her through thick lashes. He was the sort of person, Annie suspected, who was used to having a certain effect on people. She could feel something at her core softening at his smile. 'But I'm grateful. I needed a place and my old landlord – well, he wasn't so nice, in the end.'

'You're welcome to the room,' Annie said. She hesitated, and then added, 'Your friend – Jim – he's told you that, hasn't he?'

'He has.' Robbie gave his funny, feline little smile again. 'Thanks. I brought my stuff down.' He looked at the mess of cups and bowls in his big, slender hands. Annie nodded. There was something kittenish about him, his dark hooded eyes and the way he tilted his head to one side.

'Put them by the sink, would you?'

She pulled on another pair of Marigolds from the stash that she had accumulated.

'My mum hates it when I've got dirty cups in my room,' Robbie said. 'Drives her mad. I feel bad, I don't want to annoy her. But I just forget.'

Annie wasn't sure how she ought to reply.

He was wearing thick tracksuit bottoms and any number of jumpers. Jim must have brought them for him. The bulk of the added fabric just made the painful thinness of his wrists even starker.

'You cold up there?'

He shrugged.

'I can shut the windows if you're cold.'

'It's your house. Up to you how you like it. Do you mind me making a cuppa?' He turned to look at Annie, and at once he was shy. 'I haven't really had chance to talk to you properly, but you've been so nice to me and I thought it was stupid to lie in bed waiting for you to offer me one when I could just as well make it for myself. I can give you some money for teabags and milk and . . .' His face seemed to fall as a list unfurled in his mind. 'And electricity, and water . . . Jim didn't tell me what rent you wanted. I'm really sorry.'

'Don't worry about that now.' Annie took a seat at the kitchen table. Then she did something that she would never normally have done – slipping her feet out of her court shoes and putting them up on the seat of the opposite dining chair.

87

'You're tired.' Robbie's face seemed to reanimate. 'Let me make you a cuppa. I'm a good tea-maker. One of my talents.'

Annie hesitated when he put the mug in front of her. But after a few moments, she took a sip.

They sat at the kitchen table together, talking, for a couple of hours. Annie turned on the radio in case they slipped into silence, but the songs just blurred into a background hum. It was the kind of conversation that Annie hadn't had in a long time, that had no particular direction of travel or information to convey. It constantly seemed in threat of petering out – after all, what should they have to say to each other? Yet every time silence threatened Robbie seemed to let another thought drift out – about his mum's roast dinner, about the unfolding plot lines on *Coronation Street*, about the handful of Cs he'd scraped for his A Levels. Annie had to glance at the clock when Rosie came in, astonished that so much time had passed.

Rosie went over to the kettle without saying hello and busied herself with the Nescafé Gold. The coffee was her affectation, her way of asserting difference. Annie didn't like the stale smell that it brought to her daughter's breath, but thought it was best to say nothing.

'Aren't you going to offer one to Robbie?'

Rosie turned quickly to Robbie, long enough for Annie to see the blush infusing her still-pale cheeks. Her hair – dark, like Annie's – had been cut short. Another of her new assertions of independence. It left her face looking terribly exposed, Annie thought, and anxiety surged at the back of her throat. Rosie didn't know, of course. Why should she? She was thirteen.

'I'd love one,' Robbie said, sparing Rosie the need to speak. Annie saw a flicker of something in his dark eyes. 'Lots of milk, please. And sugar.'

Annie swallowed the warning – that it would do his stomach no good. A warmth seemed to have filled the kitchen, emanating from Robbie; some undefinable kindness was being offered out. Rosie was clattering about with mugs and spoons, a little more life in her movements than Annie had seen in a while.

A new song came on the radio. 'Turn that up, will you?' Robbie turned the full force of his smile onto Rosie and she blushed again. For a moment it seemed that both speech and movement were beyond her, but then her fingers crept towards the radio dial, seemingly of their own accord.

By the time Annie left the kitchen five minutes later they were singing along to the band that Rosie liked, the one with the silly name, both of them at the top of their lungs, hands caressing the air in mirror image and seeming to leave it shimmering. Robbie's voice was horribly off-key, yet it filled the room and made it warmer, brighter. Rosie's cheeks were still flushed, but now it was with a kind of fresh, glowing pleasure.

In the hallway Annie had to bite down on the back of her hand. The sob inside her had reared up from nowhere, part gaping loss, part fierce joy at seeing Rosie's smile.

October, 1959

Annie and Rita make their way back to their usual ward in silence. It takes a few attempts – they make it as far as the thick, squat staircase, only to make a wrong turning in the Tudor wing and come out into an empty, panelled room that leads nowhere. Annie chances the occasional comment, narrating how they might have got lost and their best bet for getting back. Rita remains silent.

They finally make it to the ward nearly half an hour later, greeted by a look of bemused disdain from Matron. She reminds them that it's their lunch time, and that if they don't hurry up they won't have time to eat anything.

'I'm famished, aren't you?' Annie says. It isn't true, but Rita seems to say it before every meal. Rita only nods.

Then they're in the mess. It always surprises Annie how many nurses there are at Fairlie Hall – the maze of rooms and disconnection between wings makes it possible to go a whole day barely seeing the other staff. Then, abruptly, you are reminded that there are others, hidden from view. Mostly attendants, older men, but a few older women too. Part-time. Not trained.

Once Annie and Rita have retrieved their cheese sandwiches from the counter – this is the offering that so far they have found most edible – they make for their usual table. Before they can get there, a voice calls out, 'All right?'

Annie turns. It's the big, pink-faced attendant from the little white room. She wouldn't have expected his voice to be so soft. It's very low and gentle, slightly strained, as though raising it costs him some effort.

'Come on, then,' he says, moving over his tray, though there's plenty of space. He's sitting across from a couple of other attendants, including Anthony. 'Sit yourselves down.' He smiles at them. 'Welcome to the Queen's table.'

The Queen's table? Annie looks around, expecting to perhaps see some sort of plaque.

She glances at Rita, hoping for some indication of whether they ought to decline the invitation. Even Rita must have noticed that attendants and female nurses don't mix. But Rita offers nothing, so Annie sits down and waits for Rita to follow. After a few moments, she does.

'Haven't seen the two of you around before,' the big orderly says. Annie has to lean forwards to hear him. He reaches out a great, soft hand across the table. 'You notice anything new around here. I'm Sam.'

His grip is warm and as gentle. He looks Annie in the eye as they shake hands. She's not used to that from men.

'Annie.' She pauses, waiting for Rita to introduce herself, then adds, 'This is Rita.'

'Annie and Rita.' Sam smiles, looking from one to the other. 'Rita and Annie. Jayne Mansfield and Audrey Hepburn.' Ordinarily if someone said something like that to her Annie would feel that she ought to look down demurely and blush, but something in Sam's voice makes her feel like she's allowed to join in on the laugh.

'How long have you been on the job?'

'Brand new,' Anthony interjects in a low murmur, spooning custard onto his pudding. 'Fresh out of the packet.'

'We're student nurses,' Annie says, after a pause makes it clear that Rita is not going to reply. 'This is our second-year placement.'

'Student nurses!' Sam's cheeks seem to grow larger and pinker as he smiles. 'Very good. Very professional. Are they professional, Anthony?'

Anthony gives Annie a friendly smile that makes her want to turn her face away. 'Very professional indeed.'

'We're perfectly useless,' Rita mumbles, taking a sip of tea. 'Anthony's just being kind.'

'And you?' Annie feels that she isn't going to be able to field too many more questions about the both of them, not when Rita's being so unhelpful.

'Oh, I'm an institution. I'm practically as old as the Hall. They ought to name a wing after me.' Sam laughs. The size of his laugh fits the size of his body. Anthony joins in, and after a moment, so does Annie.

'You're tough, I can see.' Sam looks over to Rita. 'Is she tough, too?'

Annie doesn't want to look at Rita, doesn't want to scrutinise. She can't bear the idea of being disloyal, though it feels that Rita's silence is its own form of betrayal.

'Rita's a marvellous nurse,' she says. She isn't sure yet if it's true, so she follows with something that she does know for sure. 'The patients all love her.'

'Very good,' Sam says again, nodding. He takes a long pause and a bite of his corned beef sandwich, then adds, 'Don't worry about the treatment.'

'The . . .'

'The electric treatment. Earlier. Don't worry about it.'

Annie does her best to look as though she understands.

'Frightens everyone to death the first time,' Sam continues, lighting a cigarette. 'But you see the results, you really do.' He takes a puff. 'We used to inject them with insulin, you know. Whatever your problem was, the answer was insulin. Or cardiozol, sometimes.' He rolls his eyes, as if describing a long-running feud with a tiresome neighbour.

'Evil stuff,' Anthony intones, shaking his head.

'Then they'd go into a coma,' Sam goes on. 'Barbaric, it was. You only realise afterwards. Barbaric. You assume the doctor knows something you don't. But with the electric, you see the results. You really do.' He leans towards Annie and Rita confidentially. 'Dr Lewin thinks a bit differently, you know. Some people don't like him for it. But people get better thanks to him, then they get discharged from this place. They used to just throw away the key. It's like day and night.'

'And we saw the night side,' Anthony says soberly. Sam smiles. Annie is having to lean forwards to hear what he's saying, but Rita still gives no indication of whether she is listening at all. She's torn her cheese sandwich to pieces and is staring at the rubble on her plate.

'People think it's a job for little ladies, nursing,' Sam continues. 'Nice little ladies like you.' He nods at Annie. That outsize laugh again. 'Maybe it is, in a normal hospital, I don't know. Maybe it's just arranging flowers in those places, smiling sweetly at whatever Doctor says. But mental nursing ...' He looks down at his great arms, as if to confirm their wingspan. 'It's a physical job. That's what they don't realise. You need to be strong. You need to be tough.' He looks down at Anthony's slender hands, which lie on the table across from his own. 'Like us, eh Anthony?'

Anthony laughs, and Sam looks at Annie again, then at Rita. 'But you'll be all right, I reckon. You'll both be all right. And if you're worried, you can always ask me.'

Annie smiles and looks down at her plate. On previous days she's been so hungry and exhausted that she's bolted down her food without tasting it. Now she looks properly, the bread seems grey in the fluorescent light of the mess hall.

'So.' Sam wraps his hands around his mug and surveys Annie. 'What on earth are you doing here, then?'

'What do you mean?'

'Come on. Little glamour puss like you.'

'People are ill,' Annie says. 'I want to make them better.'

Sam seems to be waiting for something more. Annie feels that she ought to go on, but it's like she's hit a wall in her mind. She's slightly surprised to hear herself saying, 'It's more like a need, really.'

'You need to be busy,' says Anthony approvingly.

'That's a good trait, in a nurse,' Sam adds thoughtfully. 'You need to be getting on with something. Never sitting still.'

Annie nods, not because that was what she meant, but because she feels there's something slightly shameful in trying to explain that there are two kinds of need. She doesn't need to make people better like she needed to pass her exams, fill out her timesheets, find a husband. This sort of need is different. Need like when she first went to a cinema with a boy and watched Cary Grant kiss Grace Kelly. Need like the need for a bandage or a cigarette.

'I'm not bright,' she starts again. 'I can't talk in front of people like teachers do. I could never stand the thought of being a typist. They're not useful.'

'Useful enough job, isn't it? Typist?'

'Only as useful as the chap they're working for,' Rita chips in. Rita's interjection seems to lift the conversation back into a place where Annie can gain a foothold. 'And you?' She looks at Anthony, at Sam. Anthony just shrugs.

'They said come here, we'll pay you.' He looks out of the window, at the lashing rain. 'So I came.'

'Fancied a little jaunt, didn't you?' Sam laughs his outsize laugh.

'You're jolly good at it,' Rita says to Anthony. 'Nothing seems to bother you.'

'Old men are nothing to worry about,' Anthony says with a dismissive wave of his hands. 'Plenty of real things to worry about. I'm not going to worry about old men.'

'And you, Sam?' Annie is slightly unsettled by Anthony's sphinxlike calm. 'How did you end up doing this?'

'Oh, I was never any good after the war,' Sam says. 'I was in the invasion. I saw what those Germans did. And I did things myself.' His voice is the same but his features shift a little bit, suddenly gaunt. 'And I suppose – I suppose I was never suited to the sane world after that.' The same laugh again, but scaled back. 'I got back to Sheffield from Europe in 1946. Saw an advert for a job in the nuthouse and thought yep, that sounds about right for me. And they look after you, you know.' He nods thoughtfully, as though Annie had pressed him to say more. 'Yes, they really do. You've got somewhere to live, you've got your food given to you.' He laughs again. 'Bit like the army, I suppose. And like in the army, you've got to let them tell you what to do.' A little sniff, and his voice returns to its usual size. 'No one shoots at you, though.' A pause. 'Although Matron might if she had the chance.'

'And what about the medical superintendent? Dr Lewin?' Annie ventures. She's heard the name, the muttering, echoing through the halls, but no one seems to want to elaborate much on this elusive man, who is apparently travelling in Czechoslovakia for a conference. It unnerves Annie, feeling the superintendent's presence and being unable to define it.

'Oh, Dr Lewin?' Sam pats the air. 'He's an old pussycat. Do what he says and you'll get along with him just fine. He's nothing to be scared of. No. If you're going to be scared of anyone, be scared of Matron.' He leans closer to Annie. 'She might walk and talk like a nurse, but really she's an old ghoul. She's got her problems. I'll tell you all about Matron some time – it's quite a story. But that Mrs Danvers act that she does – it's awful.'

'I rather feel for Matron,' Rita says softly. She seems to be saying it mostly to herself and looks rather startled to realise that Annie, Anthony and Sam are looking at her. She adds, 'She makes me feel rotten about myself, but I don't think she's meaning to be cruel. You can tell that she might have been rather lovely once.'

'Once is the key word.' Sam shakes his head. 'Lots of people were lovely once.' He leans closer. 'But if you're not very careful, working in a place like this, you get hard. It's something to watch out for. You get hard, and it's not easy, coming back from that.' His voice trails off, but then, after a moment, he seems to regain something, smiling again at Annie and Rita.

'Anyway, I may not have a load of posh training like you girls, but I know the ropes. So does Anthony. You can always ask us if you need anything. Better than bothering Matron.' Big laugh again. 'She'll never thank you for bothering her.'

'That's kind, Sam,' Annie says. Sam grins.

'Oh, I'm a bit kind.' He leans closer. 'But I'm also a bit nosy. This place, it's my little realm, you see? I like to know what's going on.' He leans back in his chair, glancing from Annie's face to Rita's. 'I want to know why Dr Lewin requested the pair of you.'

'Dr Lewin requested us?' The words fall out and Annie regrets them immediately. She tries to mitigate the effect by taking a bite of her sandwich and cocking her head to one side, adding in a casual undertone, 'Well, why shouldn't he? It's his hospital.'

'It's what I heard. Attendants' grapevine.' Sam smiles. 'You'd be amazed how much you can find out that way. More often than not there's truth to it. We don't ordinarily take student nurses here, you see. They say we're short-staffed, but we're always short-staffed. Usually they just tell us to get on with it.' He leans back in his chair. 'So why did Dr Lewin ask for you?'

'I don't know,' Annie says.

'We haven't even seen Dr Lewin yet,' Rita adds. 'Though we've heard all about him, of course.'

'Yes, he's been away. But he'll be back.' Sam lights a cigarette, draping himself over the skinny metal chair as if it's a throne. 'And when he is, I'm sure he'll be looking forward to meeting the pair of you.'

Annie smiles down at what's left of her sandwich. She's just about to push back her chair and let the scraping sound fill the silence when Rita chimes in, 'That woman.'

Annie lets Sam take the question. 'Which woman?'

'The one on the gurney. The one who we gave the . . . you know.'

'The electric treatment, you mean?'

'Yes.'

'What about her?'

'Why's she here?'

Sam drains the last of his tea, and then stands up himself. 'You mean what's wrong with her?' He shrugs his big shoulders. 'They don't tell me.' He pauses and looks to Anthony.

'Saw on her notes something to do with a pregnancy,' Anthony says.

Annie stays quiet, barely processing this information herself but watching Rita's features shift as the information registers. She's gone very white now, the strawberry look draining from her complexion. 'I thought it was terrible.' Rita's voice is barely above a whisper. 'Violent.'

'It helps,' Sam says. His tone is final, dismissive. 'You'll see. Everyone feels a bit funny about it at first. You've got to push past that. Cruel to be kind. Did you know that's Shakespeare?'

Annie looks back at her sandwich. She can see the tooth marks – her own – gouged into the margarine. She's no longer hungry.

December, 1983

IF IT HAD BEEN anyone but Robbie in her house, maybe Annie would have been more circumspect. She'd put a lot of thought into the sort of landlady that she wanted to be. She had enough on her plate with Rosie, after all, and had no intention of turning into some sort of pink-cheeked, pillow-waisted charwoman.

But Robbie seemed to recognise no relationship between total stranger and intimate friend. When she was in the kitchen, washing up – he seemed to produce a tremendous amount of washing up, considering he was only one person who ate very little – he would perch on the kitchen counter, chattering incessantly. She thought about telling him to get his bottom off, that he was too heavy for her kitchen units. But it wasn't true. There was so little of him.

A lot of Robbie's talk concerned people she'd never met and places she'd never been. She was learning that there was a secret network of pubs, clubs and cafes in London. It came as a shock, after living in a city for fifteen years, to discover an entire world existing in parallel to her own. She found herself intrigued. Robbie was a great raconteur – she soon felt that she knew all the people he was telling her about. He was a funny lad, funny in a way that she'd never encountered before. His humour was as cruel as it was naive. It was irresistible.

She was always careful to wait until Robbie had gone off to lie down before getting out the kitchen cleaner and the Marigolds. She hadn't heard of a single case of a woman or child getting it – and she looked very carefully in the papers every day – but she supposed there was no harm in being careful.

Robbie had it of course. No one had said so, but it was clear to Annie that there'd been bad news. He and Jim had got in a taxi one day, at ten o'clock in the morning. She'd taken note because Jim was usually at work at that time. When the two of them came back, a couple of hours later, she let them in. There had been no reason to get a key cut for Robbie; since he'd come to her, he'd been too poorly to go out. Robbie walked straight past her and went up the stairs. She turned around in time to see how hard he was gripping the banister, how terribly his legs were shaking. Then she heard the slam of his bedroom door and a strange, muffled sound. It might have been a scream, hidden in a pillow.

Jim said nothing other than, 'Tell him I'll be round later.' He looked wretched. 'I told work I had a dentist appointment. Got to go back now.' He hesitated, and then added, 'Will you also tell him . . . tell him that what we said before, it still stands. If he'll listen.'

Then he went back out through the open front door, hands deep in the pockets of his suit, his head bowed.

Robbie appeared in the kitchen mid-afternoon, talking nineteen to the dozen as usual. Annie suspected that he might have waited until Rosie was home from school.

'How were the harpies today?' His voice was breezy as he walked in, turning the tap on with a loud hiss to pour himself a glass of water.

'Awful,' Rosie said gloomily from behind her geography textbook. 'They said my skirt looked like an old sack.'

'Bitches,' Robbie said cheerfully, swigging his water. 'Bullies are bullies. And who cares about your skirt when your face is as lovely as yours? You should get her a new skirt though, Aunty Nan. Oh, and do you have a spare key?'

'A spare key?' Annie was feeling slightly winded. It was the usual Robbie, but with all the colours turned up.

'Yeah. I'm going out. Might be back late.'

He nearly bolted from the room as soon as she'd laid the key in his hand, but she called him back.

'Jim said to tell you ...' He froze, and then looked around, his expression carefully rearranged.

'Yeah?'

'He said to tell you that it still stands.' She could not bear to look at his face, which had crumpled for a second. She picked up her tea towel and began vigorously drying a saucepan. 'If that means anything.'

Robbie nodded, and more or less ran from the room. She wondered whether he needed to cry or be sick.

Annie heard him come in at five o'clock the following morning. She lay in her bed, listening to the heavy tread of unsteady feet up the stairs. It took him nearly five minutes to get up ten steps, but she understood that she was not to go and help him. That whatever he was dealing with, it was not for her eyes.

Two weeks later, Jim rented out his own flat in Cricklewood and moved in with Annie, Rosie and Robbie. They agreed that he would take the room next to Robbie's, and for a few weeks she kept up the pretext of washing the sheets on the unused bed.

Sometimes she heard something like screaming. Not screams of pain, but of anger. Thumps on walls. At first, she thought that Robbie and Jim might be having some sort of brawl. But when she walked into the hallway, she found Jim sitting on the stairs, staring into nothing. She came down late one night, when her own bed had felt particularly cold and wide, to find Jim standing at the back door, looking out into the dark garden, smoking. As he inhaled, the glow from his cigarette lit his eyes for a second, and she saw the wetness there. He did not turn to look at her.

'Cuppa?'

It turned out that Jim never really drank tea, only coffee in a posh pressing thing, but the question was automatic. He smiled politely, lips still pursed around his cigarette, and shook his head. Annie put the kettle on to boil and closed her eyes. The white noise was all-engulfing, and for a moment she could disappear into it. Then she turned back towards Jim, and went over to stand beside him.

'George always kept up the garden,' she murmured. 'He wasn't interested in any flowers, not at first. Nothing that you couldn't eat, he kept saying.'

Jim did not look at her. It was only in the quality of his silence that she could tell he was listening. 'But then he got more and more into it. He used to stay up half the night, reading books about gardening.' She smiled. 'That was just what he was like, you see. He'd develop an interest in something and then all of a sudden he needed to know everything about it. He was never satisfied being an amateur, he wanted to know it all.' She paused. 'I'm nothing like that. I'm quite happy only knowing what I need to know to get on with things. I suppose that's a fault of mine.'

Still Jim did not speak. But he had turned his head to look at her.

'He started to understand that you planted certain flowers next to your vegetables. You needed them to attract the bees, he said. And there were insects, pests, you know, that would go for the flower instead of the vegetable. He was interested in all that stuff.'

'So you sacrifice the flower for the sake of something else.' Jim reached for the ashtray on the windowsill and stubbed out his cigarette. Annie shook her head.

'It's not like that. The flowers can take it.'

The following morning, she went downstairs to find the coffee pot warm but empty, and Jim in the back garden. A mug was balanced on one of the low walls beside a vast pile of dead clematis, which had choked out all light from the garden since Annie and Rosie had moved in. Sunshine

104

had been allowed to enter through the spaces that the dead climber had once blocked. Jim was red-faced and without a jacket. He didn't turn to Annie, but gestured towards one of the raised beds. 'That'll work for winter greens, I reckon, now it can get a bit of sun.'

He noticed her staring and said defensively, 'What? Poofs can grow veg, you know.'

Annie must have looked rather stricken, because there was a moment of tense silence before he started to laugh.

They sat in the garden – Annie drinking tea, Jim with more coffee. Robbie's old, worn cat, who had the improbable name of Marguerite, wandered out to join them.

'Hello, Mags,' Jim murmured, stretching out his hand. When Jim had brought her to the house 'for a visit' she had marched straight up to Annie, and with a look of cold fury in her eyes, jumped up and settled on her lap. For a second Annie had gone completely still, then allowed her hand to find a natural place, resting in Mags's fur.

'Jim?'

'Hmm?'

'I know it's none of my business.' She paused. 'Never mind.'

'What?' Jim drained his coffee. 'Trust me, whatever the question is, I've had worse from the doctors.'

'I was just wondering.' Annie tickled Mags under the chin, and she gave a hoarse purr. 'When you said it still stands, what did you mean?'

Jim shrugged, and picked up the secateurs. 'Only that we agreed, when we first heard about it, that if I got it he'd look after me, and if he got it I'd look after him.'

'That's a big thing to promise.'

'People make promises.' Jim began to hack energetically at the potato vine that was always threatening to encroach over the wall.

'You need to wear gloves. That's poisonous.'

Jim ignored her. 'People make promises, and that was one that we were able to make.'

Annie found herself cooking a lot. Butter and cream. Not too much meat, because she worried about parasites. Jim grew more and more stuff in the garden, and soon everything she cooked could be covered in chopped herbs, along with butter and salt. She made proper puddings – rice pudding jewelled with jam. Dark, sticky cakes spiked with ginger. Robbie and Rosie made butterfly cakes together, scooping out the centres and filling them with buttercream.

'They've got wings, look.' He let a cake soar through the air and land at Rosie's lips. If Annie had done that then her daughter would probably have shrieked that she was being treated like a child, but with Robbie she just giggled and took a bite.

For a second, Annie had frozen. The hand holding the cake had a dark patch on it, like a wine stain. She thought about seizing her daughter and ordering her to drink a glass of salt water, holding her above the toilet until that mouthful of sponge and icing had been dragged out of her.

But that didn't make any sense. She knew that. Not based on what the papers said. And she'd long since decided that in the absence of anything else to believe, she'd believe in the papers. Rosie was still eating the cake, smiling up at Robbie, her fingers covered in buttercream.

The four of them tended to spend the evenings sitting together, just watching the telly. Robbie and Jim on the sofa, Annie in the armchair, Rosie perched on the arm. The four of them could all agree on *Coronation Street*, and Rosie always wandered off when they watched *University Challenge*. Jim had been on a team for *University Challenge*, years ago, when he was a student. He said his recall was rubbish now, but he still got a lot of the questions right. Robbie was useless, but he said everything with so much confidence that Annie always expected his answers to be correct.

After *Coronation Street* one evening, Annie came down from dispatching Rosie to bed and checking that her light really was out, to find Jim and Robbie sipping clear drinks laced with ice and lemon. They had lit a tealight on the table between them, and were talking softly. Robbie was wearing the same sequinned vest that he'd worn on the first night. A third glass stood on the table, empty.

'For you, Aunty Nan,' Robbie said, with a little gesture. Robbie had nicknames for everyone. Jim was Casanova, which seemed to be some sort of joke. Rosie was Briar Rose. He'd tried lots for Annie: Annie Get Your Gun, Anne of Green Gables. Even Anne of Cleves once, when she'd been a bit short with him. That was Jim's suggestion

107

of course – posh, cultured Jim. But Robbie had immediately backtracked, saying that it was too mean. Eventually they'd settled on Aunty Nan.

They drank their drinks together, the three of them. Then Robbie and Jim went out, Robbie glittering like a dragonfly, Jim standing close by, handsome in his dark navy shirt. They were beautiful, the pair of them, Annie thought. Both of them, not just Robbie. Something in the contrast between them, the way they set each other off, that was what was striking.

'Don't wait up, Aunty Nan,' Robbie called out as they shut the door.

As the house grew quiet, Annie realised that it was the first time in months that it had been just her and Rosie here. Nice to have the space to myself, she thought. But it wasn't really true. She'd avoided being alone for such a long time – not just since George died but well before that.

There was a sort of unease that often washed over her in the moments when she was alone. The seed of it had been planted when she was a young woman, just after she'd left Fairlie Hall. It ebbed and flowed with the years, receding when she'd met George to the point that she thought perhaps it was gone forever, then crashing back when Rosie was born, in the long nights walking up and down, jiggling the baby to get her to sleep. Now, without Jim and Robbie to fill the house, the unease took her, starting at her fingertips and working its way through her bloodstream, towards her heart.

She sat up watching telly until nearly twelve, when Jim and Robbie came back. Robbie had become very dizzy on the dance floor and nearly passed out.

'Home for midnight,' Robbie said. 'Just call me Cinderella.'

He was still glittering in his vest. Annie made him tea with four sugars, and tried not to notice that his eyes were glittering too.

November, 1959

IT TAKES ANNIE WEEKS to feel that she has begun to know her way around Fairlie Hall. Weeks of hurrying, heart pounding, along corridors that lead nowhere. Weeks of believing, from the throw of the light on the floor and the look of certain carvings, that she is in one wing, only to peer out of the window and realise that she's in a completely different part of the house. Weeks of losing count of creaking stairs, of doubling back, footsteps swallowed by thick carpets. Of trying heavy doors that she's just walked through, and finding them locked.

At nursing college they were told that nurses ought to always walk with purpose, yet never hurry. But when Annie finds herself sucked once again into the bowels of the Hall, with the seconds slipping away, she often starts running. The sound of her heels cracking over the stone floors is deafening. Covered in sweat, the Hall's chill finds her.

After a certain number of these episodes, Annie realises that most crucial places can be accessed from outside. So she goes out into the wind and drizzle. The elements muss her hair, dislodge her cap, paw at her uniform. But she knows she's better off avoiding the innards of the house.

Fairlie Hall is set in many acres of grounds. There's a wood, a lake, a maze. Endless gardens: walled gardens, kitchen gardens, wild gardens. A rose garden, where the red roses still bloom bloody after the unseasonable warmth. The house is distant from the main road, linked only by a lane lined with close-pressing yew trees.

The isolation is to be expected, of course. Any mental hospital where Annie might have ended up would have been the same – at a distance from the rest of the world. But Fairlie Hall has none of the regularity of the purpose-built asylums that Annie has seen before; it splays out like the legs of a crushed spider.

The Tudor wing is the oldest part of the house, the part that Annie thinks of as its heart. The brick is the colour of burned wood; inside there is a sweet smell of rotten beams. The bars have all been removed from the windows thanks to a recent directive from the health service. Looking out of through the diamond mullion, it still feels like prison. When Annie peers through the black lines, it's as if the world has been hacked to pieces.

Wings have been added by generations of owners. Each seems to have decided in turn that the old ways of doing things were impractical, short-sighted, barbaric. There's the Great Wing, which was added in the mid-seventeenth century; this houses the acute male wards. Annie is sent there one day to collect some syringes – the once-airy galleries now filled with the same narrow iron bedsteads, forty or fifty in each room; the high walls are punctuated by lighter patches, where great portraits once hung.

111

This wing also contains the locked ward, which Annie has not had any reason to enter. Outside the door to the locked ward is the only place in Fairlie Hall where she ever hears screams, but she puts those out of her mind when she walks away.

Then there's the Queen Anne Wing, which contains recreation rooms and workshops. It is here that any visitors are guided: visiting doctors, the anxious relatives of prospective patients. Framed by graceful columns, facing out onto the gentle sweep of the lawn, everything is calmer here. Patients who cried all night or flung their food across the dining hall at breakfast are lulled into stupor in these airy spaces. Tucked under thick rugs, the blotchy patches of red on their faces appear more like a soft, rosy flush.

Annie's patients are dispatched, after she has dealt with them, to breakfast and then on to the airing courts. Here they wander for two or three hours in thin cotton jackets; they benefit from the fresh air. Later they are taken to occupational therapy, which remains a mystery to Annie. During this time she can get on with cleaning the ward or changing over the bed linen. The attendants call out jokes to each other as they buff the floor. Rita knows them all by name and joins in. It's the first time that Annie has heard her laugh since the woman on the gurney, since the electric. There's an odd, abrasive feeling in her chest at the sight of Rita laughing and facing away from her.

Some of the patients are not suitable for occupational therapy – those with what Annie guesses is advanced dementia. It is Annie's task to take them to the library. Apparently, this is so that they can read and relax.

The library stands dead in the centre of the mess of wings. It sits beneath a glass dome, which would shed glorious light into the room if anyone had cleaned it in fifty years. It's a huge room, panelled in mahogany, and must once have been lit by the row of brass lamps that circle the inner mezzanine. But these have long been out of use. Now there are fluorescent lights; the shabbiness of the furnishings is obvious in their chilly glow. There's heavy, leather-studded furniture which no one can fit through the doors to move out. Stuffing weeps from holes in the leather. A number of ordinary chairs have been brought in and stand in a circle, facing nothing. A spiral staircase leads up to the mezzanine, and the whole room is lined with carved oak bookcases. These have kept their shine despite half a century's lack of polish. Apart from a set of almanacs and a few *Reader's Digest*s, there are no books.

Annie has not yet entered the red-brick Victorian wing, which houses the female patients.

'Personality disorders, for the most part,' Matron says. 'More difficult to manage on the whole. Not for you. Not yet.'

Annie has seen the female patients being led to and from occupational therapy. They look little different from the men – perhaps a little more restless, always looking around as if searching for something unseen.

Rita asks Matron how long she has worked at Fairlie Hall. A frown crosses her face, as if she has never been asked a question about herself before. But after a moment she replies, 'Since the first war.'

'When it was requisitioned?'

'Just so.'

Matron seems inclined to say no more, but Rita carries on. 'What was that like?'

Matron blinks. 'Crowded,' she says, with the hint of wry smile. 'We had a hundred patients in here.' She gestures. Annie gazes down the gallery. She cannot imagine cramming more bodies into this room.

'All shell-shock, of course,' Matron continues. 'After the war we kept some of them on.' A short pause. 'In fact, some of them are still here.'

May, 1984

THERE WAS A STAIN on Robbie's face.

It started at his temple, small, like a mistake. Then the
stains started to multiply, leeching across his forehead.
For a while they had been hidden by his sweep of blond
hair. He'd had a hairdresser friend come over and cut it
specially; he'd trimmed Rosie's while he was at it. Annie
swept up the trimmings and wondered whether she ought
to burn them. But then the impulse passed. Jim had all
the up-to-date information – he'd taught himself to read
proper medical studies. You couldn't catch it like that.
Not that you'd know that from the papers.

The haircut worked well for a while, but one morning
Annie came downstairs to find Robbie curled on the
sofa. He was beautiful, Annie thought. Not like a boy is
beautiful, or even a girl. Beautiful like a painting.

'I'm ugly,' Robbie whispered. For a moment Annie
froze. Then, taking out her hankie, she knelt beside
Robbie. She swabbed at his eyes carefully, like a wound.
They were thick with a green crust.

'Don't be daft,' she said.

He lifted his head from the sofa. Within the pink
patch where he'd pressed his face to the fabric, she

could see that the stain had multiplied again, seemingly overnight. They now engulfed one eye and half of his right cheek. Annie knew that the only thing that mattered was that she did not look away. From within the stains the eyes still looked out, dark and kittenish.

'I'll frighten Rosie.'

'Rosie adores you,' Annie said. She was starting to feel a little frightened herself, but hiding fear was all part of the muscle memory. 'I haven't seen her hanging on someone's every word like that since her dad died.'

'I'm twenty-three years old,' Robbie said. 'And I'm no longer beautiful.'

Annie felt that perhaps she ought to say something rather stern and old-fashioned, about how it was only skin-deep anyway. But there was something in her, a faint memory of what it was like to be young and crushable. So she just said, 'Jim won't think so.'

It was then that Rosie stomped in, her pyjama top on over her new school skirt.

'Toast,' she said to the room. Robbie leapt up and busied himself at the toaster, his back to them.

'Sit yourself down.' He pulled out the chair for the kitchen table, his face still angled away, and draped a tea towel over Rosie's lap like a waiter in a fancy restaurant. 'Orange juice, ma'am?'

'No thanks.'

'Don't talk rubbish. You need to be in peak physical condition for your maths test. How else are you going to grow up and become the first non-evil female prime minister?'

'I don't want to be prime minister.'

'Well, whatever high-flying job you end up doing.'

'I don't need a job. I'm going to marry George Michael.' Rosie was smiling now – an unusual sight in the morning. Robbie was smiling too, but a different sort of grin.

'None of that,' Annie said sternly. 'I know your theory.'

'What theory?' Rosie looked from her mother to Robbie, seeing him full in the face for the first time. For a second Annie saw her body stiffen, but then she just held out her glass. 'Fine. Orange juice. Jam on my toast, please. What theory?'

'Time will prove me right,' Robbie said, serving Rosie's toast with a flourish. 'Jim doesn't believe me either. But you'll see.'

'I'm scared to touch him,' Jim said from the kitchen doorway. It had been an odd, tense evening, with Robbie laughing too loudly at everything Rosie said and telling a long, rambling story about people that none of them knew. Annie wanted to get rid of the dregs of their dinner. Everything felt a little too late, like the evening had got away from them and they were already in the thick of night, without even realising it. He hovered uncertainly near the doorway.

'You're scared . . .' Annie had only heard half of what he was saying over the swoosh of the tap as she rinsed Robbie's dinner plate.

'To touch him,' Jim repeated. 'I know I need to. I know he needs things. But he's so thin, Aunty Nan. I'm scared I'll hurt him.'

Annie thought back to when Rosie was born, thinking that it couldn't be that you just held a baby with the same clumsy hands that you used for everything else. But then George had just picked her up. He'd made it look easy.

'There's no special secret,' Annie said. 'Like I told you. Just be gentle.'

She wondered if Jim had worked out yet that she wasn't much use as a nurse. She knew how to keep things clean, she thought, and how to not ask questions. But that was it, really.

What would Rita have said, she wondered? Rita would ask a question. Annie was sure of that.

'How did you and Robbie meet?'

'In Heaven.' He must have seen Annie blink; he clarified. 'That club. You know, where we met you outside. We met there about eight months earlier, I suppose, on the dance floor.' His eyes slid away from Annie and stared out of the window. 'He was topless, no shoes, just these tight jeans. All this blue strobe light draped around him like a cloak. And he looked at me and . . .' He seemed to remember where he was, and trailed off. 'That wasn't what you asked. Sorry. Yeah. We met in a club. Met properly in a club. I'd seen him around.'

'And he was . . .' Annie wanted to say something, but she couldn't quite form the words.

Jim looked at her carefully. 'He was never officially my boyfriend, nothing like that. I felt like he was too young, he needed to have more fun. I don't know whether I'm really the boyfriend type. I'm not the man of anyone's dreams. But Robbie . . . he's an Adonis, for fuck's sake. I love him, if that's what you're asking.'

Annie had expected to feel shock at an admission like this. But she felt only an odd sense of relief. 'And he loves you?'

'As much as he loves anyone, I think.' Jim snorted. 'Robbie's twenty-three. He loves dance music and drugs and beautiful boys and boozy lunches and awful films.' He resumed staring moodily out of the window at the quiet street.

'Jim was different today.'

Robbie was leaning against the sink. His breathing was laboured from the effort of standing upright, but his face was shining.

'Was he, love?' Annie never called anyone love, not even Rosie. Her own mother hadn't been the sort. But she found that the word fell from her lips around Robbie.

'Different, yeah. Or maybe he was the same.' Robbie turned back to the counter. Annie realised he'd made a pot of tea. He usually let other people do things for him. 'He was like he used to be. Just talking to me. Like I'm still me.'

'Of course you're still you,' Annie said, reaching for the cutlery drawer and slapping Robbie gently on the hip to get him to move. 'Always in the bloody way.'

'How else am I supposed to get your attention?' Annie looked up into Robbie's eyes and saw their familiar gleam. 'You're a tough nut to crack, Aunty Nan. Mysterious.'

'Eh?'

'Mystery why you put up with me.'

'There's no mystery,' Annie said. 'I need the money, and I might as well be useful. As well you might. Set the table, please.'

'I'm not useful,' Robbie said softly. He picked up the tray holding the teapot, the cups, the milk and silver spoons. 'You know, everyone likes me, but it's not because I'm useful.' He sat down carefully. He bruised so easily these days. 'I was going to give it another few years of being useless, and then work out what I wanted to do. I thought, you're only young once. Everyone seemed happy for me to just stand around looking pretty.' He laughed. It was a harsh sound, harsher than anything she'd heard from him before. 'But I've never been much use. Around here or anywhere else.'

'You're no bother,' Annie said. Growing up, that had been the highest compliment that her mother could give.

He smiled. 'That's not true.'

Annie shrugged. 'All right then, you're a pain in the arse.' She paused. 'But you're still good at standing there and looking pretty.'

He said nothing. He simply put one large hand over the stains on his face, and smiled radiantly at Annie. The handsome boy was back.

120

November, 1959

IT BECOMES HARD TO tell the days apart. Annie rises after five, goes to the kitchen. There isn't much by way of cooking facilities; they're supposed to eat in the mess. But there is a little grill, and she makes toast: one piece spread with margarine. Rita has real butter, which she keeps in a dish and always offers to Annie. Annie never accepts.

Rita makes the tea. For as long as the tea lasts they exchange sleepy mumblings. Annie talks about the shift rota, or changes to the ward. Rita talks about what she dreamt the night before. The patients figure prominently. Rita knows all of their names.

Annie avoids mentioning it, but she's dreaming a lot too, of the ward. A version of the ward that goes on without end and fades into the distance, that widens and shrinks and occasionally presses in on her so tight she might be crushed. She dreams of Matron, of Anthony, of Sam. Rita is there, always, but often she's distorted, either far larger or smaller than real life. Sometimes she's altogether unseen, but Annie knows she's there. When Annie wakes she's poorly rested, as if she's put in another shift in the night.

Once the tea is gone they wash and dress. Annie washes first, Rita lingering over her morning cigarette as she stares out of the window. She sits on the kitchen counter with her slippered feet in the sink, singing along to the radio.

Annie dresses carefully. She's always paid attention to her appearance, but her dress, her hair, the powder on her nose (nothing more than powder – Matron would faint if she wore lipstick) these all *matter* now. A careful appearance stands for something more than prettiness, or even respectability. Good grooming indicates good health. So long as the curls are arranged, the apron starched, the cap set in the centre of the forehead, then she – not Annie, exactly, but the person Annie becomes when she puts on her uniform – is a beacon. An ideal.

Rita clatters about, uniform askew, blowsy curls about her face in a way that Annie cannot stop looking at, even though it unsettles her. They lock the door to their little flat and set off down the staircase. It is so steep that Annie fears she might fall on Rita, who always goes ahead.

Autumn has come and brought heavy, soaking rain, day after day. 'Good for the gardens,' Rita says every morning. They've learned to set off early, and bring a change of stockings with them. Rita likes to talk on those walks. She doesn't seem to have noticed that Annie would rather stay quiet. That she becomes something else when she puts on her uniform. But Annie has noticed a change in Rita in recent days. So she encourages the talk, sensing that it might remedy Rita's strange new reserve. She lets Rita tell her about university life. About the lecturer who took her to bed. Or rather, she says with a snort, to the couch in his office.

'He wanted to teach me about sex,' she says. They are walking along the little lane that leads from their cottage to the main Hall. It is lined with elm and all gone to bronze. 'Men always seem to want to teach me about sex.' She gestures at the expanse of flesh beneath her uniform. 'They see all of this and think they must be the first one to take an interest in me. They think their tastes are somehow unusual. A little sordid. They assume I'm a virgin and think they can make me grateful.'

Annie focuses on looking straight ahead. The colours of Fairlie Hall seem stronger today, almost overwhelming. If you were going to show Fairlie Hall in Technicolor, Annie thinks, you'd just show the green. The way it engulfs everything.

'You've slept with a man, haven't you?' Rita gives her that direct, blue look. Even in the shade, Annie feels like she's in the glare of sunlight.

'No,' Annie says.

It's true. No man has ever taken her to bed. There was a boy at a party who kissed her a lot, and took her to a quiet hallway and messed about under her skirt. There was a specific, workmanlike way that he moved her body around. It made Annie feel flimsy. No one could do that to Rita, she thinks.

Rita gives a funny little smile. Beneath their feet the grass is as thick and soft as velvet, shrubs like damask. Above, the trees, overreaching, block out all light. 'Do you think I'm a disgrace? Because I'm not married?'

123

Annie looks at her shoes. 'I expect we'll both be married soon enough,' she says. 'What one gets up to before that is no one else's business.'

'Well, neither of us are going to find a husband among the attendants,' Rita says. There's a little snort in her voice.

'How do you mean?'

'Well, they're not . . . haven't you noticed?'

'Noticed what?'

Rita pauses, then speaks carefully. 'None of them are the marrying kind.'

Annie says nothing. Whatever Rita is trying to say feels just out of reach; she has no desire to step closer.

It's Thursday. On Thursdays one of the attendants goes to the shop in Fairlie village to fulfil orders of chocolate and cigarettes. Otherwise-pliant patients can be driven to wordless, bawling fury if they are presented with a Mars bar rather than the requested Aero. Many of them are beyond speech, but still light a cigarette with the brusque grace of Humphrey Bogart. There's one patient, Bernie, who smokes eight at a time, placed in the gaps between his fingers, dragging on each in turn with systematic, thoughtful intensity.

'Been here all his life, or near enough,' Sam tells Annie. She asks why; he only shrugs.

Thursday also brings bath time. Those who are capable line up in single file, though sometimes they lose the idea of the queue and wander away. Rita keeps them in order. It's a sort of music hall act – a monologue peppered with quips, asides, breaking into snatches of song. This leaves Annie to supervise the bath itself.

The patients are so old that Annie mostly doesn't think of them as men. But stripped of their clothes there they are. Old men, but men still. Like Annie has seen in her anatomy textbook. Like she's felt, pressed against her at dances or in dark picturehouses. Some are bloated by the drugs, by a life spent sitting, by the stodgy food. Others have shrunk into nothing. Annie is starting to recognise tertiary syphilis, which sloughs flesh from bones. There are many more, she suspects, who simply can't stomach the hospital food.

The water gradually blackens as each patient takes his turn. Annie supervises them as, one by one, they get into the great metal bath. Some don't know what to do, others are frightened of the water. They kick out, fight, and then, when their strength serves them no more, cry with all the vigour and unselfconsciousness of babies. Some need Annie to wash them. She learns to do it efficiently. Some can wash themselves, moving the grey flannel over the little sagging belly, the back of the neck, the knot of genitals. Annie must watch. She has learned at Fairlie Hall that daily life is full of perils – nothing more so than a bath. A patient managed to drown himself once, while the attendant was distracted. Then, when they get up, Annie finally allows herself to turn her face away. There is something painful about the sight of their sagging buttocks.

Annie senses that on the ward there is a whole other layer, a world of systems, communications and sabotages that she can only partially understand. Some conspiracy seems to be taking place between the patients, just beyond her reach. How else to explain the sudden, coordinated bouts of wailing, the simultaneous urination, or the inexplicable strength with which the most ancient patients rise from their beds and go running down the ward?

'Sometimes I just long to throw down my mop, kick over this bucket, and scream,' Rita says one day, after they come onto the morning shift to discover that one of the patients has urinated in the corner of the ward in the night. The smell has already grown stale. 'Have you ever done that?' She's smiling, a smile that Annie has not seen on her face since before the day with the electric therapy. 'Really screamed with everything you have in you?'

'I expect so,' Annie says, lifting the bucket of dirty water. 'When I was a child and I wanted something.'

'You ought to try it some time.' Rita stands up straight, the mop leaning at her side. She lets her head fall back and opens her mouth slightly. Annie wonders if she really is about to scream, scream until her face is red and her hair is damp with sweat. But instead she drops her head back down and looks to Annie.

'I really think you ought to try it,' she says again.

Time works differently on the ward. The patients' motions are so sluggish that it's as if a camera reel has been slowed down. Annie often doubts her watch. Yet other processes seem sped up. The water in the flower jugs grows foul and brackish strangely fast. But Matron insists on the flowers. And the only moments that Annie

126

has time to think are standing at the end of the ward, holding an enamel jug of water under a tap.

It's hard not to think about bacteria all the time. There's a filthy piano in the patients' common room, with half the keys missing. There's also a record player, though the records have been removed. Sam said that a patient smashed one up and tried to use the splinters to cut his arms. The cuts got infected and they ended up amputating. Some of the patients are allowed to work in the walled garden – the ones that can be trusted with garden tools. Annie thinks of fox dirt, of bacteria in the soil, of the rotting corpses of birds.

But Rita is keen on occupational therapy. There's a patient called Andrew, she tells Annie. Left to his own devices he sits on a chair by himself, rubbing at his arms until they become raw.

'They just sat him down next to the compost heap and told him to tear up any big bits,' she says, eyes shining. 'He was there for eight hours, would you believe? Pulling his funny faces, but hands just working, working, working.'

Annie thinks of the compost heap, of potato peelings and carrot tops and rotten flowers, and shudders.

'He settled at night straightaway,' Rita says. 'I think he was proud of his day's work.'

Annie smiles. She can't deny that a bit of activity in the day seems to make the patients easier at night. She has to get them all down before they hand over to the night shift at eight o'clock, when a hard-faced nurse whose name she doesn't know arrives. Annie tells her who's settled and who's restless. The night nurse nods and retreats to the nurses' station and a cloud of cigarette smoke. Annie doesn't trust her to settle the patients properly, not when there are syringes on hand.

Then there are the evenings with Rita. They eat in the mess, usually with Sam and his various hangers-on, and arrive back at the flat about quarter to nine. They fall into bed an hour or so later. The food in the nurses' mess is no good, but Rita always seems to conjure something sweet to eat with a cup of tea when they arrive back at the flat. The nights are so dark that they need a torch to walk back to their cottage. Annie likes those times when, huddled in their coats and too tired to talk, they see the mist of their breath illuminated in the torchlight.

'Ectoplasm,' Rita says. It's the same joke every day, but Annie always laughs.

It's the third Thursday – that is to say, the third bath day – when Annie is called off the ward by Matron.

'You need to change the linen in the side room down there,' Matron says, indicating a distant door on the long corridor. Something about the way she says it sounds deliberate. Annie knows not to allow any question to enter her face and nods briskly.

'And . . . ah . . .' Matron calls after her, her voice a little tight. 'Please talk to the patient, Nurse Graie.' Annie pauses momentarily but does not turn around. Is there a slight uncertainty that she detects in Matron's voice? 'The medical superintendent left clear instructions – he is particularly eager that you talk to the patient.'

Annie nods again. Even though she's not looking towards Matron, she does not let her face change.

The patient doesn't move when the door opens. He is a man of about Annie's own age, or perhaps a year or two older. He's lying on the bare mattress. The sheets are on the floor next to the bed. There is a familiar, unpleasant smell. When Annie stoops to gather the mass of sheets, armoured against the stench, he lifts his head a fraction. He makes an attempt at a smile.

'Morning, nurse.'

'Good morning.'

The patient looks like he might ordinarily have a round, pink, comfortable face. Yet he has clearly lost a good deal of weight in a short space of time. Now he has the look of a half-finished sketch. But the eyes are alert. This patient doesn't look like the type to soil a bed, but Annie supposes there are all sorts at Fairlie Hall. They aren't all fragments, remnants of a bygone era, more senile than really mad.

'Lovely day,' the patient says, directing his eyes towards the small window. Rain is falling outside. The drops seem to suspend in the air for a moment before hurling violently against the pane.

Annie nods. She notices a trace of Cockney in his voice. A nice voice, she thinks. She lingers a few moments, not wanting to use a tone like Matron's to tell him he needs to get off the bed. But he's already lifting himself on shaking forearms, head lolling. On instinct, Annie holds out both hands and he takes them.

'Very kind,' he says. 'Can't thank you enough.'

Annie looks at the floor, stepping carefully so that neither her polished shoes nor his bare feet land in the mess.

'I won't be a moment,' she says, shaking out the fresh sheet. She forms the hospital corners in brisk movements. She's grateful to say something in truth, something straightforward. She can change a bed over now, easily as breathing.

'Oh, there's no rush,' he says. He's moving very slowly towards the window. It's peculiar, Annie thinks, to see young healthy limbs bent into the shape of an old man. His breathing is laboured too, she notices. Perhaps he's a heavy smoker, though she can see no cigarettes.

He's made it to the window now. He looks out, holding firmly onto the sill. Annie carries on making the bed. For a few moments she lingers over the sight. There's something so calming, she thinks, about a wrinkle-free sheet. The eye can rest on the expanse of whiteness. The mind can grow calm.

'Would you tell Dr Lewin,' the patient says, as she's laying a last smoothing hand over the pillow, 'that I am feeling better today. Really much better.'

There's something anxious in his voice. She turns to him.

'It's Paul, by the way,' he says.

She nods. There's something desperate about him, something that doesn't fit.

'It's ever such a relief to be here,' he says softly. She nods again, gently taking the hand from her sleeve and holding it for a moment in her own. 'Ever such a relief to be looked after. It's given me hope, after so long thinking that I'd never . . .' He doesn't seem to be able to get to the end of the thought. To spare him, Annie nods again. She steps away, perhaps a touch more sharply than she'd intended. 'Only . . .' His hand shoots out with the strength of the young man that he is, despite his wasted body. 'Don't tell anyone, eh?' He lets go of her wrist, lies down on the newly made bed, rolls over, and says to the wall, 'I'd rather they didn't know I was here.'

May, 2020

I WAS GOING THROUGH the photos Jim sent again when the doorbell rang. I thought it was probably a delivery man. I hadn't actually ordered anything, but Rosie occasionally sent things that she'd decided I, as a woman of a certain age, ought to want. Lavender soap, Marks & Spencer's shortbread, things like that.

But it wasn't a delivery man. Paul was standing on the doorstep. I saw the look on his face and immediately let him in.

'I didn't want your neighbours to see,' he said. I shrugged.

'Maybe they'll think I'm shagging around,' I said. I nodded towards the telly. 'Everyone else is, it seems.'

We stood on opposite sides of the room. I'd never been so aware of my own body before, the way that it seemed to want to breach its own barriers. My hands twitched with the impulse to reach for him.

'Let me make you a cup of tea, Paul.'

He half-shook his head.

'Come on, Paul. You look terrible.'

He did. I'd never seen him like this before, but looking at him I immediately thought of myself in those first days after George died. He was completely without his plumpness, his pinkness, without life. He looked like an old man, any old man.

I made him tea the way he likes it, and gave a show of wiping the mug handle before I set it in the middle of the coffee table. I cut him a slice of cake, too. You can't disinfect cake, not even for show, but I thought putting it on a paper plate might have the right effect.

'I had to come,' he said simply.

'I know you did, love.'

'I had to talk to someone about her. Alec—'

'He's not the right person to talk to about Rita,' I interrupted. Paul's face seemed to bloom with relief. I knew he couldn't bear to say anything disloyal, not about Alec.

'The thing is, Annie, she was my wife.'

'I know.'

'I loved her.'

'Course you did.'

'I know we always say it's a sham, make all those jokes. I know all that.' He looked down at his shaking hands. He made to reach for the mug of tea, then seemed to think better of it and clasped his hands back in his lap.

'You were together sixty years, near enough. You stayed together.'

He shrugged. 'Of course we did. We raised Lizzie, didn't we?'

'You did it beautifully.'

The tears were pouring down his face now. 'She saved me, Rita did.' His face was shining with tears.

133

'She helped you,' I agreed. I'm not sure that Rita was someone who could save anyone, not fully. I'm not sure that anyone can do that really. But Paul's always believed in that stuff, in being saved. And it's none of my business to insist otherwise. 'She might just as well have said you saved her.'

He didn't stay for long. He'd cycled all the way from Earlsfield, where he and Rita had lived for thirty years or more. He's stayed fit, maybe thanks to Alec. After he'd stopped crying we talked a little bit. He didn't seem to mind lockdown that much. Since he retired from the civil service, more than a decade ago now, he's thrown himself into hobbies. Writing a local history, biking around Surrey, coaching kids' football. He's missing the football, he says, but everything else isn't that far off from how it always was.

Except that Rita's gone.

I showed him some of Jim's pictures, the ones with Rita in them. He stayed away from the house in those days, even when she was around a lot. I suppose, like lots of people then, he didn't want to see what was happening. I can't fault him for that.

July, 1984

ANNIE AND JIM STOOD side by side in the little room, studying the pile of clothes and books on the bed. Annie thought of the little bag they'd given her at the hospital, with George's things. His key and wallet, his library card and comb. She stepped forwards and smoothed out the sheet. She'd made up the bed.

'Is there anything you want me to take care of?'

Jim stepped forwards and picked up a jumper – the softest one, of pale blue wool. He screwed his fists tight into it for a second, then folded it carefully and put it on a chair by the door. 'The rest, I suppose. Do you want any of the books?'

Annie shook her head, and he laughed. 'I know. Rotten taste.'

He picked up a paperback from the top of the pile. *Giovanni's Room*, by James Baldwin. 'I bought this for him – thought he'd find it improving. He never read it. Serves me right.'

'I'll give it a read,' Annie said.

'Don't know if it's your sort of thing, Aunty Nan.'

'You never know. I like all sorts.' She looked down at the bed. 'What shall I do with the rest?'

'His mum?' Jim's voice is careful, neutral.

'Doesn't want it.'

'Charity shop, I suppose.' He picked up a fistful of brightly coloured shirts. 'If they'll take them.'

'Give them here,' Annie said. 'Rosie can have them for her dressing-up box.'

She took the mess of clothes from him and began folding them up, piling them on the bed. Rosie didn't really dress up much these days, hadn't done for a while. But Annie would put the shirts in the old wicker hamper anyway.

The colours separated, the shirts stopped looking like fury and became beautiful. Beautiful and enormous. Robbie had weighed less than six stone when he died.

Annie had barely finished folding when the cat jumped on the bed and settled on the pile.

'No respect,' Jim said. He paused, his lips pressing tight together, then said, 'I'm not sure what to do about Mags. My flat's too small for her.'

'Do about her?' Annie went over to the wardrobe and took out the sequinned vest that Robbie had been wearing the night he came home. 'She's happy enough here, isn't she? We've already got the cat flap.'

Jim sat down on the bed. 'Thanks, Aunty Nan.' He lay back and closed his eyes. 'No one told me how tired I'd feel.'

Annie sat beside him. She had forgotten that herself until now – those days after George's death, days when Rosie had been at school and she had done nothing but sleep. You have to metabolise the shock, she'd learned.

'Get plenty of sleep,' she said, putting her hand on Jim's shoulder. 'Eat, sleep and move.'

Russ tilted his head to one side, squinting. 'Go and stand in the light by the window, Nan. Wait, no, never mind.' He crossed the room to the light switch and the room was dropped into darkness. 'Stand next to that lamp.'

Jim came in. He looked the same as ever in a white T-shirt and dark jeans. His one concession to dressing up was his hair, which had been gelled. He looked handsome.

'What're you doing to her?' He put a hand under Annie's chin and his eyebrows moved upward, a small smile forming. 'OK. Not bad.'

'I'm trying to do a Liz Taylor thing. Pre-booze Liz, obviously. She's got the right eyebrows. But her eyes aren't blue like Liz's so . . .' Russ shrugged with one shoulder. 'There's a limit to what I can do.'

Russ had arrived at the house with swollen eyes and his makeup kit in a wheeled suitcase. Annie knew that he'd always been wary of her. When he brusquely told her that he was going to do her face, it was clear that he wasn't offering her a favour.

'You look great, Nan.' Jim gestured towards the bathroom door. 'Go and take a look.'

Annie plunged her hands into the pockets of her dressing gown, suddenly afraid. The last person who'd done her makeup had been Rita, back at Fairlie Hall. But when she looked, the reflection in the cracked bathroom mirror was nothing like that evening with Rita. Other than the lips – they were red, Annie noticed, but a softer red. There were none of those stark, sharp lines, not in this face, blurred by the years.

Russ had done something – seemingly given Annie new eyes. There was a music and harmony to the lines of her face that Annie had never seen before, the sweep of her eyebrows answering and rhyming with the arch of her mouth, the curve of her cheeks, which were softly blooming and no longer haggard. Above all, those eyes were lined with a set of lashes like cobwebs, framing something ancient and intriguing and seductive. The woman in the mirror looked like she knew something, and Annie wanted to know it too.

The only dress that Russ would accept was the one that she'd worn to George's funeral, and he'd pinned the hem up a good bit. With some black stockings, and heels, she couldn't deny the effect.

'She could do with some sort of veil,' Russ said, coming into the bathroom and folding his arms across his chest. 'For a bit of drama. It'd work with the red lips. Look, you can have a bit of mine.' He reached behind him to catch at the length of black lace that was draped across a comb at the back of his head. 'Pass me your scissors, Nan.'

He expertly cut along the grain of the lace, forming a strip about eight inches wide. He looped this into a soft bow, and began to pin it onto Annie's head. He stepped back, his kohled eyes narrowed again.

'Yep. Good.' He reached out to slightly alter the drape of the lace. 'Nice. You look like someone's mistress who's turned up at his funeral to cause trouble.'

It was clear that this was intended as a compliment.

There was talk of calling a minicab, but Russ insisted that they get a proper black cab. ('Closest thing we're going to get to a hearse today.')

'Maybe I should have gone Old Hollywood too,' Russ said, licking his thumb and swiping carefully at the edge of Annie's mouth. 'I really like how she's turned out.'

'You look gorgeous, and you know it,' said Jim. He sounded slightly bored by the conversation. 'Spanish widow suits you. Full melodrama.'

'Don't be such a stick in the mud. You know Robbie would have loved it. He'd have *died* for it.'

There was a silence, and then a peal of uncontainable laughter from Jim. Annie reached out to take his hand in hers, though whether she was trying to repress that wild sound, or to comfort him, she wasn't sure.

'You've got to admit, it's a bit funny,' Jim said. The laughter had disappeared from his voice as abruptly as it had come. 'No one used the word *die* more lightly than Robbie did. Absolutely bloody constant. It was like anything between zero and a hundred *offended* him.'

'Apart from you,' Russ interjected. 'He liked you, for some reason. You're as dull as a weekend in Worthing.'

'I have hidden qualities.'

'I can only presume.'

Robbie's mother had told them that they weren't to go to the funeral. At least, Jim and the rest weren't. She'd said Annie was welcome. But Annie said no, thank you.

Instead it was agreed that they'd all go down to Heaven, the nightclub where she'd seen Robbie, Jim and Russ on that first night. The dance floor was being used more and more as a place for vigils, a sea of candles.

'We're going to celebrate him,' Jim said. Annie saw him wince slightly. 'That's the kind of thing that people I can't stand say. A celebration of his life, no black, no lilies, whatever.' He sighed. 'It's stupid, but I want it all for him. I want Mozart's Requiem and "The Lord Is My Shepherd" and ashes to ashes and dust to dust.' His voice trailed off. 'But he hated all that stuff. You know what he's like, he wants all sorts of ghastly *Top of the Pops* rubbish playing.'

The instructions were for a candlelit vigil, and then a party. Annie stayed to place her candle on the floor. She tried to keep watching it, but her eyes lost focus for a second. When she tried to find it again, she realised that she had no idea which candle was hers among dozens, maybe hundreds of others on the dark dance floor.

When everyone started dancing to 'Tainted Love' she went to stand outside. Rosie had been dancing in a circle with Russ and a group of others, all holding hands. Annie watched her daughter for a moment. Something had changed in her in the past year – her short hair looked fashionable with new, abrupt cheekbones. The jeans clasped her waist differently. Annie did not know this girl, and had the feeling that she was not capable of knowing her, not really.

They kept on dancing. Someone beckoned Annie onto the dance floor, but she shook her head. This part wasn't for her. She'd done her bit, been useful.

When they'd rung around, the undertaker initially wouldn't take Robbie's body. Jim was on the phone, white-faced, his voice shaking with rage. Annie took it off him.

'Now look here,' she said.

'Eh?' The voice on the other end was cold, but as soon as the undertaker heard Annie his tone shifted into a sombre intonation. 'I beg your pardon,' he continued, in this softer, oilier manner. 'To whom do I have the pleasure of speaking?'

'I'm his – I'm the deceased's . . .' She thought about saying mother. 'I'm his landlady.'

She thought about shouting at the undertaker. It would make her feel better. But then she looked at Jim. He looked exhausted and somehow cramped, as if he didn't know whether to sit or stand. There was a flesh-memory in looking at him, in remembering how there was no position that could make the ache of a grieving body bearable.

She took a very deep breath. 'My name's Annie Reynolds,' she began. 'You were ever so helpful when my husband George died.'

Something in the quality of the silence seemed to ease slightly.

'I've been recommending you,' she said. It was a preposterous thing to say, but then a soft, creaky 'thank you very much' at the other end of the line told her that she was onto something.

'Really, Mrs Reynolds?'

'Yes, recommending you to all my ... er ... widow friends.'

Jim looked up. To Annie's astonishment, he started to laugh.

'Yes,' Annie continued. It was a question of keeping her voice serious, of making it just believable enough. 'I'm in a sort of ... widows' group, you see. We get together and share tips, how to handle it all. Ever so useful.'

Annie kept on talking. There was a knack to it, the right cocktail of traits: martyrdom, respectability, a bit of stupid middle-aged woman thrown in. All the while Jim was laughing silently, crouched on his haunches, shoulders racked.

'All right, Aunty Nan?'

Jim was standing beside her. He had an unlit cigarette in his hand. She gave a little nod and angled her body away slightly. She remembered it well, the longing to get away from everyone, the way that it was so hopelessly entangled with the terror of being alone. She heard the soft click as Jim lit his cigarette.

'Had to come out,' he said, sucking hard on the end of it. 'They're going on about what a brilliant singer he was.'

Annie might ordinarily have kept quiet, but something in Jim's voice invited honesty. 'He was dreadful, wasn't he?'

'Brilliant performer. Couldn't hold a tune to save his life. But he *would* try.' Jim let out a laugh that sounded like it had been inside him for a long time. 'Utterly dreadful.' He paused a minute. 'I'd give anything to hear him again.'

'Yes. Course you would.'

Jim gave a great sniff. 'It's driving me nuts.' Annie said nothing. 'Every time I have the tiniest sniffle I think that's it, I've got it. I've got fucking hay fever. All that blossom on Cumberland Street, it's killing me.' He paused and sighed. 'I suppose I'll go back to my own flat now.'

'Rosie'll miss you.'

Rosie hadn't cried since Robbie's death, but she hadn't really spoken much either.

'I'll miss her,' Jim said. 'I'll even miss you a bit.' He smiled, and for a second Annie thought she saw something of Robbie's dazzling quality in the smile.

She waited until he had finished his cigarette, then nodded out onto the street. 'I'll get a taxi from here.'

It had been three days since Jim moved his things out. Annie had spent the first two cleaning. She stripped Robbie's bed and wondered for a second if she ought to burn the sheets. In the end she just chucked the lot in the washing machine.

Then today had been all about Rosie. Taking her to the swimming baths, out for tea and cake, just the two of them. They'd watched *Mary Poppins* together on the telly – Rosie said she was too old for it, but she'd watched it all the same.

And now the girl was in bed. Annie made herself a pot of tea and toasted a couple of crumpets. Lots of butter. She carried tea and crumpets over to the sofa – hers again now – and lay with her feet up, putting the telly on.

It was a relief. There.

It was a relief to have her house to herself, a relief not to be worrying about what might happen in the night, to not have to put on a special calm, nurse's face to talk to Jim.

Robbie had died at three thirty-six in the morning. Jim on one side, Russ on the other. Annie stood in the doorway. She'd never seen someone die before.

They covered him, then went downstairs to drink a glass of wine. Annie offered to call his mother, but Jim said he wanted to do it. He waited for a while. Finished his wine and washed up the glass.

She sat beside him while he dialled, leaving her hand lying on the table next to his. She heard the stiff, 'thank you for calling', and then the silence when Jim put the phone down. She felt Russ stirring beside her, and went to pour more wine. She hadn't really stopped moving since that moment.

The doorbell rang just after she'd taken her first bite of crumpet. Annie went slowly to the door.

Jim stood on the doorstep. A younger man, who Annie guessed from his complexion to be an Indian, stood by his side. He was slender, but other than being wrapped up against a mild night he looked healthy enough. Yet when he turned his face to look fully at Annie she saw the lesion blooming across his cheek.

'This is Vic,' Jim said, gesturing. 'He's been chucked out of his flat. Any room at the inn, Aunty Nan?'

November, 1959

'DO YOU SEE GHOSTS?'

Rita turns her head languidly, and rolls her eyes at Annie's expression. 'Don't look at me like that. I'm not talking about some Hammer flick with Christopher Lee. I mean ...' She points out of the window, at a figure standing across the road. 'Do you see him?'

They are sitting in the tea shop in the village. Rita puts her teacup back in its saucer and looks again at Annie.

'Of course I see him,' Annie says. 'He's there, isn't he?'

'Of course he's there. I'm not saying he's not there. But look at him. Properly.'

After a moment Annie looks from Rita back to the man outside. She studies him. The young man is very thin and pale – not alarmingly so, but there's something of the troubadour about him. A sensitive type, she supposes. Otherwise, he's as solid as anyone else.

'Stop looking at me like I'm going mad, look at *him*,' Rita presses. 'Look at the cut of his suit, all those long lines. They don't make them like that anymore.'

'Maybe it's his father's suit. Maybe that's just what he's got.'

'He doesn't look at home here at all. He looks like he's off to dance a Charleston in some mad jazz club.'

There's a pleading note in Rita's voice; Annie looks. Yes, she supposes, there might be something a little unusual about the chap. As if he doesn't quite belong in the scene. She thinks of the photographs of Stalin that she saw in the papers when she was younger. Her mother had said they'd been doctored, and shaken her head. ('Frightening, isn't it? The way they make them look so real. You've got to look right up close.')

So Annie looks closer. And yes. Perhaps the light is falling differently on this man's face. The light of some other age.

The man disappears around the corner and Rita leans back in her chair, picks up her teacup and looks entreatingly at Annie. 'Don't you see people like that? People who look like they're in the wrong time.'

Annie frowns at Rita. Is she joking? The good thing about working in the mad house, Annie is starting to think, is that it makes you feel pretty certain that you aren't yourself mad. But there's something in the brightness of Rita's look that unsettles Annie, makes her wonder if she ought to be careful in her reply.

'Come on, don't look at me like I've lost the plot,' Rita says impatiently. 'You're not like the girls at school. He's different, isn't he?'

In a sense, Annie thinks, yes. She shrugs.

'I see them all the time,' Rita says dreamily. 'Well, not *all* the time. Maybe one every other month or so. These girls in pinafores – they look like old scullery maids.

147

Sometimes,' she leans close, and Annie finds herself mirroring her, 'you see a young man. A young man in a greatcoat, and he's got this look about him, like he knows he's going to be sent off into the meat grinder in France. Like the poor chap wants to take everything in before he goes.' Rita gives a little laugh and pours them both another cup of tea. 'I've always imagined they're people who never got seen properly the first time around, you know? So they have to keep showing themselves until someone really *sees* them. Do you believe in ghosts?'

Annie hesitates. It feels like a trick question. She has never been the sort to negotiate with reality – things just are as they are.

'No,' Annie says. She lets a little smile form on her lips, part of the old school uniform. 'I mean, of course not.'

Rita, who had been waiting very intently for her answer, turns away with a shrug. Annie can see that she's hurt, perhaps more by the smile than the words.

'That's to say ...' She carries on hastily, unsure of where she's going. Rita turns half back. Annie thinks of the severed hand in the vegetable patch of her mother's garden. 'I believe ... I suppose I believe that when something happens in a place – well, the place changes, doesn't it?'

'So you believe in haunting,' Rita says, nodding. 'But not ghosts?'

'No, not ghosts.'

Annie senses that she has disappointed Rita, but Rita does not appear to dwell on it. Instead she stands up. 'Better be off. I need to post a letter.'

It's as if none of the things that once shocked Annie can touch her anymore. When a patient screams that she's a cunt or waves his dusty old member at her, or lurches out of Anthony's grip to try to smash his head against a wall, all she feels is a sort of weariness.

Occasionally she changes the bed linen for the young man in the side room. Once they sent Rita in to do it. As Matron was walking past, Annie a few steps behind, peals of laughter emerged from the room and filled the corridor. After that, Annie is sent in again. The patient – Paul – keeps telling her to pass on to Dr Lewin that he's feeling much better.

One day Dr Lewin arrives back from his speaking tour in Czechoslovakia. Annie sees him in the corridor just after lunch. He's all soft lines: great white beard, gently curling white hair. The flesh is pale, but interrupted in places by reddened cheeks, a delicate red mouth. Eyes, round and blue behind their spectacles. His white-coat-clad bulk reminds Annie rather of a cloud. He moves along the thick dark carpet with a gentle, rolling gait.

'Matron!' His voice is familiar, ebullient. Matron turns in one of her jerky, economical movements, and gives him a nod. 'Dr Lewin.'

149

'Returned, as you see, from my travels.' He inclines his head, slightly breathless. 'I hear you've been holding down the fort admirably.'

'I do my best, Doctor.'

'I take it that these are the new student nurses?' He smiles at Annie and Rita. Matron says nothing, barely inclines her head in response.

'Marvellous. My dears.' His blue gaze floats over them. 'Welcome to our profession.'

Annie makes some sort of affirmation. Rita remains quiet. Dr Lewin continues, 'Perhaps I have surprised you.'

Annie gives a small smile.

'Are we not, after all,' he continues, 'governed by the usual distinctions between doctor and nurse?' He leans closer. 'I say not. Such distinctions are nothing compared to the gap that exists between us and the rest of the medical establishment.' He widens his eyes slightly and then leans back, as if to survey the impact of his words. 'I am sorry to say,' he carries on, 'so many of my colleagues are bound by very old-fashioned assumptions. They think there is the health of the body and the health of the mind, and never the twain shall meet.'

He spreads his arms, looking around at the heavy ebony panelling. 'You may have heard some peculiar things about the role of the mental hospital, now we've all been gobbled up by the Leviathan of the health service. Ghastly naysaying, small-minded pencil-pushing. I tell you.' He leans towards them. Annie catches the stale sweetness of his breath. 'You

150

are entering into an area of medicine that is thriving. Flourishing. And of course . . .' He smiles, revealing teeth that look yellow against all the white hair, '. . . graced by your presence.'

Annie can't say why, but her uniform seems to have suddenly grown tighter.

'Matron,' he says, turning back to her birch-like figure. 'You can spare your two new trainees for a cup of tea, can't you?'

Matron looks disconcerted. 'They're needed for the rounds,' she says.

Dr Lewin glances at his wristwatch. 'But that isn't until five o'clock, is it? We have a *little* time.' His voice is as soft as before, but it seems to ring out a bit more. Matron gives another of her almost-imperceptible nods and turns abruptly away.

They follow Dr Lewin down the long, ebony-panelled corridor. Annie expects to go through the heavy doors into the main wing, but Dr Lewin turns, his movements more agile than Annie expected, and opens a door that at first glance seemed part of the panelling.

'I'm in the old wing,' he says over his shoulder. 'All the way up at the top. I told them to put me there. Force me to take a little exercise. Doctor, heal thyself, and all that.' Even from walking down the corridor, his breath has grown heavier. Annie and Rita follow him through the narrow door.

'This is the original wing of the house,' Dr Lewin says. 'Built in 1533, would you believe? In admirable condition.'

151

Annie cannot agree. The corridor seems to lean in from each side, so close that she feels jostled by the dark timbers. The floor tilts at an angle that makes her ankles twist in their shoes. When Dr Lewin unlocks an office at the end of the narrow hallway, Annie feels herself half-falling into the room, as if launched in by the house itself.

The doctor's office is lined with leather-bound books in scarlet, midnight, forest green, and warmed by a fire that feels a touch too large for the little iron grate. Annie wonders whether the fire might be smoking into the room; breath does not come easily. Rita is still standing in the doorway, looking uncertain.

'Come on in, come on in!' Dr Lewin gestures from a little table by the gabled window, where he is adding tea to the pot. He opens the window and takes a little bottle of milk from the place where it was chilling on the outside ledge, then pours some into a china jug.

'My lair, as it were,' he says. 'Welcome.'

He questions them a little about their nursing studies, and does not seem at all dismayed by how little they know.

'You learn on the job, you see!' He leans back in his chair and takes a great gulp of tea. 'I've seen it happen, over and over. Young nurses enter the profession frightened out of their wits, thinking they don't know enough. But it's practical. Your role is to act. No substitute for experience. It's all a question of learning to take direction. Acting, you see, not thinking.'

152

He looks from one to the other. Rita still hasn't sat, but this doesn't seem to concern him. He takes a long moment to look her up and down, and then smiles.

'You're the university experiment?'

'Not an experiment, as far as I know,' Rita says. Her voice is low but clear. Dr Lewin does not seem to hear her, or else is not interested. He gives a courteous smile and turns back to Annie. 'Marvellous,' he says. It's not obvious what he's referring to; Annie gives her habitual encouraging little smile.

'Do you know . . .' he says, and then stops and turns towards the window. 'Well, there's no harm in you knowing, is there?' He mutters the last part to himself, and resumes staring out of the window.

'I often find myself, in my profession,' he begins; his voice has a rhythm to it, as if treading familiar paths in his speech, 'surrounded by men far more interested in talking about changing the world than actually doing it.' He turns back to the room, and seems to address himself mostly to Annie. 'If I might be so bold as to ask, have you ever participated in psychoanalysis?'

Annie shakes her head. She knows a bit about psycho-analysis, of course, from her nursing course and, more extensively, from the films. Images of couches, of men in black suits. Of money.

'I thought not.' Dr Lewin gives a swift, indulgent smile. 'Why should you? The preserve of the elites, I fear. Those intent on bankrupting themselves. No scruples, no scientific grounding and, I'm afraid, my

153

dears . . .' he sits back down and leans forwards in his chair, 'no evidence.'

His blue eyes are fixed meaningfully on Annie. She is bewildered. Is she supposed to be defending psycho-analysis?

'I think it helps some people,' Rita says. Dr Lewin does not seem to notice.

'I am a rebel,' he says, then smiles. 'A rebel in the academy. A rebel in need . . . of some assistance.'

His hand moves to rest on a book that lies on his desk. Annie squints to look at the title. *Schedules of Reinforcement.*

'Talk is not enough,' Dr Lewin says softly. 'You see it all around you, don't you?' Annie looks uneasily at the walls of the office, then offers a little nod. Dr Lewin seems pleased. 'I suspect you've already started to feel it?'

'Feel what?' Rita's voice is oddly loud.

'I needed to catch you at this early stage in your training,' Dr Lewin continues. 'You've seen what we do here. We pump our patients full of chlorpromazine to make them more docile. I suppose you've assisted in this already. At some point you will be holding the needle.' He gives a sad little smile. 'The patient will resist for a few moments and then fall backwards. Limp.' He stands up and looks out of the window, then abruptly turns back to look at them. 'Have you encountered a gentleman on the ward called Bernard?'

'Bernie?' Rita says. At the same time, Annie responds, 'The chap who smokes a whole packet of cigarettes at once, you mean?'

'Just so.' He gives her a little bow. 'You wouldn't know it to look at him, but Bernard is only forty years old.' An indulgent little smile. 'Now, I know that sounds terribly old to young things like you, but . . .' he sighs, 'being on the wrong side of sixty myself, I can assure you that Bernard is not so very old. More tea?' Annie shakes her head. 'Poor Bernard was put into this place at the age of twelve. His crime? He stole a pint of milk.'

He adds a splash of milk to his own replenished cup and continues, 'I have spoken to him at great length, and I suspect that there is little, if anything, wrong with him. He is merely institutionalised.' Annie looks over to the window, where outside the wind is pulling at the oak trees, and notices that they have started to shift from golden to flat, dead brown. She sees Bernie's pink, pudgy hands, barely visible in the swirl of cigarette smoke.

'Bernard's been with us for so long that he cannot survive in the outside world.'

He stands, and plunges his hands deep into the pockets of his white coat, looking down at the two of them. 'I refuse to create more Bernards.' He shakes his head. 'It is cure, not pacification, that is my goal.'

He sighs. 'In this respect I diverge from my peers, from psychiatric medicine, from the Academy itself.' Another great sigh. 'I feel a greater responsibility to my patients than to these professional bodies. I ask you . . .' he turns his bright gaze on Annie, then Rita in turn, 'to join me in my little tearaway. I ask you to participate in an experiment that will justify my methods.'

He leaves a gap, as if expecting Annie to say something. She has no notion of what might be suitable. 'The particulars of this experiment . . .' He pauses for a long time, then gives a small smile and seems to depart from his intended course. 'The particulars of this experiment are hardly suitable for discussion with young ladies. There is a certain delicacy . . . I must respect it. All I ask is that you enact my will, even when it seems peculiar to you, even when it defies some element of your training.' His eyes are fixed on Annie. 'Sometimes it is the training – the institutions themselves – that are wrong.'

Annie feels that he is somehow expecting her to look alarmed.

'Isn't it remarkable,' he says, going back over to the window and looking out at the deer park that lies beyond the walled gardens, 'that this view has scarcely changed in the four hundred years that this Hall has stood? Yet this unchanging place might alter the course of medicine.'

August, 1984

ANNIE AND RITA NEVER quite lost touch.

They never arranged to meet, yet they kept bumping into each other when they'd both moved to London. Christmas shopping on Regent Street, a walk in Richmond Park, the National Gallery on a Thursday afternoon. Rita would appear, and somehow Annie was never surprised to see her.

Over the years Rita started wearing stovepipe jeans, blouses tied up to show her midriff. She grew her hair long and cut a fringe; her eyes looked out all the bluer. They always said they would arrange to meet; they never did. Nor did it ever occur to Annie that they might not see each other again.

For a few years Rita really did disappear, but even then she sent postcards. Yugoslavia, Marrakesh, Goa. She never signed them 'Rita and Paul' but always wrote in a 'we'; a settled, unquestioned 'we'.

On the night that Vic arrived at the front door, Annie sat with her address book in her lap for a long time, open to Rita's name. She still had Rita down as Blythe. She had no idea if she used Paul's surname. But then Vic came in to ask for a glass of water to take his pills, and she got distracted. The next morning had been the usual flurry of bedsheets, getting Rosie off to school and explaining to her that yes, they'd got a new lodger.

All Rosie said was, 'I get the first shower.'

It had been a joke between her and Robbie, complaining about who used the most hot water, but she wasn't laughing now.

'I have to go to school.' She folded her arms across her blouse. 'I'm not going without a shower. I don't want to smell.'

'You don't smell, darling.' Annie tried to say it quickly, just to indicate that the very suggestion was absurd, but she could see from the change in Rosie's face that it had come off as dismissive.

'I need the first shower,' she said again, and her voice was rising now. Annie tried not to wince, thinking of Vic upstairs. He'd been very polite, but it seemed like he'd barely slept. 'And he can't use my soap. He'll have to get his own.'

'I'm sure he's brought his own soap.'

'Someone's been using my soap.' Rosie's voice was louder still.

'I borrowed it,' Annie said quickly. It might have been true – she couldn't actually remember. Everything was such a haze these days, and she was so tired. For all she knew it could have been Jim, but he had enough on his plate without fielding the fury of a fourteen-year-old girl.

But her response – intended to soothe – seemed to only provoke Rosie further.

'Nothing's just mine!' She seized her backpack, shouldering it and making to storm from the room. She slowed slightly on the stairs, as if hoping that Annie would call her back. But all Annie could think of to say was, 'You've got lots of things that are just yours.'

When she was Rosie's age she'd still shared a room with Eddie. There had been barely a foot between their two little beds.

Rosie didn't turn around. 'Fine.'

She said it calmly. It might have been easier – jolted Annie out of her exhaustion a little more – if she'd shouted, or said something dramatic. But her tone was odd – tight and resigned. After she'd slammed the front door it took Annie a good five minutes to break the odd stupor, to get back into motion. But there was a new lodger now. She was needed.

Something similar happened when Jim later turned up with Graham, and Davey, and Mackie. That same itching in her fingers, the row with Rosie, the desire to hear Rita's voice. Somehow, Annie had five lodgers now. Vic – whose real name was Vidur, but he went by Victor – Graham, Mackie and two Davids – one David and one Davey. She never asked Jim why he'd brought these people, but she'd said she wanted lodgers and that part was true.

When Lee arrived, carried in a chair by three friends and almost too weak to speak, Annie said he'd have to go to hospital in the morning, but for the time being he could have her bed. She worried all night, lying on a mattress in Rosie's room. They'd just lain him on her slept-in sheets; her own body might have exuded something that would be the end to the wreckage of his immune system. She paced outside the door at six, and finally knocked. She knocked again, but he didn't answer. When she went into the room, she found that he was dead. She got Rosie ready for school before ringing up for them to come and collect the body.

Vic was healthy for a long time. When he was well, he sat in the kitchen listening to the radio, dancing and persuading Annie to dance too. When he felt weaker he'd sit down, but keep dancing with his chest, shoulders, arms. He was a vegetarian, and taught Annie to make some delicious, cheap things with lentils. This was a relief; Annie would have swiftly run out of ideas on how to feed him otherwise.

When he faded it happened very quickly. He seemed to rage the whole time. Just as his limbs had struck out to the beat, they now flailed in fury. Jim said he'd heard of it happening, a kind of dementia setting in. Annie wasn't sure that this was what was happening. He seemed lucid enough, when she looked into his eyes. Just incandescent with rage.

There was a lot of that in the house in those days. Between Vic's fury, Rosie's seething and Jim's moody silences, Annie often felt as if she were on a raft all by herself, floating in the middle of a stormy sea.

When it became obvious that there wasn't long to go, Jim rang Vic's parents. Vic insisted that there was no point; when Jim told him they were coming his face went very still. His father sat outside in the car, but his mother came in and held his hand, and cried. Keith, his lover, hovered by the door the whole time. Mackie settled at the foot of the stairs, quiet and watchful as a cat, offering reassuring smiles whenever Keith turned to look at him.

There was a change in Vic after his parents' visit. He seemed to grant himself a reprieve from his anger, to let himself rest. He took some water from the sponge that Keith pushed gently against his tongue.

'Am I doing it wrong?' Keith asked. Annie could see that the stick was shaking slightly. A drop of water fell from the tip and splashed onto Vic's cheek.

'You're fine,' Annie said. She could take over, she thought, but there was no need for that. 'Just be gentle.'

Vic made a soft, almost purring sound when Keith washed and dried his hair.

'Looking good?' It must have taken him some effort to speak, rolling his head towards Annie, but her responding nod seemed to give him some burst of energy, for then he smiled, a luminous smile. He reached out one long hand to touch Keith's cheek.

'Thanks, babe.' A frown distorted his features, his skin stretched tight over his skull. 'You need to sleep.'

'I can sleep later.'

'Don't be stupid.' A long breath in, a long breath out. 'You just met my mum. Anyone would need a lie-down after that.'

'Someone needs to keep an eye on you.' Keith was looking longingly at the pillow next to Vic's, but his voice was resolute.

'Aunty Nan's here.' Vic looked at Annie again. 'She's a nurse, don't you know.'

Keith nodded, then sighed. He got into bed beside Vic, fully dressed beneath the covers. 'Just for a few minutes. You'll wake me up?'

Annie said nothing, but Vic said, 'Course she will.'

Keith closed his eyes. His face was tense, as though he remained watchful still. Annie realised how young he looked – there was still some baby fat there even despite the dark rings beneath his eyes. He lifted his arm and placed it very gently around Vic's waist. 'That OK?'

'Course it is.'

Annie took the seat that was still warm from Keith's body. She could tell from Keith's breathing that he'd fallen asleep already. Vic's was so intermittent that it was hard to tell, but his eyes were closed too, a half-smile on his face. His lips were so dry that they'd cracked slightly. In the centre of the still-soft mouth was a tiny fleck of dried blood – maroon.

After a minute, Vic spoke.

'I had a dream about Grace Kelly last night.' A long breath out. 'Taken from us too young.'

'She was lovely,' Annie said softly. 'When I was a young girl I used to copy all her clothes.'

She stood up, careful not to jolt the bed, and crossed to the chest of drawers where they kept the box of rubber gloves. She pulled out a pair and placed them carefully on her hands.

'In my dream she was wearing like . . .' another laboured breath in and out, '. . . a kaftan sort of thing. Probably too hippy for the real Princess Grace. And we were by a

pool in this villa. I think it was in the South of France.'
Breath in, breath out. 'Not that I'd know. I've never been.'

Annie picked up the tub of Vaseline from the little cluster
of medicines. 'It sounds like that old film. *To Catch a Thief.*'

'I must have seen that on telly.' Another breath, shal-
lower this time. 'A long time ago.' His hand moved just
slightly, pulling the cover closer under his chin. 'Anyway.
We were relaxing by the pool. Drinking kir royales. Just
chatting. That was the dream.'

'Sounds nice.' Rain was starting to fall outside, washing
away the dregs of the evening, easing the passage into the
deep of the night. 'Wouldn't mind a trip like that.'

Applying a touch of Vaseline to her gloved hand, she
pressed it to his parched lips with the tip of her ring finger.
The mouth seemed to relax in relief, and Vic gave a little
smile. Another tiny ruby of blood welled at the split in his
lip.

'She was nice,' Vic said. His breathing was very faint
now. 'Taken too young.'

It seemed that he might have fallen asleep after that.
Annie took a tissue from the bedside table, dabbed away
the little drop of blood and applied more Vaseline. Then
she removed her gloves – very carefully, the way she'd once
been taught – and placed them in a plastic bag along with
the tissue.

For a long while Annie listened to the rain. She could
hear footsteps outside in the garden: Jim, working away
by torchlight, pruning the roses. Annie must have
nodded off herself then, in the chair.

When she woke again the heaviness of the dark told her that there was nothing left of the day, that they had strayed far into the silence. She remembered the feel of this time from the months after George's death. It sat lightly around her, the night.

'You know,' Vic said, and Annie jumped slightly, 'I don't know anyone who's died.'

Annie said nothing.

'My ex's friend got ill. I knew him a bit. And my grandma in India, when I was a kid. But I don't remember her.'

His hand moved lightly over the cover to find Keith's. Keith slept on, a slight snore in his breath. 'He's still out like a light,' Annie said.

'Good.' She could barely hear Vic's breathing now. It seemed to come and go, as the wind outside ebbed and flowed with the drum of the rain. 'When I was growing up my parents told me it was a cycle. Death. Rebirth.'

'Do you believe that?'

'Never thought about it much.' A slight smile. His eyes remained closed. 'Thought there was plenty of time.' He took an odd, rattling breath.

'We've got time now.'

'I tried to ask my mum more about it earlier.' He paused for a long time, as if he'd lost the thought entirely. But after perhaps a minute, maybe more, he added, 'She just started crying. I didn't push it.'

He shifted slightly, and Annie understood instinctively that he wanted to roll over a little, towards Keith and the window. She stood automatically, lifting his bones in the tender places, guiding his shoulders until he settled. 'Maybe Princess Grace has come back already.' His thumb moved very slightly, stroking Keith's hand. 'Maybe she's something else now.'

For perhaps an hour, maybe longer, all was silent. Annie drifted in and out of sleep. Then, with a swiftness that Annie was not expecting, Vic opened his eyes. In the stretched expanse of his face his lashes were full, thick and soft. There was still a shine in his eyes, a light. 'If Keith gets ill, you'll take care of him.'

There was a command in his voice, Annie could hear it. She nodded, but she was not sure if Vic could see her, so she said, 'Yes.'

'Like he's taken care of me.' A whisper-breath, in and out. 'Promise.'

'I promise.'

'You've been nice to me.'

'It's the least I can do.'

'You do it well.'

Annie nodded. Her eyelids were so heavy now. When Vic said, 'Is Keith still asleep?' it cost her a great deal of effort to open her eyes and check. She nodded.

'Good.'

When Annie woke up, the room was laced with silver-grey light and Keith was awake, staring blankly at the ceiling, his hand gripping Vic's so tightly that it might crush it, and Vic was gone.

November, 1959

THE EVENING OF THEIR encounter with Dr Lewin, Annie and Rita end up listening to a programme on the radio – something about the Bomb. Chilly in her bed, neither awake nor asleep, the Bomb grows larger in Annie's mind. It becomes, somewhere between midnight and two in the morning, a problem that it is her job to solve. When she sleeps she dreams of winter greens spattered with blood and armless hands lying in the dust.

Annie often wonders if she ought to spend more time thinking about the Bomb. It's something to do with atoms, which she doesn't know about. But she knows about cells. She understands that the Bomb attacks every cell in your body. It's an ending more final than anything else that can be imagined. You can't see the radiation, she's read that in the papers. But that doesn't mean it isn't there, waiting to detonate in every cell.

So she has slept poorly. When Matron tells her to change the bed linen in another side room, it barely occurs to her that she has not been in there before. Nor was she aware that it was occupied.

Rita has mentioned in passing that she's been in to see Paul a few times.

'Just to chat,' she says. 'It's rather nice to talk to a chap of our age, don't you think? He's in an awful state, poor love. Asked me if I'd bring him a Bible.'

'What did you say?' Annie is wary. 'He doesn't think he's Jesus, does he?'

Rita laughs. 'Do you know, I had one of the old boys tell me he was John the Baptist the other day. I thought that was terrifically funny. If you could be anyone, why would you go for the chap who plays second fiddle?'

'Did you say that to him?'

'I did. He said it was a fair point, but he still asked me if I wanted to be baptised. I said maybe after I was finished giving out the tea.'

'And?'

'And we left it there, didn't we?'

'And . . . and Paul?' There is something pulling at Annie about this man in the side room. 'Did you give him his Bible?'

'Matron said it was all right.' Rita shrugs. 'I don't mind what he does with it. I asked him if he wouldn't rather have something a bit jollier, but he just laughed.'

She speaks so calmly that the question that has been playing at the edge of Annie's mind – the question of what might be wrong with Paul – seems crass and babyish. And now Annie is being sent into another side room, to speak to another unknown man.

'Oh, and Nurse Graie?' Matron pauses, her oddly youthful, pink mouth contorting slightly. 'You may need to prepare yourself for the smell.'

167

Annie stands for a while grasping the door handle. Once she has summoned her courage, she opens the door sharply.

A wave of foul air engulfs and enters her, forcing her to throw her head back and clamp her eyes shut. When she opens them she sees that a man of about thirty-five is on the bed, very upright. Annie can tell he's tall, even though he's sitting. His shoulders are broad and his head held carefully. His face is very pale. Annie can see in the fluorescent light that there is a scattering of freckles across the aquiline nose. Perhaps some Scots blood, she thinks. Aristocratic Scots.

His breathing is quiet and regular, as if the smell isn't bothering him at all.

'Hello,' she says.

The man turns his head at her greeting. He makes no other motion. The bed he sits upon is neatly made. He has combed his hair and washed his face.

'I'm to change the bed linen,' she starts to say, but by opening her mouth she begins to retch. 'But I . . .' She looks over to the far corner of the room. Beneath the window there is a mess of vomit, and worse besides.

'Just a moment,' she murmurs faintly, then walks out of the room as fast as she can without running. It takes only a minute to fetch the mop, the disinfectant and the towels, but nearly ten more to force herself back into the room. The man does not look up when she enters, nor has he moved. She hastens to clean up the source of the smell, holding her breath.

There's a small window. She glances at the man. Thin as he is, there's surely no way that it could make him a danger to himself. It only opens an inch or two.

'I'll get the key to the window,' she says.

He regards her with mild interest. 'Will you?'

'Of course.'

Arranging her face as best she can, she turns towards the bed. 'Would you stand up so I can change the bed linen over?'

The man turns to look at her. He moves very slowly. It's odd, she thinks, but she could swear that she detects some little note of pity. Something about his expression, a twist at the corner of the mouth. Perhaps, she starts to suspect, his is a subtler delusion than the other patients on the ward. Something just as powerful, but less easily identified.

'As you wish,' he says. There it is, the insolence. Annie feels the urge to take a step or two backwards, but stands her ground.

The man rises. She can see, as soon as he sets his feet on the floor, that his whole body is shaking. For a second, she thinks he might overbalance and reaches out an arm to catch him, but he manages to stop himself at the last moment, and clasps his hands behind him, moving to stand stiffly by the door.

He's very thin, Annie thinks. Not emaciated like the syphilitic patients, but very thin.

'Why are you doing this?'

Annie looks down at the clean bed linen in her hands. 'Because it's Tuesday.'

'No.' He shakes his head, impatient. 'Why are you doing this? Making me ill, and now treating me like an invalid?'

'I . . .' Annie has no idea what she's supposed to say to this. After fumbling for a moment, she settles on, 'I'm a nurse.' A pause. 'And you were ill already.'

The patients do this sometimes. They're convinced that they'd be fine if it weren't for their medication. 'We're just doing our best to help.'

She wrestles with the sheets for a few moments. The man just stands there, staring straight ahead as if she weren't in the room at all. She thinks of what her grandmother always told her, about her youth, when she was a housemaid in a great estate. How the great family made such a study of ignoring the maids and footman. It was as if you weren't there at all, her grandmother said. As if you were a ghost.

'I don't soil the bed,' he says abruptly, as she's gathering the sheets into one mass. He speaks very clearly. 'I know that's what you want, but I'm not going to.'

Annie doesn't respond, but looks over at the mess under the window.

'Best ventilation,' he says. 'Even with the lock, that window barely fits in the frame. You can feel the draught.' Then he turns his head, very sharply. 'What is your name?' The tone is imperious.

'Annie,' Annie says. She flinches inwardly. An elementary mistake. 'I mean . . . Nurse Graie.'

The man nods slowly. He seems uninterested in her mistake. 'Annie,' he says. Then, 'Nurse?'

'Yes?'

Her voice is far breathier than it ought to be, her speech too hurried for her own comfort.

'Would you be so good . . .' He looks her directly in the eye. His irises are a fine, bright hazel, like a walk in woodland. '. . . as to ask Dr Lewin if I might have some more paper? And another pencil.' He turns his head to the little table in the corner – one could hardly call it a desk, but there's a little stool in front of it. On the top of the table is a good-sized sheaf of paper, and Annie can see the closely-written lines of pencilled script. She hesitates, then nods.

'And you might as well ask him,' the man adds to her back, as she turns to leave the room, 'whether he has reconsidered my request to have use of a fountain pen. I give you my word of honour that I'm no danger with it. Not to myself. I just prefer the way it feels, writing with ink.'

Annie nods. She cannot leave the room quickly enough, nearly tripping on the trailing bed linen as she goes.

'Matron.' Annie wonders when she will get the right gait for this place. If she walks fast enough to appear purposeful, she finds herself a little out of breath. Too slow risks the sin of malingering.

Matron is standing in the centre of the corridor holding a clipboard. Her body is entirely still apart from her right hand, which moves across the page with a peculiar speed. She does not look up until Annie is right in front of her.

'I was wondering if I might have the window key for the side room?'

Matron returns to her writing, a single tiny crease forming between her downturned eyes. 'I see no reason why you should have cause for that.'

'The patient soiled the room, Matron' Annie says.

'I'm aware, Nurse Graie.' She does not look up. 'Hence my advice to prepare yourself for the smell.'

Annie baulks for a second, but then thinks of Rita. She can keep talking, keep asking questions, she tells herself, and then eventually all will become clear. 'Well, Matron' she says, trying not to sound frightened, 'I've cleared up the mess, of course, but the room's still very stuffy. I thought it best to . . . air it out?'

Sister Schneider was evangelical about the benefits of fresh air. A stout Bavarian woman, she had insisted that every window on every ward be flung open at all hours, even when the sky was thick with snow. As far as she was concerned, the significance of penicillin, iodine and insulin all fell at the feet of *lüften*.

But Matron makes no move. Her expression does not change. It's only the caving-in sensation that Annie feels in her chest that makes clear the magnitude of her mistake.

'You cleared up the mess,' Matron repeats. Her voice is soft and, Annie thinks, oddly beautiful. The sort of speaking voice that you might expect an opera singer to have. Annie nods.

'Speak up, Nurse Graie.'

'Yes, Matron, I did.'

'And did I ask you to clean it up?'

'No, Matron.'

'Did I ask you to open the window?'

'No, Matron.'

'Did I ask you to undertake any task at all, save the changing over of the patient's bed linen?'

Annie knows better than to look at the floor, but knows just as well that if she meets Matron's gaze she will be scorched and cry out. So she fixes her eyes on the window frame, just behind Matron's shoulder. The watery sun has sunk out of sight behind a copse of trees; gloom is spreading across the sky like an ink stain.

'No, Matron.'

'It cannot be undone.' Matron's voice is so quiet that Annie almost has to strain to hear it. The way she said it made it seem like a terrible sentence is being pronounced.

'I . . .'

'Speak up.'

'I'm sorry, Matron.'

To her astonishment, something in Matron's face seems to soften just a fraction. 'We'll say no more about it.' She starts to walk away, then pauses.

'I suspect that you might have a question, Nurse Graie.'

Annie's instinct is to turn away. But she stands firm.

'You may ask, if you wish.' There is something indecipherable in Matron's features. Annie draws in a breath, waiting for the trick, but it does not come. So she speaks.

'If we're not cleaning up the mess, then why are we changing the bedding?'

'All patients have their bedding changed weekly. It's hospital procedure.'

Annie nods, as if she understands. Then she finds, to her surprise, that part of her *does* understand. If they were to start changing the bed linen on days other than a Tuesday, then who knew what would follow? As she has this thought, a sense of peace overcomes her, so powerful that she thinks she might cry with relief. When she comes back into the side room with the fresh linen, she does not look at the man again.

'I'm afraid I can't open the window,' she mutters to the bare mattress. He is standing behind her, very still. There is a pause.

'I see.' Then, just as she's plumping up the pillow and straightening up to leave, he speaks again. 'Ask Dr Lewin about the pen though, will you?'

June, 1985

ANNIE STAYED AWAKE LONG enough to see Rosie off to school – Rosie had been spoiling for a fight, but Annie couldn't face it and just accepted the glowering silence instead. Once the front door had slammed shut she went to ring Vic's mother. Her address book on her lap, she rang the funeral director next, and the council, and then, to her own surprise, she turned the pages until she found Rita's name. Rita had sent a card when George died. No words of sympathy, no platitudes about what a wonderful husband and father George had been. Just a single scribbled line: *give me a ring when you're ready – all my love, R.*

Well, Annie thought, I'm more than ready now.

Rita arrived an hour later, with a tin of homemade biscuits.

'They're awful,' she said, watching Annie attempting to arrange them on a plate. 'Paul says he likes them, but he's a rotten liar.'

She'd picked up mid-conversation. Annie didn't mind – she'd barely slept. The sugar in the shortbread seemed to bring her briefly back to life. Mackie made it easier and harder by wandering in, his short flower-patterned dressing gown showing his thin, lesion-patterned legs.

'Keith's sleeping,' he said. 'And Jim rang. Apparently Vic's family are OK with us going along to the cremation.' He paused. 'Men only though. Sorry, Aunty Nan.'

'It's OK, love.' Annie leaned back on the sofa, closing her eyes. With anyone else she'd need to explain, need to hide the parts of herself that were depleted past their strength. But it was only Rita.

'Got lots of lodgers, have you?' Rita had waited until after Mackie had left the room to ask.

'It's good income,' Annie said. 'But never mind that.'

She asked after Paul, and Lizzie. Lizzie was off at university now, Rita said. She'd thought about nursing but Rita had warned her off it.

'Eats its young, that job does. Paul wants her to be a teacher, because he never could.'

There was a silence after that.

'And how is Paul?'

'Same as ever.'

Annie looked up quickly. Rita's expression was cheerful, but Annie could detect a certain meaning there that was unmistakable.

'It's been lovely for him, ever since Lizzie went off to university,' Rita continued. There it was, the same note of hidden emphasis. 'He's so much more social these days.'

Annie swallowed. A crumbled remnant of biscuit caught in her throat and she felt like she might choke. She thought of Paul, out dancing, part of the night. She couldn't picture it, she realised. Perhaps it was because when they first met she only ever saw him in his pyjamas and dressing gown. She couldn't picture him as part of the world that belonged to Robbie.

But it had to be said, and there was no way to say it subtly – you could never count on Rita to pick up on implications. She must have it out.

'You mustn't sleep with Paul.'

Rita's weather-beaten face creased for a second, but then smoothed out. 'Er, thanks, Annie.' And then quickly, as if for appearance's sake, 'But he's my husband, you know.'

'I know.' Annie nodded emphatically. 'I'm not questioning that. But really, you mustn't sleep with him. Because there's this disease.'

'I've read about it.'

'The papers don't know the half of it.' She says it very sharply, almost snapping. Rita stays quiet, and she resumes. 'We don't know what causes it but I'm starting to hear that it's probably . . .' Annie was, absurdly, about to say *marital relations*, but then she remembered that Rita was a trained nurse and managed 'sexual intercourse'.

'Right.'

'Of both kinds, Rita. You know what I mean. Paul's still . . . he does, doesn't he?'

'Of course he does. And of course I know. And Paul and I . . .' She trailed off. 'No. You're right. I'll tell Paul that he needs to be careful. That we need to be careful.'

'Lizzie needs her dad.'

'She does.' A pause. 'And I need my husband.'

Annie tried to take one of the biscuits, just for something to do with her hands, but most of it had crumbled away by the time she lifted it to her mouth.

'So your lodger has it?'

'All of them.'

Annie hadn't expected to answer so honestly, but it was different, talking to Rita. She wasn't expected to be a mother, a housewife, around her. She wasn't even really expected to be decent.

'They're very young,' Rita said softly. Her eyes clouded over as she turned back to Annie. 'And what do you do? You look after them?'

Annie shook her head. 'No, no. I'm just the landlady.' She explained how Jim brought them to her. 'Then they go into hospital for outpatient stuff, but they don't want to go in as inpatients because, well . . .'

'. . . They won't be treated properly.'

It was such a relief not have to explain herself from the very beginning. 'There's not much that I can do, other than make sure they take their medications. They get their diagnosis and the doctors, well . . . They're just saying the obvious things. Rest. Exercise, but not too much. Balanced diet. Don't go mad on the booze, cut out the fags. Don't share a toothbrush. Don't share a razor.'

The medical advice that they'd gathered from doctors had been scant and uneven. Jim warned everyone, 'Don't tell people, they might get nasty. If you tell your GP you won't be able to get life insurance.'

Most of their information therefore came from a few small, scrappy, but impressively informed organisations. 'The doctors don't know anything really,' Annie said. 'We know more than they do.'

And, Annie had learned, often it was a case of not doing. Not wincing when she saw the thin, stiffened, sarcoma-spattered limbs. Not turning her face away when she heard the coughing. Not trying to talk them out of it when they wanted to call their mothers, or talking them into it if they said they didn't. She kept an eye out, of course. Not just for the pneumocystis pneumonia and the lesions, everyone knew about those. But for the creeping skin conditions, the thrush. The little things. Sometimes it was clearing away the empty wine glasses and the ash trays, providing pints of squash and fried slices for the hangovers, pretending not to smell the herbal tang of the pot they smoked in the afternoons.

'Something more needs to be done,' Rita said. 'Not you, I mean.' She leaned forwards to scoop up a rough clump of crumbs. 'By the health service. The government.'

'People are trying,' Annie said.

It was true. Jim had started using her phone a lot. He offered to pay for the bill, but she said it was all right. At first it was just to ring around after someone had died, but later he started calling the local MP most days. He'd sit at the kitchen table, a cigarette fading to nothing between his fingers, eyes glazed. Annie bought a longer cord for the phone so he could sit on the garden step and look out at the roses while he waited. Eventually, after many nights sleeping on the sofa, he'd started renting one of the rooms in the house again, the smallest one at the top. It was easier that way, and Annie was relieved to have someone else there at night.

They talked for a while longer. Rita's eyes grew enormous listening to Annie. There was relief in telling someone about how the boys would come home from the GP with stories of stickers on their file marked 'warning'. Relief in not having someone ask how that could happen, because of course they both knew it so well.

'Do you do much with them? Keep them busy?'

Annie wrinkled her nose. 'Like OT, you mean?'

The thought had occurred to her, but she wasn't sure where to start. Jim wanted to have them all gardening, but one of the hospitals had warned against it. Too much bacteria in soil. So Jim worked the garden alone, occasionally helped by Rosie. He grew beans, tomatoes, cucumbers, and Annie chopped them into salads.

'I'm an art therapist now,' Rita told her.

Annie bit back her initial response, *what's that when it's at home*, and said politely, 'That sounds lovely.'

'It suits me,' Rita said quietly. 'You've got to find the thing that suits you. You can't expect to find it right away. But I found this. Joined the association when Lizzie started school.' A pause. 'You seem like you've found what suits you.'

Annie felt her mouth tightening. In a sense, of course, she knew that Rita was right. But looking at her kitchen, at the sheets drying on the rack, at the vegetables laid out for chopping, she couldn't help but think – really? This is what I'm made for?

Rita smiled at Annie. 'You don't look any older.'

She looked different and the same, Annie thought. It was if the whirlwind around her had shifted shape and colour and yet, at the centre of it, there she was, unchanged. She was tanned – not in the fashionable way, but from years in the sun.

Annie looked down at her hands. They were dry and chapped with scrubbing, like they'd once been from all the cleaning at Fairlie Hall. 'I feel a lot older. Rita, I—'

'It always amazes me,' Rita interrupted, 'how young we were then.' Annie looked up slowly, and when she met Rita's gaze she was surprised to see the warmth there. 'You do so many silly things. When you're young.'

'I shouldn't—'

'But I'm glad,' Rita interrupted again. 'It all ended up as it should. With me, and Paul, and Lizzie. We've found a way of living that suits us.'

Rita appeared at the door the next morning, lugging a great bag of clay in one hand and a portable potter's wheel in the other.

'Creative,' she said, bumping the bag of clay behind her into the kitchen and setting out the wheel with a clatter. 'Tactile. *Meditative.* They'll love it.'

Annie wasn't so sure. There was something in the way that Rita shepherded the lodgers over to the kitchen table, doled out clay, spoke in a voice that was a touch too loud

181

and eyes a touch too bright, that unsettled her. Or perhaps it was merely that she was picking up on something among Mackie and the others that felt a little resentful.

Rita told them to make whatever felt right, to think of the clay as a means of self-expression. Mackie dutifully produced a sort of flower, David a cat, and Davey a cock and balls.

'Gorgeous.' Rita clapped her hands together. 'Cheeky sod.'

But Annie could see she looked a little deflated.

Something relaxed after Rita went home for the evening. While Annie made the chilli con carne, Mackie sat at the kitchen table, pressing his thumbs into a lump of clay, his eyes half-closed.

In the following weeks, Annie's kitchen became a production line of wonky vases, ashtrays, some brave attempts at mugs.

'I'm making an urn,' said Davey. 'To put me in. To remind you of me.'

'Why?' Graham chimed in. 'Because it's bent?'

'It's asymmetrical,' said Davey with dignity. 'You can put me on the mantel.'

When the clay was finished and ready to fire, the men disappeared. Graham to the doctors, Davey out to lunch, David and Mackie to lie down.

'The gang's back together,' said Rita happily, sluicing bits of clay from between her fingers. 'It's a proper therapeutic environment. We're helping.'

'We're not making anyone better,' Annie said. She said it despite herself, not to get at Rita, but because some days it seemed to well up inside her and threaten to choke out every other thought.

Rita said nothing for a moment. She watched as Annie pinched a little piece of clay from the table and passed it back and forth, worrying it between her fingers. Then she said quietly, 'You don't know that, Annie.'

'I do.' Annie could feel the raggedness in her throat. It had been there since she woke up to find Vic dead, and now it threatened to tear open. 'I've had three go now. There's no recovering from this.'

'Perhaps you've just had bad luck. Some of them will start getting better, I'm sure of it. I've been reading the papers.' Rita leaned forwards confidentially. 'There's a whole theory going around that lots of people are infected and most of them just fight it off naturally, you see? No drugs, no nothing. And it's just that certain people are more vulnerable. And once we work out what it is, we can cure them.'

'And if we can't?' Annie closed her eyes. 'What then?'

Annie sensed Rita withdrawing from her a little. 'We've got to be hopeful, Annie.' There was something reproachful in her tone. 'You ought to know that. You can't just write people off.'

'I'm not writing them off.' Annie's eyes were clenched now, and leaking. 'I'm just—'

'I think you're just tired,' Rita interrupted. 'It's ghastly, being back in all this medical stuff. I don't know how you stand it. But Fairlie Hall taught me something. You saw it today – these chaps don't need drugs and chemicals.

183

They need art and good food and a cosy home. The things you're giving them.'

Annie wanted to nod, but something forced her into stillness. It was as if another old, familiar acquaintance had entered the room and sat on the sofa between them. Being together reminded her of being apart.

Rita seemed like she would have been happy to stay for dinner. 'Paul's out tonight. He's met this chap, Alec. Complains about him a bit, says he's a slob. But they're always together, so . . .'

Annie could feel the invitation in her mouth, pushing at the back of her teeth. But not tonight, she told herself.

'I'd invite you to stay,' she said awkwardly. 'But I've got to help Rosie with her homework.'

It was mostly a lie. Annie had never been much help with Rosie's homework, being no good at academics. And with the constant parade going through the kitchen, there was always someone on hand. It was just as well – Rosie's teacher had sent a letter home not long after Robbie died, saying she wasn't paying attention in class, and a steady stream of letters had followed in its wake. They'd stopped recently, but Annie suspected that they were merely no longer being passed on.

Jim was a computer programmer, whatever that meant, apart from the fact that he understood maths. Better still, he understood it enough to be able to explain it clearly, so that even when she was standing with her back to the two of them, at the sink or chopping vegetables, little by little she came to understand it too.

'How old's Rosie now?'

'Fifteen.'

Rita shivered. 'Awful time.'

Annie looked at her in surprise. 'She's happy enough, I think. Well, there's been losing her father, but she's coping. Coping splendidly.'

'I'm sure you're right,' Rita said quickly, with a smile. Annie said goodbye to her and agreed that they would speak soon, and it was only when she'd shut the front door that she realised what bothered her about Rita's expression. It was the smile that she used when she was saying something too kind to be true.

Annie went into the living room that night to find Davey and Jim sitting on the sofa, a great pile of Robbie's shirts between them like a third person.

'Rosie chucked them out,' Davey said in explanation. Jim didn't move. 'Said she's too old to dress up.'

Annie said nothing. One of the shirts was lying languidly on top of the rest; she could almost see the long limbs spread out.

'Suppose she's fifteen now,' Annie mumbled. 'Young lady. I keep forgetting.' Her knees suddenly felt like they were threatening to give out, and she dropped down beside Jim on the sofa. 'She's cross with me.'

Jim reached out to lightly pat Annie's knee.

185

'We're just gathering more and more bags of stuff,' Davey said. 'There's a whole bin liner of Vic's bits and pieces in my room.'

'Send them to the charity shop,' Jim said flatly.

'Are you joking?' Davey scoffed, but there was no real anger in his voice. 'I'm saving them for when I've lost a few pounds.' He stared down at his knees. They were as skinny as a little boy's.

'Sorry about Rita earlier,' Annie said. She knew she was being pretty transparent about changing the subject, but there was something about Davey's carefully light tone that made her feel like she might lose her composure for once. 'I know she's a bit ...'

'Oh, she's fine.' Davey gave a half-smile and rolled his eyes. 'She's doing her best. She made us laugh.' He picked the top shirt off the pile and laid it in his lap, smoothing it out. 'It was nice to make something again.' Davey had worked in the theatre. Building sets, designing costumes. The long hours were too much now. 'Are you sure you don't want this, Jim?'

He lifted the shirt up, the sleeves flapping gently.

'I'm not exactly going to wear it, am I?' Jim's voice was deadpan these days – it was rare to hear any expression in it. 'You can have it if you want.'

'Not to wear.' Davey laid it back on his lap, caressing a silky trim with his middle finger. 'But there's some lovely colours here.'

May, 2020

I WAS MAKING SOUP when I looked out of the window and saw her. For a moment I kept stirring the onions for my soup, somehow incapable of reacting. Then my whole body seemed to jolt.

She looked like a Victorian doll. Reams of soft black curls, enormous grey eyes, a little flounced pinafore. Three or four years old. But she was looking around her in that frantic way. I darted out of the front door, no coat, barely remembering my keys, but slowed my walk to an ordinary pace before she could spot me.

'Hello, my love,' I said, in my best nurse's voice. 'Where's your mummy, then?'

She was looking around her, taking in all the black and white houses. I understood what was happening. In the Grid, all the streets look exactly the same, crisscrossing each other, but you're never quite where you think you ought to be. Even cab drivers, with the Knowledge under their belts, hate the Grid. The little girl looked anchorless, too frightened to even wail. I took her hand.

'Is your mummy nearby?'

She nodded, and tears leaked out of her vast grey eyes. I wondered if I ought to phone the police. I'd not brought my mobile with me, and besides, it seemed a bit much. Her frantic mother might only be a street away. If I took the child into the house to fetch my phone, I might make everything worse.

'I've got an idea,' I said. I led her to the nearest street corner. I'd a good view in all four directions. 'Why don't we wait here? Then we can see Mummy coming.'

The little girl nodded. I watched her looking from one road to the other; I could see the panic growing.

'Have you seen the blossom on the trees?' I directed her attention upward to where the blooms spread above us in a thick pink roof. The grey eyes lifted in the small peaked face. For a moment the tears, which had been falling thick, seemed to freeze. One little hand drifted up, reaching.

'Would you like to get closer?'

She nodded. I lifted her up. I haven't held a child for such a long time. I'd forgotten it, that sense of yielding trust in their weight. She put one hand on my shoulder, the better to push herself up in my arms, reaching to crush the petals between her little fingers.

'Pretty?'

She nodded again, a smile stealing into her lips.

'Livy!'

A woman was hurrying towards us. Beautifully dressed, even in these days. Barefoot, terrified.

'She wandered out while the Ocado delivery was arriving,' she said to no one, her voice shaking as she dashed across the road without looking and snatched her daughter from my arms. She clutched at Livy's head, weaving her hands through the thick hair, then seemed to remember the rules, and took a big step back. I did the same.

'Thought it must have been something like that,' I said. I was doing my best to sound calm, comforting, though I felt a little shaken by the suddenness with which the weight had disappeared from my arms. 'No harm done. We've been looking at the flowers, haven't we, sweetheart?'

The child, reinstated in her mother's arms, seemed to have remembered her own panic, and started to cry.

'Thank you,' the woman said, but it wasn't gratitude in her voice.

'Bye, Livy,' I said. The woman had already turned away. She was small, in her elegant vest top and cashmere tracksuit bottoms. Even the weight of such a little girl seemed to bend her out of shape. Livy's grey eyes remained fixed on the blossom as her mother carried her away.

Where exactly did I go wrong, I wondered, as I padded back to the house. I was still in my slippers. Was it picking her up? Taking her hand? Did my calm make the woman feel stupid? Or was she just angry that I'd been there at all, that there had been a witness to her moment of sickening failure?

When I got back into the house the kitchen was full of smoke and the onions had blackened and stuck to the bottom of the pan. I ran cold water over them, and steam filled the kitchen with an almighty hiss.

I told Rosie about it when she rang. I was pleased to have a story of my own, to match the tale of the people on her street who'd stood at their garden gates to sing 'We'll Meet Again'. It irritates me, all the stuff about how whatever this is, is like the war. Even the war wasn't like the war, not the way they talk about it now.

But Rosie was furious. 'You shouldn't have done it, Mum.' A pause. 'You know full well you shouldn't have done it.'

I wasn't expecting to hear that venom in her voice, the same as in Livy's mother's. 'Well, what exactly should I have done, then?' I replied, rather tartly. 'Let the little mite wander into the road and get run over?'

'Obviously not. No one's suggesting that. But it was mad to hold her hand, pick her up. Completely mad.' I could hear her shaky breath distorting the line. 'It's making me worry about your judgement. What if she makes you ill?'

'What if I make *her* ill?'

'Oh, don't talk rubbish.'

'What was I supposed to do?'

'You could have stayed in the house and rung the police. You could have gone into the street and talked to her from a distance.' Her voice was rising. 'You could have got that couple next door to sort her out. All sorts of things. You know full well, Mum. Don't pretend you don't.'

'I did what anyone would have done,' I said coolly.

'I wouldn't have picked her up.' Rosie sighed. 'Do you need to come and stay with us, Mum?' Her voice was hard now, tight. 'I don't think you're coping on your own.'

'What're you on about?' I felt a hot surge in my chest; at the same time my fingers became cold and numb, like I might drop the phone. 'I'm coping fine. I'm not the one who couldn't keep a proper eye on her own daughter, for heaven's sake!'

'Yes, because you were a perfect mother, weren't you?' Rosie's voice was icy. It knocked the breath out of me for a second, but then I gathered myself.

'I don't know what you're referring to,' I said. My hands were shaking madly, as if to compensate for the composure of my voice. 'I think all this must be getting to you. We're all upset, aren't we.'

I said the words but I didn't let the question enter my voice. 'Anyway, I'll speak to you later.'

I put the phone down. I thought of the little girl and her vast grey eyes, her cloud of black curls. In those moments when I'd stood at the window, seeing her and not seeing her, the only thought in my head had been, 'ghost'.

June, 1985

ROSIE ARRIVED HOME, HER hands laced with bruises. Her eyes – dark beneath the tangle of her new perm – were watchful, raging.

'What's happened?' Annie's voice was shaking, but she managed to gently pick up the injured hand. It looked like someone had been pinching her girl. Rosie just looked up at her, sullen. 'Has someone been hurting you? The other girls?'

'No.'

'Darling, you need to tell me.'

'Of course they haven't!' The words burst from her, her gaze hot with fury. 'They won't touch me!'

'What do you mean, Rosie?'

'They say I'm dirty.' Her cheeks were all tears now. 'No one will hang around with me. They say I'll make them sick.'

'And I hope you told them that that's nonsense?' Annie could hear her own voice rising sharply, tipping just above the edge of what she could control. She knew she must have sounded sharper than she intended, because Rosie took a step back. 'You know that's nonsense, don't you? You know there's no possible way of you becoming sick?'

'I told them that it doesn't work like that.' Rosie's voice was caught somewhere between fury and misery. 'But I don't even know how it *does* work. And they don't care, anyway.'

Annie had found, to her own surprise, that when it came to the illness, she somehow knew exactly where her own limit was. How much she could bear in a day, when she needed to go outside for a cigarette and when she could carry on. But in the face of Rosie's distress she felt that she knew nothing, could do nothing at all of use. So she asked Rosie what she wanted for her tea, sending her up with bowls of soup for David and Mackie. She waited for a moment until Wham! started to come through the floorboards, turned up loud.

Some of the neighbours had started to complain about noise. Usually it was her tenants dancing, sometimes someone left a record player on late. Often though the bumps were falls – the men getting up in the night to go to the loo and then collapsing. Some of the children on the street started to say that there was a poltergeist in the house. There were talks of white, skeletal faces at windows, malevolent-looking eyes.

Annie didn't blame them. She knew how tempting it was, believing in ghosts.

She often dreamt of the first boy. That was what she called him, in her mind, even though after him there were no numbers, only names. That bundle in the corner of the waiting room, the great fleshless hollows of his face carved out by the harsh light, the automatic jerk of his head when the nurse drew near, but never near enough. The expectation of help. Annie often wondered what sort of person he might have been.

May, 2020

ROSIE RANG ME BACK about an hour later. I could tell she'd been crying.

'I know you're independent, Mum,' she said, before I could get a word in. 'I know you do brilliantly for your age, but I worry about you.' Her voice broke. 'I worry all the time about you getting ill.'

'I'm not going to get ill.' I tried not to sound impatient; I didn't want to set her off again. 'How can I get ill when I never see anyone?'

I thought about Paul, how he'd stood at the other end of the kitchen only the day before. I had no idea how careful he was being, and what Alec was doing. I pushed down the feelings of guilt that threatened to come rearing up.

'There's a solution to that, Mum. I keep telling you, you can come here. It's allowed, because you're alone. And we can quarantine you in the flat and—'

'Rosie.' My voice was under control now, gentle. 'I know you mean well, but I can't do that. You know I can't. If I come and live in your granny flat I'll get old.'

She said nothing. What she was thinking didn't need saying.

'I've seen it happen,' I carried on. 'People lose their independence. It's the easiest thing in the world, it's like gravity. You've got to keep on fighting.'

'Yeah, well, you've always been a fighter, haven't you?'

'Rosie, I don't want to have a row with you.'

'What about me?' I heard the rupture. 'What about what I might lose? Mum, you know what it's been like for me. What it's been like ever since I was little. All that loss.'

Now the anger came flaring back up.

'You loved having a full house. You loved having all the boys around.'

'Exactly, Mum. I loved them, and then they died.' It was too late, she was off again now. A great sob. 'Like Dad.' Her crying engulfed the phone line like static. 'Did you ever think about me, when you were doing all that?'

An acrid, sour taste filled my mouth. 'I knew you were safe. I knew you couldn't get it.'

'Did you? Or did you just decide that you knew? Did you actually know for sure?'

For a moment, I stumbled. What exactly did I know at the time? I remember scouring the newspapers for any sign that anyone other than a gay person or a haemophiliac had become ill, and telling myself that on that evidence Rosie could not get sick. I don't remember thinking that way about myself – I think I did assume it was a possibility for me, but not her, somehow. Never her.

I don't think Rosie noticed my hesitation. She snatched in a breath, between sobs. 'Anyway, you knew they were going to die, didn't you?'

196

'We didn't know for sure. Not at first.'

'But then you did know. You must have known at some point that it was all only going one way. And then you could have stopped it, Mum. You could have stopped it, but you didn't.'

'You were a child back then, Rosie.' I swallowed, but the foul taste was still there. 'I wouldn't expect you to understand.'

'I understood what it was like being bullied because of what you were doing.'

'So what should I have done?' Now I was shouting. I can't shout like I once did, full-throated. It cracked, sounded pathetic, and I suddenly wanted a glass of water. 'What should I have done?'

'I don't want to talk about this anymore, Mum.'

'You were the one that brought it up.' My hands were shaking so much that my wedding ring clinked against the glass as I filled it up from the tap.

'We're all upset, aren't we?' she said. For a second I couldn't say quite what disconcerted me about her tone, and then I realised that it was *my* voice she was using – specifically, my nurse's voice. 'It's not good for people, Mum. All this time to sit and ruminate. You get obsessed with things.' She paused. 'I can't stop thinking about the past. Are you the same?'

'I need to make something for my dinner,' I said. The sink was still full with the blackened ruins of my soup. I could hear Rosie heave a sigh, heavy with the traces of her recent tears.

197

'OK, Mum,' she said. I heard the resignation in her voice, and the triumph and shame competed somewhere in my chest. 'I'll call you again tomorrow.'

'OK. Bye, darling.' It's so funny, how I could say those words in the same bright voice I use every day. 'Have a lovely evening.'

November, 1959

ANNIE ASKS MATRON FIRST.

'We don't allow patients to have pens,' Matron says, her face contracting. 'They could be a harm to others. To themselves.'

'How could he harm himself?' The question is out before Annie can stop it. 'That is to say, he doesn't seem . . . And there's no one else in the room.'

'He's been given plenty of pencils. Dr Lewin was clear about that. He's to have pencils.' Matron pauses. Annie thinks that the patient could probably do a fair amount of harm with a pencil if he had a mind to. But she supposes there must be a logic to the rules.

'There's nothing to stop him from writing if he wants to,' Matron continues. She lingers for a second. 'Letters, I expect,' she mutters, seemingly half to herself. 'A letter to his mother, perhaps. They're fond of their mothers. Is there anything else, Nurse Graie?'

'Nothing else, Matron.'

'I must telephone the New York office.'

The naked body is grey with dirt, the old man's face shadowed with beard though Annie shaved it only hours before. The eyes, Annie supposes, are dark brown, but they seem, from the stool where she is sitting beside the iron bath, to be the colour of charcoal. 'I must telephone,' he says again, in a distracted, querulous voice. 'I'm worried that some of my interests aren't being looked after, and with this economic climate . . .' He breaks off, staring into the distance. He does not seem to notice when Annie takes him by the hand and leads him forwards. He does not look at the bath or at her as she lifts the greyish rag to wash him. It's only when she says, 'Well done, Albert,' that he seems to notice her, and says in a calm, clear voice, 'Shut up, you dried-up old whore.'

The sudden blow of his words seems to demolish her composure. Guilt returns, sitting in her chest at a rolling boil.

She asked Matron. Matron said no. That ought to be an end to it.

She's sent back to the side room. This time it's to change the flowers in the enamel jug. The smell is as bad as it was the previous day, but it seems to choke her a little less. He gives a sardonic grin as she comes in.

'For me?' He looks at the hyacinths in her hand. 'You shouldn't have.'

She gives him her generic smile and lifts the old flowers out of the water. The stems are rotten-sweet. He nods at the fresh posy in her hand. 'Hyacinths. Interesting choice.'

'I'm sorry?'

'Some flowers are toxic, you know, if you eat them.'

She stares uncertainly down at the stems in her hand. 'Bad for dogs,' he continues. 'Horses, too. You're in trouble if a horse eats a hyacinth. Heart failure. Humans are all right though.' He gives the small, twisted grin. 'Just vomiting and diarrhoea, nothing to write home about.'

She stands, uncertain, her hands full of blooms.

'Oh, put them in the vase, I'm not going to eat them,' he snaps after a few moments. He shakes his head. 'It's just rather fascinating, the way you lot carry on.'

But Annie's attention has shifted to a small bloom of scarlet on the inner white of his wrist. 'Hold on. I'll be back in a moment.'

'You're off, are you?'

She ignores him and hurries out. As the stench of the side room falls away she is overwhelmed by the scent of the hyacinths. She realises that she never did put them in the jug. She abandons them in the waste bin of the supply cupboard before hurrying back to the side room, gauze and tape in hand. 'You've got a cut on your wrist. I need to patch it up.'

'Beg pardon?'

Annie doesn't want to hurry him, but it's becoming difficult to remain in the room with the smell. 'Come on then. We don't want you to catch some nasty infection.' She's trying to make her voice pragmatic and commanding, but it sounds more like she's begging. He gives her a look out of the corner of his eye, then seems to take pity. He holds out his arm. Annie sees the small red graze on the inside of his wrist, no more than an inch long. He notices the way that Annie's eyes linger and says, with some irritation in his voice, 'Oh, it's nothing like that. I was just trying to force the window open – which I wouldn't have had to do if you'd given me the key, like I keep asking – and I slipped and grazed it.'

'Bit of a sting coming,' Annie says, soaking a pad of gauze with iodine and swabbing at the wound. The blood has turned brown and the graze has started to scab over. He continues to look at her insolently. Once she has finished tucking the bandage into place he gives a curt, almost involuntary, 'thank you, nurse.'

Just as Annie is stepping out of the door, he mutters something. She pauses to take a breath of the cleaner air from the outside corridor, then turns back. 'I'm sorry?'

'You've made me look like I really belong here now.' He raises the arm with the bandage, as if in salute. 'Well played.' For a moment his face distorts, but then it rights itself. 'Did you ask Dr Lewin about the pen?'

'The pen?'

'Yes, the pen. It's a simple request. Dr Lewin mind, not Matron. She'll be no use at all.' He stands up from the bed and takes a few slow, considered steps to the little table in the corner. 'If I could have a desk – a proper one – and if the whole place could be cleaned up, I might have a chance of getting a full draft done while I'm here.'

He gives that twisted little smile again. 'Marvellous to be free from distraction.'

'A pen?' Dr Lewin settles back into his chair, a slightly dreamy look shifting onto his face. 'A pen. Interesting.'

'He says he prefers it to a pencil. Oh, and he told me to thank you for the supply of paper.' Annie lingers, unsure if she ought to take a seat. It's as if the strings of her apron, the laces of her shoes, the tails of her cap are all held in Matron's distant hand. She feels thrown off balance by her own insubordination. But something about the way he asked made it seem – not urgent, not exactly – but like the request had a particular weight.

'Naturally!' A great smile on Dr Lewin's face. 'Why shouldn't the man have a pen, for heaven's sake? What sort of intolerable old prison camp are we, that a man shouldn't have a pen?'

'Matron said a pencil was fine. She said . . .' She doesn't finish, but looks down at her own wrists.

'Don't think I'm encouraging you to doubt Matron's judgement, you know,' Dr Lewin says. His voice, gentler than previously, is less ebullient. 'She's marvellous at what she does.' He sighs. 'But she's been here too long. It happens to the finest nurses. They stop feeling.' He nods at Annie. 'They find it difficult to change course.'

'She thinks he wants to write a letter to his mother,' Annie says. Her voice is barely above a whisper. Dr Lewin is giving her his gentle, enquiring look. 'But he talked about . . . about a book.'

'A book?' Dr Lewin seems surprised, but pleased. 'And why should he not?' His smile broadens. 'You wouldn't have heard of him – anyway, he writes under a pseudonym – but you might be interested to know that our man in the side room is, among other things, a rather distinguished novelist.'

He nods again, as if she were doubting him. 'Spy thrillers, but a cut above. Extraordinary prose style. I took one of his down to Cornwall last summer and truly – splendid stuff.' He leans back in his chair, seemingly overtaken by a charming thought. 'One wonders . . . people did all sorts of things during the war, you know. I've often thought that perhaps . . .' He seems to shake off the thought and laughs. 'Well, at any rate, he's marvellous.'

'I thought . . .'

'You thought perhaps he was delusional?' He smiles kindly. 'Understandable. I suppose you've got that chap who thinks he's the Duke of Windsor on your ward. But no, our man really is a writer. I expect he's spending the time here cooking up his next adventure. Enormously clever, wonderful plotting. Where he gets his ideas from I'd love to know – perhaps he'll tell me, if I ask. But then again . . .' He sighs. Outside the window, the sun drifts behind a cloud. 'But then, perhaps Matron is right after all. A chap like that, a clever chap – he might start making all sorts of demands if we yield on the pen.' He seems to shake himself out of a dream, and gives Annie a businesslike nod. 'Yes. We'll leave it as is. If he truly has something that he wants to write then he'll get on with it, pen or no pen.'

Annie nods. She's unsure whether she's being dismissed, but thinks it best to turn and leave. As she makes to go, however, Dr Lewin speaks again.

'One day, you know, I'd love to conduct a study on the relationship with artistic output.' Annie turns back to Dr Lewin. His eyes are sparkling. 'It's undeniable. It's part of what made the whole criminal hypothesis so implausible. Look at Wilde, for God's sake.'

Annie has a vague memory of a funny school play, and nods. Dr Lewin does not seem to see this. 'And if it were possible, so to speak, to cure the condition without curing the creativity – for who knows what it is that gives man the impulse to create?' He seems to drift away, his eyes resting on something unseen. Annie puts her hand on the doorknob, and the creak of the hinges seems to revive him. It's as if he's woken from a dream, standing sharply and coming round the desk to look down at Annie from above his glasses. Annie realises that his breath has the same sweet stench as the rotten flower stems.

'Nurse Graie.' He pronounces it 'grye'. 'Annie.'

Annie wonders whether the use of her Christian name is some sort of trick, that if she makes any response she'll find herself reported to Matron.

'Matron tells me that you've been getting on well here,' he says. He looks Annie up and down. 'Adaptable. Marvellously adaptable.'

'That's good to hear, Doctor.'

'There are some nurses who have no interest in advancement.' He casts a hand towards the window, indicating that Annie should look outside. She walks over, and out on the lawn she can see Sam standing there with a patient. The patient is drifting between the flowerbeds, and Sam is watching him with the air of a patient dog owner.

'Mental nursing can be a fascinating profession,' Dr Lewin says. 'But you need to stay at the forefront of things, you understand? Otherwise you end up like Matron.' He jerks his head in the direction of the ward. 'Hardened, you know. Seeing the same things over and over, patients passing through with little hope of improvement.' He leans closer to Annie. 'I can help you, you know.' He widens his eyes, his voice low and coaxing. 'I can involve you in some of the most exciting mental treatments in development in Britain.' He smiles, and Annie notices again the odd softness of his pink lips. 'Perhaps assisting in a leucotomy. Wouldn't you like that?'

Annie realises, slowly and then all at once, that Dr Lewin's hand is on her waist.

At first it seems that this can only be a mistake, but then his hand moves downwards, across her backside. She stays, all stone. Very quietly, she hears him breathe, 'Good girl.'

She cannot look at him. She can scarcely look at anything. There is only the window, the grounds of Fairlie Hall, and that strange, sweet-stale breath.

'I thought I'd better let you know straightaway that there's no chance of a pen. I've been told to tell you no.' She says it to the wall above his head. She's been dreading saying the words, but as soon as they're out a sense of peace floods her. Her gaze drops down to him. His eyes are very dark in his white face, hands resting lightly on his knees. He nods – once, slowly.

'From Matron?'

'From Dr Lewin.'

At this he seems to grow stiller, though his hands clench at the material of his pyjama trousers. Then he shrugs. 'I suppose it's an affectation, really. I can get on all right with a pencil.' This muttered to himself. Then his eyes go back to Annie. Sharply – 'Are you all right?'

Annie takes a small step back. She feels her mouth contract, her eyebrows furrow, the ice harden in her throat. 'What do you mean?'

'You looked a little . . .' He shrugs again. 'Never mind.' He holds out his bandaged wrist. 'You were wanting to muck around with this, yes? By the way, is that other nurse coming around soon? The blonde one?'

'Nurse Blythe. I don't know. And I'll look at your wrist tomorrow,' Annie mutters. She turns to half-look at the mess beneath the window and allows the disgust to enter her voice. 'You're fine for now.'

He waits until she's at the threshold of the door to call out, his voice mocking, 'Fine, am I?' For a moment she is stone again. 'I thought I was supposed to be ill?'

She is walking along one of the oak-panelled corridors. The boards of the floor and the panels of the walls, the ceiling, are all one. Annie wonders whether she is walking on the floor at all, or rather the ceiling. Perhaps the two are shifting and interchanging with each step. Gravity behaves differently in Fairlie Hall, or maybe it is just more ruthlessly like itself.

She looks down. She is carrying a pile of soiled sheets down to the laundry room in the basement. Matron sent her.

Yes, that's it.

The door to the basement is disguised in the panelling, like the door that leads on through the house and into Dr Lewin's office. Yet instead of turning into a corridor beyond, the ground falls away. One has to be very careful, leaning into the dark to rummage around for the light switch. And then, there it is – a wooden staircase flooded with light, radiant as jaundice.

Annie has felt, since she last left the stinking side room, that there is nothing to her. Like she is yet another goose feather, waiting to be blown away. Her feet make little noise on the steps as she descends, no creaks.

There before her is the great white hamper, almost as tall as Annie herself, into which she places the dirty linen. The smell is sharp and animal, of bodies and sweat.

Something shifts in the shadows. A denser darkness, moving within darkness. And again, Annie is all stone.

A vast, black, bulky creature is moving beneath the stairs. Annie can hear its staggered, laboured breathing so loudly that she feels it stirring at her skin. She wants to scream, but her mouth seems to have sealed itself. She presses a hand against it, though she doesn't have enough oxygen in her lungs to cry out. The bulk shifts again, its breathing growing faster.

Then she hears a voice – a man's voice that she recognises. It says, 'Stop. Someone's there.'

A great face, like a waxen moon, peering out of the gloom. Then, two more eyes, reflecting the scant light deeper in the dark.

Annie turns. She flees back up the stairs, her heels hammering against the stone floor, the echoes all in her ears. Nothing else to be heard, nothing else to be thought but that slow, terrible rhythm, those low juddering breaths.

July, 1985

ON THE YEAR TO the day after Robbie died, Annie and
Jim took bottles of spumante up to Hampstead Heath. It
had been an odd morning, with yet another row with Rosie,
which fell into a tense, strained silence when Davey came
down to show them the 'secret' he'd been working on. A
patchwork quilt, made of Robbie's shirts, Vic's shirts.

'It's not finished yet,' he'd said. 'We'll keep adding
to it.'

Annie looked down at the quilt, ran her hands over it.
She'd thought, in her time, that she was clever with a needle
and thread, but this was something else. Davey had put
the colours together in a way that she'd never have thought
of and could barely understand, beyond seeing that it was
beautiful. He'd combined disparate fabrics and textures
but allowed connections to form between them, paisley
giving way to embroidered velvet and then at the centre a
patch of bright blue silk, like the view from a skylight.

'It's beautiful.' It didn't feel like enough to say that, so
she tried again. 'You're so clever.'

'I liked making it,' Davey said. He shrugged, like it was
nothing, but there was a certain tension in his shoulders.
'And like I said, it's not finished.'

Rosie had stormed out at that point, slamming the door. Davey hadn't said anything but it was obvious he'd been upset, and Jim was distant, and they'd almost cancelled the trip they'd planned. But Annie, acting on instinct, felt it was right to gently insist. Jim needed to get out of the house that day, to move. Of that much she was sure.

So they got the tube together, and then walked for a long while. Annie found herself growing a little out of breath, walking up the hill. Her exercise these days consisted of running up and down the stairs with trays and bed linen, and little else.

Jim showed her the place where he'd had his first real encounter with Robbie.

'Usually the anonymity is part of the fun,' he said. 'You see some young god, and you think yeah, why not? Why shouldn't I have that, for a few moments? It's like you see how much beauty there is to go around, all just there for the taking.'

'But not with you and Robbie?'

'Oh, with me and Robbie for sure, that was all it was to begin with.' He poured out the spumante. Annie had brought her crystal flutes, a wedding present, wrapped in handkerchiefs. 'But then we kept meeting each other. It's a small world, you see people, but there's something different when you turn around at the bar and there he is.' He leaned back on the bench, seemingly seeing something that Annie couldn't. 'I'd see him in other places, too. Not just gay places, like that time in Heaven. Just

211

in the greasy spoon, having breakfast. He sold me an album in Tower Records and we didn't say a word to each other, but I couldn't stop smiling when I was walking away from him.'

Annie stayed quiet. It was the question that seemed to rear up again and again, she thought. When to speak, when to be silent. If she could work that one out, she thought, perhaps everything else would make sense.

'It's not good that he's dead,' Jim continued abruptly, after a long break. 'It'll never be good that he's dead. But now he's gone and they've stopped talking about him so much, stopped making up all that crap about how he was a saint and a brilliant singer, I can remember him the way he was.'

Very gently, Annie said, 'And how was that?'

'A nightmare.' A laugh came volleying out of Jim. He carried on laughing for a few seconds, only half in control. 'He wasn't very nice to me a lot of the time, you know.' Jim ground his cigarette into the paving slab with the toe of his shoe and absentmindedly deadheaded a rose. 'I was a pity fuck in the beginning. And then . . .' He shrugged. 'I think he liked that I'd do what he asked. He was just so gorgeous, you know? Like a Greek god. When you see someone that beautiful it's hard to believe you're allowed to look at them. And for all his bravado he liked the attention.'

'Robbie? Attention?' Annie let out a laugh of her own. 'D'you think so?'

'And I'm so old and fat, I was thrilled.' Jim patted his stomach, and Annie shook her head. She thought Jim was

212

as handsome as anyone, but he never seemed to want to hear that. It certainly wasn't true that he was fat. Where once there had been a pot belly was now an absence, swathed in the same soft black T-shirt. He seemed to catch Annie looking, and shook his head. 'Don't worry, it's just stress. Stress and gardening.' He took his pack of cigarettes out of the pocket of his jeans, and then seemed to change his mind and replaced them. He wandered towards a nearby rosebush, tugging restlessly at the stems. 'It'll catch up with me eventually, I expect. I'm not different from any of the others.' He started to pull harder at the blooms, petals drifting to his trainers.

'Robbie was special, wasn't he?' He said it plaintively, asking Annie to tell him that his version of the world was right.

'He was charismatic. That's for sure.'

'I'm not sure how much he liked me. And sometimes he was awful and I didn't like him. But sometimes ...' Annie heard the break in his voice and wanted to step closer, yet knew that this would be the wrong thing to do. 'Sometimes he was perfect. And we were perfect. Beautiful. And there were things about him ... the way he was with Rosie, do you remember?'

Annie remembered. What's more, she knew that Rosie did too. She'd been very quiet that morning. Her legs had looked so long, spearing out from beneath her school skirt, her face pale as she swung her backpack onto her shoulder. Robbie would probably have crowed that she looked gorgeous, grown up. Annie just wanted to wrap her arms around her, to keep the woman from burgeoning out of the girl and growing out and away. But they didn't have that sort of relationship, the embracing sort. Annie wasn't sure she understood exactly how. She understood it, the wrapping around of arms, but it never seemed to occur to her at the right moment.

'And now he's gone, and nothing will ever be quite right. Maybe tomorrow they'll announce the vaccine and I'm meant to go skipping down the block to get it and honestly ...' His voice thickened further. It was so quiet that Annie could hear the soft pat of his tears hitting the paving slabs. Or maybe it was just starting to rain. 'Honestly, I don't even know whether I'd want it. It's not like it'll bring him back.'

Annie thought of George. About that first year after he'd died, the unsteadiness with which she'd done everything. 'It'll come back, you know. Wanting life.'

'Yeah.' Jim flicked his lighter on, then off again. 'Problem is, I've never really wanted anything as much as I wanted Robbie.'

'I'm so sorry, Jim.'

'It's all right. I had him. Sort of. For a while.' He took a cigarette from his packet and lit it. 'There's something that I'd forgotten, and I've remembered it now. I've forgotten all sorts of stuff from around that time, from just after he died.'

'I know. Your memory doesn't work properly. I know.'

'I told you back then that I left my job.' He stared off into the distance. 'I lied. They wouldn't give me the day

214

off for the funeral, and I told them to go fuck themselves. So they sacked me.' He held his cigarette long enough to draw in a deep breath. 'They knew about Robbie. I tried to keep it quiet but they worked it out with all the doctor's stuff and they seemed all right with it. They all knew. They knew what we were to each other. And they knew that he'd died, and no one fucking said anything to me. No one, Annie. I felt invisible. I felt like I was going mad.'

Annie recognised it. The fury. Sometimes the anger would break in waves over her whole home. Often it was scattergun. Fury at Thatcher and Reagan, at Americans for bringing their plague. At Haiti, where the thing had found its way into the world's blood supply. Sometimes this opened out to black people more generally. Other times they were angry with science itself.

'They say there's going to be drugs. Well, hurrah. Stick it in my arms, shove it down my throat, whatever. Give it to me. But they won't, will they? The bastards.'

'Medicine does get better,' Annie found herself saying softly. 'It does. I've seen it myself.'

'So Rita reckons too,' Jim said. 'You know she told Davey she'd go to Mexico? To get him those pills?'

'Maybe she should.'

'They're snake oil. I've heard. They won't work. She knows they won't work.' He paused. 'Honestly, I think she just fancies the thrill of it.'

'She knows how to have fun, Rita,' Annie said softly. 'Not like me.' She saw Jim looking at her and smiled.

'You know me. Dull and dependable. Workhorse sort of person.'

'Nothing wrong with that.'

'Apart from not being much good on a night out. Not like Rita.'

'Rita's a scream,' Jim said slowly. 'We adore her.' A long pause. 'But if I was dying I know which of you I'd prefer to have look after me. She'd chat all day and forget to flip me over. I'd end up laughing all the time, but covered in bedsores.'

'She's a better nurse than me.' Annie could feel her throat growing tense. 'In lots of ways. She cares.'

Jim drew closer and put his arm around her shoulders. 'You care, Aunty Nan.'

'I do my best,' Annie said. It would be selfish, she knew, to make Jim comfort her.

November, 1959

'THEY'RE GOING TO BOMB us, you know.' Albert's voice is almost casual as he tilts up his chin, letting Annie run the razor blade down his neck. 'The Russians. They've got the bomb to end all bombs.' He smiles brightly. 'Then it'll be over. All of it.'

Annie taps the razor on the edge of the basin and watches the fragments of stubble settle at the bottom. 'Is that so, Albert?'

He pulls his head back, his lips thinning in disgust as he looks at her. 'Stop playing the fool,' he snaps. 'Stop pretending you don't know.'

He winces when the razor slips and the blood blooms on his cheek. So startling, Annie thinks, in that colourless room. It's starting to bother her a little less, the sight of blood.

There is a directive from Dr Lewin that the two men in the side rooms are to take daily walks. Half an hour in the grounds. Perhaps it's something to do with the pen, Annie thinks. She does her best, when Matron informs her, not to let her eyes do any questioning.

Rita is pleased with this new duty. 'Happy to stretch my legs during the day. And Paul's a hoot.' She pauses. 'Not sure about the other one though. He's terribly . . .'

'Sardonic?' Annie has never been sure of exactly what this word means, but feels that it fits Peter, with his demands and his nonsensical questions.

'Oh, I don't mind a dry sense of humour. It's just, well, doesn't he frighten you a touch? I get the feeling that he absolutely despises me. I don't think it's because of anything I've done.'

'He's probably got some sort of paranoid condition.'

Rita's face creases a little. 'I suppose. They say it's just an extreme manifestation of paranoia, don't they?' She pauses, looking a little troubled. 'I've never believed it myself. I just don't see the link. I tried to read Dr Freud, you know, when I decided to switch to mental nursing. Nearly put me off, I didn't understand half of what he was saying, but he says it all with so much confidence and he seems to think that even if you prove him wrong then actually you're somehow proving him right.' She shakes her head. 'I'm not terribly interested in the causes anyway, if I'm honest with you.'

Annie doesn't answer. Rita has a way of looking at her, so confiding and assured that the two of them share a view, that the idea of proving her wrong grips Annie with panic.

The three figures stand out against the green lawn – Rita in her stark white, Paul with a greatcoat buttoned over his pyjamas. A few steps behind – Peter. Head down, hands clasped behind his back. Annie is sure that she can hear their laughing, even through the windows. Everyone laughs with Rita.

She turns away. The ward is precisely as it should be. She walks slowly down the narrow aisle, eyes sweeping from side to side. Bedsteads at exact right angles, each wheel pointing forwards, sheets smooth as glass. Annie has measured the turndowns to the half-inch. No feathers, not anywhere. She unballs her fists and stretches out the cramp.

'You run a tight ship,' Anthony says from behind her. She jumps at the sound of his voice. 'Very fast learner.'

She nods and turns quickly away.

'Matron says . . .' Anthony begins, but she nods quickly.

'It's all right, she's already told me. I'm to see to the side rooms while they're out.'

It isn't true, she knows that on the surface. But on some deeper level she feels sure that if Matron were here then she would want Annie to go to the side rooms. To bring that same sense of order, of peace, to the places that are hidden.

She thinks she sees something in Anthony's eyes – a wariness or suspicion. But she turns away.

She's half expecting to find the door locked. So many doors in Fairlie Hall are locked, whether it makes sense or not. But with the occupant away, the door stands open. It's Thursday, so the mess has been cleared away.

She walks swiftly, purposefully, over to the table where the sheets of paper lie, neatly stacked in three small mounds. With the swift, decisive movement of a nurse taking up the fever chart, she picks up the first stack, and begins to read.

In truth, Donovan minded the confinement itself far less than he might have had cause to expect. By now, in the third week of their imprisonment, he knew every inch of Stalag IV: each clod of the dirt, each spike of barbed wire and blade of grass – for there were still a few that had escaped the press of hundreds of boots – had to Donovan some quality of a kingdom. A kingdom that, despite certain setbacks, was enhanced by the sovereignty of knowing that one wasn't likely to be shot at or blown up at any moment.

It's as Dr Lewin said, Annie thinks. He's writing a story.

She has never known anyone who makes things up for a living. She supposes that it all has to come from some-where – books on shelves, films in the cinema, plays on the radio. It's just never really occurred to her that there is a *work* there, a physical work. A work that she can hold in her hands. Work that, if she is so inclined, she might tear to shreds, or throw onto the fire. She could blame one of the orderlies.

But she carries on reading.

For some, the confinement itself might be a cause of distress, or serve usefully as a thing to be railed against. But Donovan was used to being a prisoner in so many senses that this particular manifestation gave him no especial misery. After many years in which he was obliged to be interested in so many distant matters, he finally had licence to limit his world to a stretch of ground, a mere twenty-four acres. The other fellows might occupy themselves by reading the smuggled-in German newspapers and trying to decipher what was going on – beyond the propaganda, filtered through a foreign tongue. But for Donovan, there was no requirement to do anything beyond staring at the sky.

Annie's eyes flick out of the window. The three figures are no longer walking on the lawn. Have they just disappeared from sight, or is the allotted half hour over? She has no idea. Fairlie Hall is performing its usual distortions on time.

'Ruminating again?'

Donovan turned and straightened his shoulders, the movement reflexive and brief, like a salute. The man approaching him was smiling, a steady smile. His hands were thrust deep into the pockets of his airman's uniform, a scarf thrown over his neck in concession to the bite of the German winter. His cheeks, Donovan noticed, had a particularly delicate flush.

221

'Have we met?'

The man leaned against the edge of the barracks building, two or three yards from Donovan. He was wearing his military overcoat as though it were a dressing gown, his bearing louche and relaxed.

'Might have done. Small world, I suppose.'

He alluded with his eyes to the mess of wire and potholes on the other side of the fence. 'You've been standing in this spot a lot. Casing the joint?'

Donovan watched the man keenly. The idea that this chap has perceived him before, when he believed himself little better than invisible in this place, was strange to him. It gave him a weight that he felt he had not held until this moment.

'Fairlie,' said the man, holding out his hand. 'John Fairlie.'

'Is it working?'

Annie drops the pages and they spill, frictionless and silent, over the polished floor. She whirls about to see Peter standing there, in the doorway. There's something of the outdoors in his cheeks – more colour than usual. But perhaps that's anger. When he speaks, his voice is as measured as ever.

'Wasn't planning on having anyone read it at this stage.' His voice is as chilly and harsh as the barbed wire on the page. 'You're hardly my ideal reader.' His eyes drop from her face to her shoes and back again, his mouth distorting with a cold look. 'But since you've taken the time, I may as well ask, does it work?'

'What do you mean?'

'Well.' He takes a step towards her. 'Are you drawn in? Are the characters clear in your mind? Quite simply . . .' He bends to the floor and picks the papers up, smoothing them carefully into a stack. 'Do you want to find out what happens next?'

Annie's lips press tight. She wonders if she might herself vomit. She shakes her head, not in answer to his question, but as a wholesale rejection of the situation.

'No?' He looks away from her, at the pages in his hand. 'Well, it's just a first draft, anyway. Everyone's a critic, whether they're qualified or not.' He takes a step to one side and nods at the door. Annie recognises the motion at once. He is dismissing her. In every way that a person can be dismissed. As she walks slowly from the room, her face burns.

'Nurse Graie?'

Matron's voice rings down the ward. Annie steps forwards. It is only a little after four in the afternoon, but the clocks have gone back and the ward is dark. She had been standing in the shadows, scrubbing at one of the light switches.

'Ah.' Matron sounds almost surprised to see her there. *Where else would I be?* Annie wonders. *This is what I'm for.*

'Nurse Graie.' Matron takes a step forwards. Her features are a little different to usual, though Annie cannot account for the difference. 'Dr Lewin informs me . . .' She trails off, then begins again. 'Dr Lewin informs me that you have agreed to participate in the experimental treatment that he is conducting this afternoon?'

Annie hesitates. The specific nature, time and place of her agreement had not been delineated to her, but she knows the meaning.

'You're to go to the side room where they're keeping him.' For a moment Annie's heart lurches, but Matron clarifies, 'That is, Mr Hamilton.'

Paul, Annie thinks, her thoughts thick and sluggish with relief. *Paul. That's all right then.*

'Nurse Blythe was asked to assist, initially,' Matron adds. 'But I'm afraid she was indisposed. Therefore, your presence is required.' Matron makes a jerky sort of movement, as if she has half a mind to place a comforting palm on Annie's shoulder. But instead the hand merely lingers, full of air.

There are two figures, vast and white, scarcely differentiated from the white wall. Annie's eyes refuse to focus in the gloom. But then, reality reveals itself. Dr Lewin and Sam. Dr Lewin revolves slowly, fretfully, taking stock of the little side room. Paul, very thin, is nothing more than a huddle on the bed.

'There's not enough space in here,' Dr Lewin says at length. 'We can't use the slides. Not properly. Is there no other space available?'

'Afraid not, Doctor,' Sam says. His voice is soft, paci-
fying. The same voice that he uses to speak to the patients.
'All the occupational therapy rooms are in use.'

'It's unscientific,' Dr Lewin says, in the same fretful
tone. 'We need consistency across the treatment . . . these
aren't appropriate conditions.' It's clear that he's not really
speaking to Sam, who anyway has the smile of one who
knows he'll be blamed no matter what.

Eventually Dr Lewin turns around. He makes a perform-
ance of noticing Annie.

'Nurse Grye! We're delighted!' He gives his fatherly
smile and places one hand on her back, ushering her into
the room. Paul looks up and gives a weak little grin.

'Not to worry,' Dr Lewin says, speaking to himself. 'Not
to worry at all. The crucial components are all present.
We have our medical staff, we have our medicine . . .' – he
indicates a little paper cup in Sam's hand – '. . . and we
have our patient.' He points at Paul with a careless gesture.
'No reason to delay.' He turns to Paul and speaks again
in his low, kindly voice. 'Are you ready?'

Paul is still for a moment. Then, without looking at
Dr Lewin, he nods.

'The emetic, if you please.'

Sam steps forwards and hands a little paper cup to
Paul. He takes it, hesitates, then drinks. Dr Lewin leans
in close to Annie, his lips brushing her ear as he whispers,
'Apomorphine, you see. And brandy. Two ounces.' Annie
nods as if this means something to her.

For a minute or two nothing happens. Paul's breath is slow and even, his eyes fixed straight ahead. Sam stands beside him, somehow taller than usual in the gloom. Then Paul's body starts to convulse. For a few moments his face is marble-still, beads of sweat running from his forehead. At last his mouth opens, as if prised by some unseen force. He begins to vomit.

Again, Annie feels Dr Lewin's hand on her back.

'You needn't be present for this part,' he mutters in her ear. She feels his words as much as hearing them, all wet breath. She cannot get at the meaning of what he is saying, continuing to stare at Paul as his body contorts with convulsion after convulsion.

Then Sam is there; he is leading her outside; she is back in the glare of the corridor. Just as the door closes, she hears Dr Lewin snap, 'The pictures, attendant – now!'

Annie does not know how much time passes. She stares at the white wall. She can no longer hear anything. At length, Sam comes out of the room. His face is a little pink, as if he's faintly embarrassed.

'You're to come back in,' he says. 'Doctor wants you in there.'

Annie obeys. She sidles past Sam's bulk into the little room. Inside it is as if the darkness and the stench have made the room smaller still. In the middle yet somehow apart, Paul is still hunched on the bed. He makes no sound, but Annie can tell from the shake of his shoulders – or perhaps some disturbance in the filthy air – that he is weeping.

'Comfort him, Nurse Grye,' Dr Lewin says.

Annie stays where she is, even when Sam prods her in the back.

'What are you waiting for?' Irritation has seeped into Dr Lewin's voice, all its cloudy insubstance is gone. He is harsh, almost military. 'Comfort him.'

Annie steps forwards and places one hand on Paul's shoulder. She almost recoils, feeling his humerus hard and sharp through his pyjamas. At her touch something seems to dissolve in Paul. On instinct she steps closer, sitting on the bed and putting her arms around him as he collapses forwards. Between sobs she can hear one word, over and over. *Mother*, he says, and then again. *Mother*.

She holds him, despite the stench. In a moment of detachment she is proud of her resolve, and the feeling of peace settles in her chest, like a cat curling up to go to sleep.

'That's enough.' Dr Lewin's voice again, that unfamiliar snap. Annie releases Paul and he collapses back onto the bed, still weeping. Annie glances quickly at the mop and bucket in the corner, at the mess on the floor, at the stained and stinking sheets. Dr Lewin shakes his head.

'Sam will deal with that.' He turns to Sam. 'The injection should follow in fifteen minutes. In the meantime, play the recording, please.'

He opens the door in such a way that Annie understands she is to follow him. It is only when she is out in the clean corridor that she realises that she too is filthy, that her clean dress is covered in Paul's sick. She can scarcely focus on anything apart from this, but forces herself to stare at the pure expanses of Dr Lewin's white coat as he stands before her.

'Well, Nurse Grye?'

The eyes are still blue. They look wetter than usual.

'It could have been better.' His tone isn't harsh. 'I understand that it's shocking. I know you did your best. But I don't mind telling you, it could have been better. That mother stuff. Poor chap doesn't need any more confusion. That's not who you're supposed to be.'

All of Annie's effort is going into preventing her face from crumpling. As far as anyone's concerned, she thinks, she's just there to chase goose feathers across the ward, to stop old men from drowning in their baths. To smile stupidly when Ronnie puts his red face in hers and calls her bitch. Cunt. Slut.

She thinks of Paul, grey and sheened with the sweat of nausea. Tears forced from his eyes by convulsions. It was not me, she thinks. Whatever it is that happened, it was not just me. It was Sam, and Matron too, a bit. And Dr Lewin. Dr Lewin, who has lectured in Czechoslovakia. Dr Lewin, who is famous all over the country.

'Nurse Grye?' She stops at the sound of the doctor's voice. Every part of her made frozen. But her instincts forbid standing like this, back to Dr Lewin. She turns around.

'Don't get downhearted.' Dr Lewin sounds gentle, generous even. Annie looks up and realises that his cheeks are flushed, his eyes bright. 'You're not exactly where you need to be just yet, but your cooperation was immensely valuable.' He steps closer, then seems to think better of it and smiles. 'Trust me,' he says. 'You shall, by degrees, improve.'

Annie nods.

'You're clever, Nurse Grye.'

Annie stays very still.

'Clever enough to be familiar with the work of Dr Skinner, I daresay.'

Annie forces herself to speak. 'Something to do with dogs?' She does not look at Dr Lewin, but rather at the wall behind him.

'He has done some work with dogs, yes.' Dr Lewin's voice is soft, coaxing. 'But his experiments on pigeons are what really fascinate me. No need to go into all that. All you need to remember, Nurse Grye, is that Skinner's work focuses on the relationship between actions and their consequences. Man is, after all, defined by what he does, not what he thinks or feels. At our core, we are nothing more than a collection of behaviours. You understand this, as a nurse. Some nurses might have good hearts, good motives . . .' Here he laughs, as if to make clear to Annie that she is to catch his drift. 'But really, it's all in the actions.'

Annie nods slowly.

'You can act, you know,' he continues. 'Some nurses wouldn't have the courage. Some nurses would put their own egos above the needs of the patient. Not you.'

'Not me,' Annie whispers.

'So you'll help me.' Annie hears the smile in his voice. Perhaps he notices her discomfiture, adding, 'It's nothing frightening, what I'm asking you to do. It's the most ordinary thing in the world. But it takes courage, to be a real nurse.'

His voice is so low, so soft. It's as if he's laid his hands on her again. Annie can feel her knees shaking.

'You're a real nurse, Nurse Grye.' His voice is laced with satisfaction. 'Because you're a real woman. That's what it's all about.'

May, 1987

AFTER FAIRLIE HALL ANNIE often found herself in the grip of a physical feeling that she could only describe as unease. It started out in brief episodes – moments really – but now it struck her for entire nights. When she was alone there was an overpowering feeling that there might be someone in the house with her, just upstairs, listening intently. To have her home full of young men was a relief. They came and went. Some died, some went into hospital, some found new accommodation. It was possible to pass years that way, lurching from one health panic to the next. When someone new came into the house there seemed a different promise every time, a possibility of a different ending.

Annie came into the kitchen to find Jim and Davey sitting at the table. It was the first time that she'd seen Davey up since he'd started the AZT. She wanted to say something, but she suspected that he wouldn't want her to point too much out.

'Russ came back from the clinic,' Jim said. 'He's negative.' He slurped on his coffee. 'Little shit,' he added.

'Glad to hear it.'

'He's been winding Jim up,' Davey chimed in.

'I'm not wound up. It's just that he's convinced that just because he's managed to dodge it that he's suddenly queen of safe sex.' Jim rolled his eyes. 'He's had half the boys in Western Europe, for God's sake. And there he was, wittering on about how you've got to assess risk.'

'Nothing sexier than a little risk assessment,' Davey added. His face was still wan, but his eyes were sparkling. 'You know what they say. Don't die of . . .'

'. . . Ignorance. Yeah, we all know, Davey.' Before the AZT had knocked him out, Davey had taken to sneaking up on people inside the house and then screeching in their ear, 'Don't die of ignorance!' Then he'd crow with laughter as they leapt out of their skin. Annie was grateful though. Jim's fuse was growing ever-shorter these days, but Davey seemed to have a good way with him.

They all took the laughter where they found it. These days there would be the occasional week where there were no obituaries. Then there would be an onslaught, when it became confusing to remember who had died and who hadn't. One half of a couple would go – one who'd teetered on the brink for months, in and out of hospital, sickening and then rallying and then sickening again. Then the other might go a month or two later, quiet as a cat, ill on Tuesday and dead by Friday. She heard it all from Jim.

'Anyway, Aunty Nan,' Jim continued, 'there's a chap arriving later. Fourish. Gay Switchboard sent him our way. He wants the room.'

The room that, until last week, had been Graham's.

'They'll be sending a nurse in to see him every day,' Jim added. 'I reckon he'll be all right on the first floor, don't you?'

These days Annie slept in the living room. Her old room, on the first floor, had made more sense as a room for one of the men. Rosie was still in her room at the top of the house, but at seventeen Annie knew it was a matter of time before there was yet another bed available. Another mouth to coax bites of food into, another space to be made empty, another mother to call.

'Anyway,' Jim said, 'I'm off to meet the MP.'

'I'm sure he'll be really interested in what you've got to say,' Davey said. 'I expect his majority lives or dies by your good opinion. Anyway, haven't you heard? Maggie thinks we'll sort ourselves out.' He assumed a remarkable imitation of Mrs Thatcher. 'You there, take your cock *out* of that boy this instant, in the name of God and England!'

'I wouldn't mind her money,' Jim said calmly. Two years ago, after Robbie's death, he'd been sacked. Now he was technically on the dole, but really he spent most of his time going around hospitals, or distributing leaflets at gay clubs. 'Anyway, it's not *her* money, it's the Treasury's. We just need one of those old Tory queens on our side . . .'

'Those old Tory queens are the *last* people who're going to help us,' Davey said flatly. 'It doesn't look good for them, does it?'

'They might if we show them we're not going anywhere.'

'Yeah.' Davey looked down at his wasted arms. 'That's us. Not going anywhere.' He yawned and stretched. 'You know, I'm a bit bored of AIDS. Can't we make this kitchen an AIDS-free zone?' He paused, then added, 'Well. You know what I mean. A talking-about-AIDS-free-zone.'

'You do what you want.' Jim stood up. 'I'm heading off.'

Davey nodded his goodbye and started to roll a joint with long, thin fingers. Annie let them smoke dope; some of the men said it made the nausea better. Only when Rosie was at school, though. That was the rule, and they all respected it. As they heard Jim open the front door, Davey called out, 'Just tell them straight people can get it too. They'll throw money at you!'

There was a grunt of assent, and the sound of the door closing.

'Thank God for that,' Davey muttered. 'He's turning into Pimlico's answer to Mary Whitehouse. We could all do with a break.'

'Who's Pimlico's answer to Mary Whitehouse?' It was Olu, the newest addition to the house, hovering in the doorway. Jim had found him in a homeless hostel, even though his family only lived a mile or two away. When Annie had asked if he wanted to let them know about his diagnosis, he'd shrugged and said, 'Leave it. They'd rather hear I was dead than know I'm a poof.'

'Jim.' Davey twisted the tip of his joint and went to the back door. 'He's got that . . . what do they call it? Internalised homophobia. He hates himself. That's his problem.'

There had been a row the night before. A group of them had gone off to Graham's funeral, and then out to a gay bar afterwards.

Annie had stopped counting the funerals. She no longer had a grasp on precise numbers – there were just three or four types. There were those for the ones whose families had nothing to do with any of it. In a sense, these were the best. Less black, more music playing, an iron-clad will to keep smiling, to keep dancing.

Then there were the funerals where the families had been torn by their divided duty. On the one hand, they invited the full complement of great aunts, but also felt unable to turn away the gaggle of men at the back, replete in their black sequins and leather trousers. A ragged rendition of 'The Lord Is My Shepherd', answered moments later by The Communards and 'Don't Leave Me This Way', sobs falling unevenly between the beats.

Worse were the funerals where the truth was buried, where the friends of the dead boy were allowed to attend only if they agreed to participate in the lies about rare cancers or sudden aneurysms. Where a whole person, be they spiky or shining or shy, was devoured by the Church of England funeral service and the shop-bought sympathy card. For some it was the empty crematorium, the cancer cover story, the back-garden bonfire. Most devouring and all-encompassing of all was the silence, the shake of the head, the lips pressed together, as if to speak the names were to summon the disease that killed them.

Graham's parents were that sort. They'd been allowed to attend the funeral, the boys, but they had to pretend that Graham had died of leukaemia. Everyone drank heavily afterwards.

Annie hadn't heard all of the row, when they'd all spilled back in from the club, but after a while she came down to remind them that Rosie had college the next morning and needed her sleep. That was when she heard Jim shouting. She'd stood outside the door, knowing that it wouldn't be right to cross the threshold.

'For fuck's sake,' he'd been saying. 'This isn't about politics, it's about keeping yourself healthy.'

'That's such shit, Jim.' Russ's voice. 'Everything's about politics for us.'

'Right, you're making your political statement by fucking everything with a cock and a pulse and that's somehow setting you free, is it? Right up until it kills you.' A muffled slam, like someone hitting the arm of the sofa. 'And maybe plenty of other people along the way.'

'So you're calling me a murderer?'

'No—'

'You're saying that by living my life, I'm harming people. I've heard that one before.'

'I'm not—'

'Go back into the closet, right? Safe there. Nothing can hurt you if you're crouched in the closet—'

'Shut up!' Muffled again, like someone was speaking with their hands over their mouth. Annie had hesitated for a moment longer, then gone back upstairs. She hadn't slept well that night, on the bare mattress in the room that had been Graham's.

Davey took a deep toke of his joint, and offered it to Olu, who shook his head. 'My body's a temple.'

'A temple to what?'

'Dunno. Beelzebub?'

'Suit yourself.' Davey blew out his smoke. 'You know, it used to be that fucking – sorry, Aunty Nan – that having sex with someone was you going away for a bit, into your own little world. And now it feels like you're lying covered in newspaper headlines. Like the whole world is watching, and flinching.'

'It's our own business,' said Olu. He wrapped his arms around his frail frame, though the day was warm. 'Since I found out I was HIV, I've only fucked boys who I know are already infected. Where's the harm in that?'

'I know. I mean, what's the point of being gay if I can't even fuck anyone? I didn't come to London to go to Buckingham Palace, you know.' Davey took another toke. 'Try telling that to Jim though. He's on a crusade.'

At that moment the doorbell rang.

'That'll be the new chap, I expect.' Annie was grateful to have a reason to leave the room. She didn't like hearing all this about Jim – just listening to it without intervening felt disloyal. 'Unless it's Rosie.' She checked her watch. 'Put that joint out now, please. Air freshener's on the side.'

'Might be Rita,' Olu said. 'She rang earlier. Said she was coming over. With her crystals.'

Annie didn't know Olu well enough yet to discern what he made of Rita or her crystals, and his face gave nothing away. Some of the men loved Rita, she gave them hope. Some of them couldn't stand her, and said could she please stop pretending that they weren't going to die. The previous week Rita turned up with armfuls of magazines. When Annie flicked through them, the pages flapped curiously.

'I cut out any bits that mentioned death,' Rita said earnestly. 'It's not good for them. Won't help them keep a positive mental attitude.'

But it wasn't Rita and when Annie opened the front door, her first thought was that she'd never seen a man who looked less prone to keeping a positive mental attitude.

'I've heard that you can help,' he said.

Annie hesitated. Most of her lodgers were fairly young, not many of them more than thirty. This man looked sixty, maybe older. He was dressed the way that all men of that age used to dress, in a mackintosh and tweed suit, a proper hat. The suit, the hat, the tie, all grey, the eyes green, a strange pale green as if they too were trying to be grey. He might once have been handsome, Annie thought, but in the way that a marble sculpture could be handsome, without any colour to bring the beauty to life.

'Jim told me you were coming.' She looked at the carpet bag that he had at his side. His knuckles were white with the effort of holding onto it, but his face was impassive.

'You'll take me, then?'

The voice was entirely flat and monotonous, as if he couldn't quite bear to let any hope creep into it. Annie hesitated.

'I'm not sure if it'll be quite right for you,' she said.

'Quite right is a luxury,' he said brusquely. 'I'll take what I can get.'

Annie stood aside to allow him in, and held out her hand. 'Annie.'

The man looked down at her hand for a moment as if he hadn't expected to see it, but after a moment he returned the handshake. 'Name's John,' he said.

December, 1959

Donovan lit his cigarette. It was the first from the Red Cross parcel, and the only one that he would allow for himself. The rest had already been exchanged for items that would serve him better – chocolate, tins of food, a pen for writing home. It had to be a pen – pencil was too easy to erase. If his letters to his mother were destined to be censored, then he wanted the evidence of the excisions plain to see.

But he allowed himself this one cigarette. He inhaled deeply and then coughed. He was starting to suspect that these things were not altogether good for him, despite their magnetic appeal and instant effect on morale. But perhaps being stuck in Stalag IV was simply making him paranoid.

'Creature comforts?'

At Fairlie's voice Donovan did not jump, but rather allowed himself to become stiller. He listened as the footsteps approached, but did not turn to look at his companion until he saw the packet of cigarettes offered out before him.

'Yours if you want them.' He looked now at Fairlie, who still had that soft flush to his cheeks. 'I don't smoke.'

'What do you want for them?'

'Nothing.'

'If you're not going to get anything for cigarettes then you might as well smoke them yourself, you know,' Donovan said. He hesitated, and then took the packet. 'There's much to recommend it.'

'I've always rather liked the smell of the smoke.' Fairlie stepped a little closer to Donovan, who let the butt fall from his fingers and extinguish in the snow with a soft hiss. 'But they make me cough.'

'You get past that. And I find that the time it takes to smoke a cigarette is precisely the time I need to get my thoughts clear.'

'What thoughts of yours need clearing today?'

For the first time Donovan met Fairlie's eyes. They were grey. The Polish winter was icy, but Fairlie's breath was warm.

A bell rings and Annie jumps. That signals the end to the patients' dinner – she'll be needed back on the ward. The room stinks, as usual, but Annie finds that if she averts her eyes from the mess then the worst of the smell doesn't seem to affect her. She is careful to replace the pages in the same place that she'd found them. They had been stacked neatly in the centre of the little table, all the edges carefully aligned. She can't help but wonder if Peter knows that she'd read them.

She leaves, shutting the door behind her.

'I don't think I can stand this anymore.'

As ever, when Rita begins to speak it is as if she and Annie are already mid-conversation. 'I'm tired of being a nurse.'

Annie feels almost faint with relief. If she had eaten anything that day, she thinks, then she might even vomit.

'We can't spend all our days off sitting around thinking about the ward. I want to go dancing,' Rita continues. 'Be someone else for a bit. Wear a frock that isn't white.'

'Oh.' Annie keeps her voice light. She's so good at it now. 'Yes, I suppose that would be rather nice.'

'Do you ever get the need?' Rita removes her feet from the sink, where they have been soaking alongside Annie's in hot water, and pads over to the little table to light a cigarette. 'You know, to drink and dance and just sort of thrash about a bit?'

Annie has never drunk more than a sherry or two, but she laughs along when Rita produces one of her little bottles of brandy and pours it neat into teacups. It burns her throat on the way down, like medicine, she thinks, and then has to press her lips together. Rita turns the radio up loud, and it's Adam Faith and he's singing over and over again, *What do you want? What do you want?* And Annie is giggling and putting on her green dress, the one that she made herself and reminds her of the sea, and Rita is leaning close to her to paint her face, so close that she can smell the cigarettes on her breath. She can smell the brandy too, but it doesn't make her feel sick this time.

'How do I look?' Annie hears herself saying, and she hears too the smile in her own voice, the playfulness. She steps forwards to view herself in the mirror and lurches a little. Rita holds her tight by the elbow.

'I think you look gorgeous, but you might want to change it a bit,' Rita says. 'You know how slapdash I am.'

When Annie looks in the glass, her first instinct is to scream.

In the half-light of evening, all she can see is a slash of a mouth, smudged at the edges as if it were dripping blood. The creature in the mirror's eyes widen, and Annie sees just how much black stuff Rita has smeared around them. The clean lines of her old face have been rubbed out, blurred into something dark and frightening. She doesn't recognise her own eyes. She stares at the creature in the mirror and does not know her.

Then the mouth, that hideous red mouth, opens, as wide as a wound.

'Do you like it?' Rita's white, round face appears in the glass behind Annie's. The image in the mirror seems to blur out for a moment. 'You've got such super cheekbones, such strong features, you can carry off a lot of makeup. I imagined you as a sort of Harlequin. You've come out like a mime from the Twenties, very Colette. I love it.'

She steps back from Annie and gives an odd little smile.

'Yes, it's exactly like you're a flapper or something,' Rita continues. 'Perhaps you're a ghost after all, and I've just never noticed before.'

Annie moves closer to the mirror, so close that it is as if she might kiss the creature within. Now Rita has mentioned it, she sees how the dark of the kohl, the crimson of the lips, the white of the face, carve out a sharpness and brilliance to her features that she's never seen before. Unconsciously, she reaches a hand up to caress her own neck.

'Here.' Before she understands what is happening, Rita has pushed a finger into Annie's mouth. 'Suck,' Rita instructs. Annie does as she's told. The finger tastes of cigarettes and the apples that they ate after dinner. Rita withdraws her finger from the red wound of Annie's mouth with a soft, popping sound.

'That'll make sure that you don't get any lipstick on your teeth.'

Annie turns to face Rita. She is not wearing much makeup herself, only a coral lipstick. Her blonde hair is smoothly waved for once, and Annie thinks she looks like sunshine.

'You do look super,' Rita says, in a low voice, unlike her usual one. 'And a bit frightening. Like you might devour me.'

Annie thinks of the snakes that eat whole buffalo, and lets her eyes fall down Rita's body, from the great height of the crown of her head to her feet in their high heels. Then all at once she is seized with the wish to scrub off the red mouth. She puts her hand up to her face, as if to cover it, but Rita brushes it away impatiently.

'We'll miss the bus if we don't go now. I'm not waiting half an hour for the next one.'

They run to the gates of the Hall. There's a bus stop on the lane, which some of the married attendants use every day for getting into work. The lane seems very broad compared to the Fairlie Estate with its winding pathways, and Annie feels oddly exposed. She is wearing an evening coat, which she made herself from one of the patterns in *Vogue*, but she suspects is supposed to be cut from a much thicker material. She is very cold, and sure that the rain will fall at any moment.

The bus journey is bumpy and Annie spends the whole time with her forehead pressed against the cold glass of the window, tasting the brandy at the back of her throat. It now seems horrifyingly sweet; she cannot understand how she ever drank it. When they get to the dance hall she goes straight to the ladies' room and stays there for a while, head leaned against the wall of the cubicle, the tiled floor blooming in and out of focus.

She is sick. It was the bus, she tells herself over and over as she retches, her stomach jerking violently within her smooth green dress. Everything hurts – her throat, her chest, even her feet in their high heels.

And then it is gone, and she is lucid again. She rinses her mouth at the tap when no one is looking, and goes back into the bar. She orders a cocktail, thinking that her wage now is higher than her mother has ever earned in her life.

Rita is already on the dance floor, dancing with a man who scarcely comes up to her chin. He looks frightened, but a little bit entranced. Rita sees Annie. At first her expression is a little concerned, her blue eyes soft, but something in Annie's air seems to reassure her and she grins. She gestures with her eyes to the man in her arms and mouths, *he's got a friend.*

And now Annie is dancing too. The man holding
her hand, her waist, is scarcely taller than she is. He's
wearing an old-fashioned sort of suit, cut very close to his
slight frame. He has high cheekbones, like a girl's, Annie
thinks, fuzzy with the cocktail. No, like a sprite. Glittering
eyes – grey – a cloud of soft dark hair. A mouth that is
smiling like she's something worth smiling at.

They dance through one song, then another, then another.
He says something in Annie's ear but she can't hear over
the music and she's sure it can't matter, not like the way
they're dancing matters, the way they dip and swirl and
sway, and Annie is laughing like the laughter is being drawn
out of her by some unseen force, and even as she stumbles
she knows that she'll be caught. A slow song and they draw
close; the grey-eyed man is still looking at her, into her face
as if it's a flower that's opened for him. Annie raises her
hand to touch his cheek and it is smooth, smooth as marble.
She is gripped by the desire to pull him close, to engulf
him with her arms, her green dress, to devour him whole.

She smiles. Will he be frightened by her smile, by whatever
remains of the red mouth that Rita gave her? She doesn't
care.

'Annie?'

A hand on her shoulder. Rita is here. She was wearing
makeup after all, Annie thinks, with that same strange,
distant lucidity. She was wearing makeup after all, because
now it is all dried onto her cheeks. Her partner stands a
few feet off, looking bewildered.

'I want to go home now, Annie.'

Home? For a moment Annie thinks of Heartsease Terrace, of her mother crouched in her armchair like an old spider. She thinks of the hand in the vegetable patch.

'Has something happened?'

'Nothing. I just . . . I'm not myself tonight, I'm afraid. Thought a dance would make it better but . . .' She breaks off, forcing a smile. 'Come on, it's the last bus back to the Hall soon.' Rita is using her own nurse's voice, wiping her tears, but the black tracks remain. 'I want to go home.'

Annie hesitates, the room swelling and fading again with the effect of the cocktail. She makes to turn back to the grey-eyed man, but he's gone.

May, 2020

PAUL RANG ME AT half past seven. He knows I'm an early riser. I started asking him the usual sorts of things, but he interrupted me.

'Alec and I are going to get married.'

For a moment I stared out of the window. A slim young woman was running past, her long braids tied high on her head and flying behind her. A little boy of seven or eight ran a few steps in her wake. I supposed that she must be trying to tire him out a bit before homeschooling.

'Annie?'

I remembered the phone at my ear. 'Married? What're you getting married for?'

I didn't mean it to sound harsh; I was just surprised. Paul and Alec had been living in their own way for so long that it hadn't occurred to me that they'd even want a change. Besides, in every way that mattered, Paul had been Rita's husband.

But Rita was gone. I knew that. I'd downloaded Zoom so I could follow along with the funeral. I'd seen Paul in his beautiful pinstriped suit. He hadn't cried, but he'd held tight onto Lizzie's hand and stared at the coffin all through the service. When they started to shut the curtains as the coffin lowered into the furnace I'd slammed the laptop shut.

And now he and Alec were going to get married. Perhaps my old brain just wasn't able to make language anew, even now. A man having a husband. Perhaps I'd never truly understand those words.

'We just thought, why not? Alec's younger than me. I won't be around forever. There's all sorts of medical decisions that we think about more these days, don't we?'

I winced at the 'we'. I thought of Rosie. It would all fall to her, in the end.

'And we like a party, don't we? You might as well celebrate whatever there is to celebrate, and, well ...' Trust Paul to witter. Eventually he trailed off and just said, 'Because we can, all right?'

'That's ... I'm pleased for you, Paul. Congratulations.'

'You don't sound convinced.'

'Don't I?' I fumbled the phone. 'I'm thrilled for you. That's lovely, lovely news.'

It was the way he said it. I wasn't used to anyone declaring with any certainty that they were going to do anything. People don't talk about the future as a definite thing, not these days.

'We're going to do the legal bit at the registry office, obviously, but we'll do a symbolic ceremony too.' Paul coughed. 'In July. At the Fairlie Estate.'

The phone call suddenly made sense. 'The Fairlie ... you mean at Fairlie Hall?'

'It's a boutique hotel now, you know,' Paul said. There was a peculiar defiance in his voice, one that I couldn't remember ever having heard from him before. 'They do everything. Diptyque toiletries in the rooms. That guy from *Masterchef* has a bistro where the . . . you know, in that Queen Anne sort of wing. Anyway, it's hardly the same place these days. We stayed there a couple of years ago, Alec and me, and he just fell in love with it. There was a huge fire in the late Nineties, you know, and the Tudor wing was totally—'

'Paul, have you gone—'

'No, I haven't gone mad,' Paul interrupted, and there was steel in his voice. 'I'm just ringing to ask if you want the sort of room with a bath in it.'

'You mean a room with a bathroom?'

'No, a room with a clawfoot bath inside the bedroom. It costs extra. Do you want one?'

'Why does it have to have a bath inside the bedroom? Paul, are the hotels even going to be open?'

'They're taking bookings,' he said stubbornly. 'Do you want a room with a bath or not?'

'I . . . I'll need to have a think about it.' I stood in the middle of the living room with the phone to my ear, revolving slowly in a circle. 'Do you think they'll even be letting us do weddings in July?'

'Don't know, do I?' His voice became light, almost blithe. 'That's why the hire was so cheap. But we're used to not knowing what's going to happen, me and Alec. We ought to be good at it. We've decided that there is no time to waste.' He hesitated, and then said with an unfamiliar brightness in his voice, 'It'll be an adventure.'

An adventure.

Marrying George was one of the least adventurous things I've ever done. It was probably because it all seemed so safe and simple that the possibility of anything happening to him truly never occurred to me. And then it did, and something in me was turned on its head, blown wide open. I'd thought I'd been so clever, so safe, so orderly in my choices.

And then he died and the things I thought made sense stopped making sense.

I waited until I put the phone down to let myself laugh.

It'll be an adventure, he'd said. Well, that was true enough. These days, going to the big Sainsbury's in Pimlico instead of the little Tesco at the end of the road feels an adventure. Returning to Fairlie Hall, with sixty years passed, feels like something else.

December, 1959

'Nurse Grye.'

Annie has not seen this room before. It isn't long and bedstead-lined like the ward. Nor tiny and narrow, like the side rooms. It's a cube, a place in which to be. Chairs pointing at nothing. A white wall, a projector. Matron says the room is used for occupational therapy. She says that they used to do screenings here, of films. Not anymore. She didn't say why. The room is suffused with the saccharine light from a bulb. No daylight; the heavy curtains are pulled across. But someone has left a gap, and Annie can see a fillet of the world beyond. A sky, grey but bright, so bright it might as well be blue. The grounds of Fairlie Hall, green.

'Nurse Grye, the emetic, please.'

Annie looks down at the paper cup in her hand.

It is not me doing this, she thinks, as she hands the cup over. *If it wasn't me it would be someone else. That means it isn't really me at all.*

The patient takes the paper cup from her hand. He looks up at her. His eyes are dark brown. Almost black. All shine; she can't see any expression.

He says, 'Some water, please.'

Annie looks to Dr Lewin. He gives a little nod.

'Water,' she mumbles. 'Yes, water.'

When she hands him the cup he looks at her unblinkingly. He takes the pills in his mouth. Then he holds up the little cup of water, as if to toast Annie. He drinks.

Dr Lewin gives the smallest twitch of his fingers; the light shuts off. Annie can no longer see the patient's contortions, but she can hear the retching. She thinks of what he said to her. When he is sick, she does not look away.

Projected on the wall: images of men. Not men the way they're supposed to be. Men showing expanses of skin. Men looking at the camera through their lashes. Men smiling, men with dark, soft eyes, men with their heads turned to show the expanse of long, smooth necks.

The retching continues. The smell is growing terrible.

It strikes Annie that at no point has Dr Lewin done anything. He only stands there. The greater the flurry and the noise, the stiller that he becomes. Sam is by the door, with a bucket and a mop.

Eventually the retching falls quiet.

'Now, please, Nurse Grye.'

Annie steps forwards. She has a clutch of clean cloths in her hand, in the other a basin of warm, soapy water. She wipes the patient's chin. His eyes are glassy; he looks away from her.

'Speak to him, Nurse Grye,' Dr Lewin says, in the same imperious tone. 'He needs to be soothed.'

Annie opens her mouth. She can think only of a single sound, a mother-sound. 'There, there.'

Could words mean less, she wonders?

Dr Lewin puffs out some air. It's clear from his face that he finds her unconvincing.

As she washes him with water, the patient complies. He lets her dress him in clean pyjamas, not taking any of the weight of his own limbs. She must use all her skill to manoeuvre him. He does not look at her.

'There now,' she murmurs, stepping back, staring at the buttons on his soft, laundry-scented flannel pyjamas. 'Isn't that better?'

She thinks of those men with their soft eyes, in the pictures.

'Much better, thank you nurse.' He stands. His face is grey. Sam leads him away, back to his room. Dr Lewin puffs out his breath.

'A little better today, Nurse Grye,' he says. 'A little better. You understood, I think, what we talked about last time. This question of actions and consequences.'

Annie nods.

'And you've contemplated, I think, my observation that often to be a good nurse and a good woman is one and the same thing?'

Annie nods again.

'I'm glad. This means that we can proceed.'

And then he explains to her what she is to do. It's so simple. So elegant – half science, half art. And yes, Annie thinks, she understands now. Finally, after all these weeks in the dark, she is in the full glare of the light, and she sees everything. She sees that through the retching and the stench and those dreadful pictures, there is a world where everything is still, sweet-scented, clean. She sees too that in Fairlie Hall there is a sort of kindness that she has not understood before, a form of kindness that lies on the other side of cruelty.

July, 1987

SHE ALWAYS WAITED UNTIL the partner was ready before she called the funeral director. You could never guarantee that the parlours would let them in to take a last look, so Annie made sure they could do it in the house, if they wanted to.

It felt like a scant offering. When she'd gone to see George he'd been in his best suit, the tie he'd worn for their wedding. He was dressed for the occasion. She couldn't imagine saying goodbye to him in his pyjamas, like they were rushing away from each other still half-asleep.

It was Davey who'd gone this time. Davey, who had had them all laughing only a day ago. Who'd held them all in the palm of his hand, who'd got Rosie through her English O Level. She'd tried ringing Steve, his lover, but just got the answering machine message that he and Davey had recorded together. *Leave us something interesting to listen to or fuck right off*, Davey had said in his smooth, wry voice.

And now John had developed pneumocystis pneumonia. Antibiotics had worked last time, but he was much weaker now. He was refusing to go to hospital.

She couldn't exactly say that she had warmed to John – there was something in him that seemed to hold everyone at a distance. Perhaps it was the accent – cut-glass, like an old film. Perhaps it was the way that he never let anything enter his expression without a moment's calculation. He seemed to deliberate over the simplest things – a simple thank you or excuse me had an odd weight when it came from John.

And yet, for all his reserve, he was immovable on this.

'I simply do not wish to go into hospital again,' he said, his voice low and a little hoarse from the latest intubation. 'I can't choke down another ghastly institutional cup of tea. No more polystyrene.'

Perhaps that was what made her a little uncomfortable when John was around. He always seemed like he was taking inventory, and there was always something missing.

Annie was standing, with Davey's slippers in her hands, staring into space, when Jim came in.

'Your neighbour's lovely,' Jim said. 'I knocked on her door to tell her that her bins had been got at by a dog. She screamed at me through a crack in the window to go away.'

'That was bound to happen,' Annie said. 'She's been taking her bins right into the road.' These days people didn't even want to put their rubbish next to Annie's. 'What did she say?'

'She called me a . . .' His fist balled for a moment, but then he leaned against the counter and laughed. 'Called me a friend of Dorothy. Or words to that effect.' His eyes lingered on the sink for a second, and then, without warning, he picked up a bottle of kitchen cleaning spray and started to wipe down the countertops.

'I'm going to have a word with her.'

'Don't be daft, Nan.' He didn't pause in his motions. 'She's just some mad old trout, they don't listen. We'll just play our music really loud tonight and—'

'I'm not having her speaking to you like that. She insulted you.'

'Well. She's not wrong. Does it still count as an insult?'

'I'm not having it.' A kind of cold fury had surged up in Annie. She felt that if she didn't move, speak, it might break her apart. 'You live on this street, same as her.'

Jim went still, looking down at the counter. Then he said quietly, 'Do what you like.'

Annie went to put her shoes on. As she opened the door she heard Jim calling from the kitchen, 'It won't change anything.'

'I've told you, if you come anywhere on my property, I'm calling the police this time, and they won't take kindly to the likes of you!' Pauline Murgatroyd's voice was shrill through the letterbox.

'It's me, Pauline.' Annie managed to control her own voice. 'I'd like a word.'

'Oh. Annie.' Mrs Murgatroyd's voice calmed a little. She opened the door, and made a show of taking a big step back. 'I've been meaning to speak to you.'

'Have you now.' Annie's voice scarcely sounded like itself. 'That's just as well.'

Mrs Murgatroyd's eyes were very pale and dry-looking. 'Now, I know you're a good Christian woman, Annie. All I can think is that these queers are taking advantage of you.' Annie swallowed hard. 'I see them, coming and going. The things they wear. Noise at all hours. And I know, I know,' Mrs Murgatroyd continued, 'who am I to judge? I understand you need lodgers.'

'If anyone's been playing music loudly, I'm sorry.' Annie felt rather shaky. 'I do tell them. Rosie's the worst culprit.'

'The music's the least of it.' The large pale eyes blinked. 'I'm worried about your safety, Annie. I can hardly sleep for thinking about little Rosie, in the house with all those . . .' She seemed to search for a word that was bad enough, and when she wrung it out she made the word *'men'* sound obscene.

'I'd never let anyone in the house that could be a danger to Rosie,' Annie said coldly.

'I'm sure you're doing your best.' Mrs Murgatroyd swallowed, as if to keep the bile down. 'But I don't mind telling you, I don't agree with that sort of thing. The lifestyle.' She smiled. A calm, beatific smile.

The smile awoke a physical memory in Annie. That little hit of pleasure, that implacable sense of peace. The sense of being washed clean by . . . not hatred. Nothing as hot as that. Contempt, the sweeping peace of contempt. The way it left everything feeling fresh and bright and empty.

'It's against God,' Mrs Murgatroyd said.

Annie thought of Jim, staring at the wet, filthy pavement outside Heaven.

It's stupid, but I want it all for him. I want Mozart's Requiem and 'The Lord Is My Shepherd' and ashes to ashes and dust to dust.

'Against God, is it?' Without thinking, Annie seized one of the blood-red geraniums from the window box and yanked it out by the roots. 'Believe in God now, do you? That's very bloody convenient.'

She knew she must look a madwoman. She found she didn't care. 'Oh you're thrilled, aren't you?' Annie took another fistful of geraniums and flung them at Mrs Murgatroyd. For a second the old woman stood there, covered in petals and frozen in shock. Then, with a snarl that astonished Annie in its inhumanity, she slammed the door shut.

Annie wasn't finished shouting. 'You're thrilled that they're dying, aren't you? Thrilled to think you were right all along, eh?' She hurled another fistful of geraniums, the potting soil splattering over the paintwork of the door. 'Thrilled because you think that every one of your nasty, cruel impulses was on the money!'

She picked up the window box and hurled it with all her might into the paving stones, where it shattered. Bloody geraniums lay all over Mrs Murgatroyd's porch. 'Well, good luck to you,' she roared at the closed door. 'Good luck to you, living like that!'

She didn't know how long she would have stayed out there if Jim, shell-shocked but laughing, hadn't come out to usher her inside.

He made two cups of tea and poured out a large pair of brandies. 'Take your pick,' he said. Annie went straight in

260

for the spirits. At first Jim sipped his tea; then when there was a little space in the cup he poured in his own brandy.

'You know,' he said, in a low, contemplative voice, 'in America, they're talking about tattooing us.'

Annie didn't look up at first, but after a few moments she forced her eyes to meet his. 'They're talking about enforced quarantine,' Jim carried on. 'You know what that means. Same shit. Again.'

'I'd thought we'd worked it out,' Annie said. Her voice was shaking. 'Took us longer than it should have done, but I thought we'd got the right idea now. About all that stuff. Hating people.'

'I'm not sure that they hate us,' Jim said. 'Well, that old bat does.' He nodded towards the street. 'But she's weird.' He shrugged. 'Most of the time I think most people just aren't very interested. You know. They've got their lives.' He sniffed. 'That's most of the time. Then I have these dark nights when I think, maybe they really do just want to wipe us all out. Would it really be so surprising? If they killed us and made out we'd done it to ourselves?'

Annie thought of Fairlie Hall. The way that they used to send the patients out of the way into the freezing airing courts, with nothing but thin cotton jackets.

'I don't think it's anything as organised as all that,' she said. 'I think it's just gravity, pulling us all down.'

January, 1960

ANNIE DOESN'T MIND THAT they had to wait for the rain to stop before she and Peter could go out. Today the walk needs to be different. The conditions must be right. Besides, she likes the way the soaking, sloping lawns look after the deluge.

'You look different,' Peter says. He touches his own head to indicate her hat – her new hat, made to go with the little flared navy coat that she's wearing over her own dress. It feels different, being in Fairlie Hall in civilian clothes.

'Thanks,' Annie says. She has no idea whether he intended it as a compliment, but it seems generous to take it that way. She smiles, but he is not looking at her.

'Have you ever noticed that?' Peter points halfway down the shrub border. Annie shakes her head.

'Noticed what?'

'The rest of the rose bushes are white. This one's yellow.'

Annie shakes her head again. There's a look in Peter's eyes, a sort of triumph.

'Funny, isn't it?' She gives a little laugh. 'I bet the gardener felt a silly bugger when he realised.'

She waits for a reply, but he just goes over to the Christmas roses and puts his face close to them, lingering for a long while. Annie watches. She might ask him to pick one for her. Would Dr Lewin approve of that?

'Use your judgement,' he'd said. 'I can't tell you how best to be a woman.' He'd smiled, those teeth yellow against his white beard.

When Peter withdraws his face from the flowers, it's wet with raindrops.

He looks much better, Annie thinks. The lines of his face are strong, like a drawing in pen-and-ink. But he's still pale and thin – thinner than he ought to be – under the suit and mackintosh. She can picture well what he looks like beneath the clothes, all the bones spearing out.

'Beastly weather. Always beastly, in this place.'

He's staring back at Fairlie Hall with a look that reminds Annie of the rain-crumpled flowers.

'Pretty, this view, isn't it?' She steps a little closer. He stays very still. 'That's the Tudor wing that we can see from here. From Henry the Eighth's times. He came here on his progress, you know.' One of the grounds-keepers had told her that, his face shining with pride as if the honour still enriched the soil of the Fairlie Estate.

Peter seems to take no notice at all. 'Dreary, muddy sort of place,' he mutters.

'Oh, don't be such a misery.' It's time to take matters in hand, Annie feels. She closes her grasp over his arm. 'Let's enjoy the sunshine, eh? It won't last.'

Annie likes the way he looks down at her. It makes her feel like a film star, ornamental and delicate. She smiles at him.

'You might ask me something about myself,' she prompts. She tries batting her eyelashes, but feels foolish.

'Might I?'

When she's been out with men before, they've rarely bothered with asking her about herself. Annie has learned to make a game of it, checking her watch at the beginning of the date and then again at the first moment that the chap asks her a question. She doesn't just want Peter to be as good as them. She wants to teach him to be better.

'All right then.' He plunges his hands into the pockets of his mackintosh and resumes walking. 'Why did you become a nurse?'

Annie does not reply but rather quickens her pace slightly, raising a hand in greeting.

'Oh, hello Ronnie!' They have reached a walled kitchen garden. Winter greens, kale, radishes, all peering out from the damp earth. Annie remembers her mother's vegetable patch, and for a moment the Christmas roses shift from deep pink to scarlet. A few yards off, Ronnie is pulling gently at the fronds of a carrot, as if he might be able to persuade it out of the earth.

'How are you today?'

Ronnie says nothing, but continues caressing the carrot-top.

'You seem to be doing a grand job,' Annie continues cheerily. 'Keeps you out of trouble, does it?'

Ronnie begins to clutch at the earth more restlessly, like an uneasy sleeper worrying at his bedsheets.

'Take good care, Ronnie,' Annie calls out.

Peter is looking at Ronnie with an expression that Annie has seen plenty of times before. She knows it's best not to give that look a name. She glances upward at the sky. All day it has changed, from one moment to the next.

'It'll be raining again before you know it,' she says, in her brisk nurse's voice. 'We'd best be off for that cup of tea.'

He looks at her, for the first time his face unsure.

'Oh, come on,' Annie says, linking her arm with his. 'It's not far. It's ever so nice inside. Warming up, that's what you need.'

Annie likes it when they pass through the front gates unchallenged. It makes her stomach warm and twist when he looks at her enquiringly, following her lead as she sets off confidently for the left fork in the lane.

As they're walking, down comes the rain. They begin to run. Annie can feel her hat wilting on her head, but she laughs. You might as well laugh, she thinks. The press of the rain, through her clothes and onto her skin, makes her feel a way she hasn't felt in a long time.

He laughs too. Annie realises she's never seen him laugh before, only ever that cold, sardonic smile that isn't really intended as a smile at all. It fills his face and makes him still more handsome. By the time they've arrived at the tea shop they're just looking at each other, laughing in a cycle that needs no origin.

He pauses inside, eyes moving around, lingering on a man at a table by the window. There are only a few other patrons. Admittedly, it's a funny time of day, and funny weather, to be going for a stroll and refreshments.

'Come on,' Annie says again, and this time she slips her hand into his. 'Let's warm up.'

They order tea for two; Annie, a buttered toasted teacake. She feels bad for ordering food if he isn't eating, but she missed breakfast. When she suggests he get something too, the Hall's paying, he shakes his head. He stares at the cup of tea in front of him for a long while before adding sugar. It makes Annie want to draw him close.

'What do you think you'll do, after it all?' She takes a sip of her tea. It tastes bright and burnished, like the copper kettles on the shelves around the top of the room. He picks up a packet of sugar, rips it open, and stirs it into his tea.

'Oh, I don't know.' He rubs a hand over his eyes so hard that Annie half-expects to see the inky lines of his features blurred. 'Go back to my flat, I suppose. Go back to how things were.'

'Except different,' Annie prompts.

'Yes.'

'Because you've got hope now.'

He takes a sip of his tea, pauses for a second, and then spits it out. Annie seizes the napkin from her lap at once and begins dabbing at his shirt. It won't do for him to pick up a stain.

'That's not sugar, it's bloody salt.'

Annie frowns. 'Are you sure? Why should it . . .' The packet says sugar, clear as day.

'Taste it,' he insists, holding his cup out to her. Annie shakes her head. 'Taste it,' he says again, his voice rising, at the edge of control. 'Go on!'

The other people in the tea shop are starting to look over. Annie can feel her shoulders shrinking in embarrassment. But she can't bring herself to take the cup he offers, to put her lips where his have just been.

'I believe you,' she mumbles, taking instead a large gulp of her own tea. But that lovely coppery taste seems to have disappeared.

For a while she stares at her lap, no longer liking the idea of her teacake, knowing it's getting colder with each passing minute. He's looking at it too, with an expression of nausea.

'So,' Annie says. There's a long silence. A new expression seems to cloud Peter's eyes, like fog rolling in over the sea.

'Did you know that Fairlie Hall was an army training camp during the war?' He lights a cigarette.

'You were there?'

'Oh yes.' He nods, the smoke from his cigarette blurring out the movement. 'For three months. We used to do artillery drills on that little hill, by the copse.'

'How old were you?'

'Eighteen.'

'Young.'

'First time away from home.' He lifts the lid of the teapot to look inside, but doesn't pour himself another cup. 'Terrifying.'

Annie says nothing.

'But the chaps – we looked after each other. Or rather, they looked after me.' He begins to laugh softly, staring somewhere past Annie's shoulder. 'There was this one fellow – well, he used to have everyone in stitches. Kept the platoon together. We all adored him. Called him Auntie – he was forever knitting. Little warmers for your throat. Bed socks. That sort of thing.'

He takes his cigarette from his mouth and looks at Annie. 'Bullet through the lung in France. Choked to death. I was holding him.' He stubs his cigarette out. 'I suppose that's what nursing is. Holding people.'

Annie closes her lips sharply. He's still looking at her closely, and she feels the need to defend herself.

'I'm not sure about the emetics, you know,' she says. 'I think we could probably do it differently, just with the pictures and the tapes. But I'm just a nurse, you know. They don't ask me.'

He's staring at the remaining wisp of smoke from his cigarette.

'It's Sam who administers everything.'

A muscle in his neck twitches. He looks down at his cup of tea, then pushes it away from him. He's getting tired, Annie can see that. But all things considered, he really is so much better.

She pays. She wonders whether she ought to do it differently, to let him feel more like the man. But Matron did give the money to her.

They walk slowly back down the rain-soaked lane. When they get to the gate of the Hall he stops. The set of his body, his broad shoulders, his tall, slim-hipped figure, his handsome face – they're all so resolute. But the voice is wrong. It cracks, like the voice of a little girl.

'Don't make me,' he says. 'Please.'

Annie pauses. She wants to put her arms around him, but that would be too much for him, she's sure. Besides, she's not clear on how far the whole thing is supposed to go.

'Don't be silly,' she says, for the dozenth time that day. An hour before she might have linked her arm through his again, but something inside her is beginning to reassert itself. 'They'll have cleaned out your room now.' She lowers her voice, as if talking to a frightened animal. 'You're in recovery now. You're so much better. It won't be like it was before.'

He's shaking his head. She closes her hand around his upper arm in her nurse's grip.

'You chose this,' she reminds him, gently. Dr Lewin had told her to remind him of that.

'Please,' he whispers. 'Please.'

The attendants cleaned the side room while they were out. Once again, the room is spick and span. Annie sees a glimpse of it before Matron locks the door. A fresh sheet, shining white. His face, so pale, so handsome. Eyes like blots of spilled ink.

He needs to end his treatment slowly. Little by little, that's the trick.

Matron is walking up the corridor, the keys to the side rooms jingling at her belt. She halts.

'Well, Nurse Graie?' She raises an eyebrow. 'How did it go?'

'Oh, well! Very well!' Annie feels her chest catch and tries to raise her chin. She knows she's twittering. 'I thought we got on very well. We liked each other.' She feels her cheeks burn.

'Seemed healthy? Vigorous?'

Annie thinks of the way he inhaled the scent of roses, his eyes closed, and nods.

'Able to interact with you . . . as a woman, so to speak?'

'Oh yes.' Annie thinks of the young man in the dance hall, the young man with the grey eyes. Of the way he disappeared. 'Better than most, I'd say.'

'No sign of any homosexual tendencies?'

Annie looks at the floor, her heartbeat loud in the quiet of the corridor. 'No.'

Matron gives a sharp nod. 'Good. Dr Lewin will be pleased. He can be moved to convalescence, in that case. See to it, please.'

She reaches again for the bunch of keys at her belt. 'Help me with the other chap, would you? He's still got two more emetic administrations to go.'

Paul is not lying or sitting in his bed, but crumpled there, like an abandoned umbrella. 'No more pictures,' he mutters.

'No,' she agrees. 'Not today.' But she doesn't know if it's true. That's Dr Lewin's business, not hers.

Annie tries not to notice that he's lying in his own urine, his own sick. His excrement. It does seem strange, after what they were always taught. Hygiene above all else. But, as Dr Lewin says, sometimes it's right to go against instinct.

There's no need for Annie to hold him down anymore as Matron prepares the syringe. When the needle enters he doesn't flinch. He raises his arm so that Annie can take his blood pressure, opens his mouth for the thermometer, yields his chest so she can listen to his heart.

October, 1987

As Annie had expected, John had deteriorated rather quickly. He had been such an ordinary-looking man. Now he looked like a ghost, or a sage, with those enormous eyes in the hollow face. The lack of any colour elsewhere about him seemed to heighten their green. He said very little; several of the other men didn't like him much. Annie once found Jim sitting in his room, the two of them drinking coffee together, but for the most part John kept to himself. Rosie didn't like him either.

'He's too *still*,' she'd said, shivering a little. 'He just looks at everything and never moves.'

'He reminds me a bit of my father,' Jim told Annie. 'That generation of men. They saw things in the war, and it made them different. I think he's in a lot of pain, but if he is he wouldn't tell me.'

It was the third bout of pneumocystis pneumonia.

'He's strong,' Alie, the visiting nurse, told Annie. She was a young girl, not that much older than Rosie. They'd asked her not to wear her nurse's uniform to come to the house so the neighbours didn't notice her so much. She always came in Doc Martens and rock band T-shirts. 'You'd never know it, but he's had tuberculosis before.

In a POW camp, he told me. How he's still going I've no idea. Grumpy git, isn't he?'

Her bluntness seemed to pierce the tension in the room, and Annie laughed. The truth was that she felt for John. She knew nothing of his background, but imagined him growing up in some enormous manor house, perhaps somewhere near the sea. She couldn't expect him to be pleased about it, ending his days in her odd in-between house in Pimlico.

Annie knew better than to ask how long it would be now. Not knowing, she was coming to realise, was the natural state of affairs. One was tempted to ask for numbers and estimates, but those questions were only ever a comfort blanket and had nothing to do with reality.

'I'll be back tomorrow,' Alie said, finishing her tea. 'See you then.'

'See you, love.'

Later that night, Jim came downstairs with a scrap of paper in his hand. A number, he said, that John had given him. A number for an old friend.

Annie was upstairs when Jim let the friend in. One of the boys had had a bad night and she needed to change the bed over, so she only caught sight of him while she was standing on the stairs with her arms full of dirty sheets.

Her first thought was that he'd never put the weight back on.

Or perhaps, she thought, in the seconds before he caught sight of her, he'd always been that thin. Maybe the time at Fairlie Hall hadn't really changed anything.

When he saw her, it was clear that he didn't recognise her. Not at all. Why should he, Annie thought dully, as he passed her on the way up the stairs with a brief nod. She'd been a role, not a person, then; it wasn't so different now. With her flowered dress, her hands in their Marigolds, her eyes clouded by a lack of sleep, she looked no different to any other tired woman of middle age. Why should she expect to be seen, really seen, by someone like him?

He emerged from the room some minutes later, his face flat and blank. Annie was standing by the front door. Perhaps that was why he noticed her the second time. She wasn't doing anything, so she couldn't be mistaken for the cleaner or the charwoman or the maid. She was just standing, not looking at him.

He seemed as if he was going to walk past her, but then he paused, his hand on the door. He looked down at her. It occurred to Annie that after all these years, there were some things that could never change. One of them was the way that he made her feel: as if she were shrinking. In her mind, she could hear his voice again, from the last time she saw him. How he'd pleaded with her, how he'd begged. And how she'd stood there, a low thrum of pleasure in her chest, as she said nothing, did nothing.

He looked her full in the face for a few seconds. Then he left, shutting the door quietly behind him.

January, 1960

'WHAT'S THIS?'

Peter has stopped short. Annie glances over her shoulder to look at him. For a second she has the impulse to take him by the hand and lead him forwards. But just as she reaches for him, she looks down at her own sleeve, remembers her uniform.

'It's the convalescent ward.' She folds her hands in front of her. Calm and tolerance, that was the role. 'You're being moved.'

'I'm a convalescent now?'

'It's a good thing.'

He's staring at her. She wants him to look at her the way that she's seen Paul looking at Rita. 'You're not in that little side room now, you're on a proper ward. To rest.'

'A rest cure? Is that what I'm supposed to need?'

'You're already cured.'

There's just a touch of laughter in his eyes, a laughter without mirth, like the lick of blue flame. Annie looks away. 'I'm to hand you over to the Ward Sister here.' She hesitates. 'I don't expect I shall see you again.'

He looks at her. The laughter is gone and there is nothing in his eyes.

'Perhaps I'll still be able to accompany you on your walks.'

'What about my things?'

Annie knows well what he is referring to, but she says, 'You'll get your personal clothes and so forth back when they discharge you.' She's heard Sam say it to someone; it seems as likely to be procedure as anything else. 'It'll all be waiting for you when you leave.'

'Don't be silly,' he snaps. Annie frowns. 'My papers. I need my papers.'

She feels her lips tighten. 'I expect you'll get them back soon.'

She knocks on the door of the convalescent ward, which is unlocked by a very small, wispy Ward Sister. Annie realises that she was expecting to see some slightly modified version of Matron. This woman has very bright blue eyes and cheeks like crab apples. Her eyes move from Annie to Peter, who is standing several yards behind her. Her lip twists; as she moves past Annie to place a clawed hand on the sleeve of Peter's pyjamas, she snaps, 'You need to stick closer to your patients.'

Annie feels that she ought to be used to reprimands now. But perhaps she has only learned to handle them when they issue from Matron's lips.

'My papers,' Peter says again, seemingly propelled forwards by whatever strength exists in the frame of the Ward Sister. 'You'll get them for me, won't you?' The haughty, wooden quality seems to be splintering out of his voice; just before his face disappears behind the

276

closing door of the convalescent ward, his eyes catch Annie's.

'You'll bring them for me, won't you, Nurse Graie? You'll bring my papers?'

Annie says nothing. There is a pleasure, she feels, as the door closes, in seeing him like that. She closes her eyes to the low hum of it as she walks away.

She finds the bundle of papers beneath the mass of used bedsheets on a trolley outside the side room. An orderly has heaped everything together. With the papers safely in her hands Annie steps back. Peter has been true to his word. The used sheets aren't soiled. They never have been, not once.

The orderly emerges from the side room, his face contorted with disgust at the smell. He has dark skin, though not as dark as Anthony's. Annie guesses that he might be an Indian. He says something.

'What?'

The Indian repeats his words, and Annie understands them the second time. 'Matron said those were all for the incinerator.' He is eyeing Annie with distrust.

'Dr Lewin told me that I was to give them to him,' Annie says. The attendant shrugs and picks up his bucket, which is full of filthy water. Beyond him, Annie can see that the little window has been opened. She can feel the icy breeze.

Walking away from the side room and the attendant, Annie feels as though a little candle had been lit inside her, like the flame is growing by the second. Is that how easy it is to get what one wants in this place? You simply have to speak with a certain authority?

Besides, she thinks as she tucks the papers under her arm, it isn't as if she really lied. Hadn't Dr Lewin said that he thought Peter might be working on his next masterpiece?

It's Annie's lunch break now. No one will miss her, she thinks. With her uniform huddled about her she makes her way out into the grounds. Behind the walled garden, on a freezing iron bench, she sits down and begins to read.

Donovan has been liberated from the camp. Liberated and recruited as a spy by John Fairlie, using his language skills on a posting to the newly-created East Berlin. Annie reads on, so fast that she can barely take in the details. It's the story itself that absorbs her, of course, but there is a strange hunger that she feels every time Fairlie's name is mentioned. She turns the page, and finds that the next chapter is loose, a letter. She keeps reading until something forces her to slow down, until her eyes catch on a single, barbed phrase, and something inside her is punctured forever.

October, 1987

'JOHN'S DEAD,' PETER SAID, as soon as he saw Annie on the doorstep. It was clear that he wasn't really speaking to her, but to himself. Behind her the traffic continued to roar along the busy Earl's Court Road as if nothing of consequence had happened that day. Then, for a second, Peter's eyes focused on Annie and he spoke with cold fury. 'Isn't he?'

Annie stood there, a girl of twenty again. Her hands were shaking as they closed around the handbag that she held in front of her like a shield. She nodded. 'Would you let me in?'

He looked at her with an expression of blank indifference that seemed to come from exactly the same place as it had twenty-five years ago. It landed in the same place too, between two of Annie's ribs and deep in the cavity of her chest. She breathed in, the handbag shifting against her.

'I've some things of his to give you.'

Once he'd stood aside to let her in it was as if the disparity between them suddenly dissolved, and he was the one left shaking. He led her down a narrow passageway, staggering for a moment and putting a hand onto the wall of the hallway to hold himself upright.

Annie followed him to a room with a small, lit fireplace, lined with books on three sides. On the fourth was a window onto the street, though this had been obscured by heavy velvet curtains.

'I've no idea how he got it,' Peter said. He had almost collapsed into an armchair in front of the little fire. He didn't invite Annie to sit down. She remained standing in the threshold.

'Never thought he'd be the one to go first.' Peter spoke low, almost as if the air had been let out of him. 'He's not the type to sleep with just anyone, you know,' he continued. He was still looking blankly ahead.

'It doesn't mean anything about him,' she said gently. It was one of the things that she found herself saying a lot. 'That he got it.'

'No.' For a second he seemed to slip out of his haze, and those dark eyes drilled into her. 'No, I suppose you're not in the business of judging, are you?'

She gave a little half shrug. She found herself saying, 'Judge not, that ye be not judged.'

His lip curled at this. 'Just what we need in the mix. Religious fervour.'

'Some people find that religion helps,' she said. She wasn't one of them, and she hoped that was clear from her voice, but it seemed important not to dismiss it entirely. 'People find help in all sorts of places when they lose someone. Someone they love.'

Peter's eyes were still on hers. 'Nobody told me that we could love, you know,' he said softly after a long pause.

'All right, I went to public school, I know my Greek. But I was never sure about Achilles and Patroclus. War's different, you see. It makes everything different.'

Annie thought of Matron. She hadn't thought of her in so long, but now that great bonelike face reared up in her mind so sharply that it was as if there was a photograph before her. She would be dead by now, of course, she realised. Dead, or very old. Nearly ninety.

Poor Matron, Annie thought. No real use in peacetime.

'War changed things for a lot of people,' she said. She knew how mundane it sounded, and knew too that Peter had never expected anything more than mundanity from her.

'People thought that prisoner of war camps would have been places without love,' he said, staring at the fire. 'But in all that mess, in the confusion, we were free.' He shifted fretfully in his armchair, and it struck Annie that the handsome young man was old now. 'Free for a moment.'

They were silent again for a long while. Then Annie heard a noise coming from another room and jumped. It sounded like someone was moving around the kitchen. Peter shook his head.

'It's just Edward,' he said. Perhaps he saw her slight surprise, because he added, 'Yes. I'm with someone these days.' He smiled, perhaps the first genuine smile she'd ever seen from him. 'We're both in rude health, if that's what you're wondering. It's all cups of tea and doing the crossword together. Pure domesticity. He's younger than me. There are things he doesn't remember.' He paused.

281

'That's a good thing. I could never be with someone again like I was with John.'

'He fell into a coma, just after you visited,' Annie said. Peter nodded, very slightly, his eyes fixed on something unseeable to Annie. She reached into her handbag, closing her fist briefly over the paper within, screwing it up inside her palm, before drawing it out and smoothing it between her two hands.

'I read this to him.' She can barely hear her own words, but they seem to snap Peter out of his trance. He focuses on her, on the paper. Miraculous, to her, that he does not recognise it, after so long.

'What?'

'I read this to him,' she repeats. Her hands were shaking. 'Your letter. I don't know if he could hear me, but I thought I ought to, just in case.'

She placed the sheet of paper on the table between them. It still crouched in the crumpled shape that it had taken on when Dr Lewin threw it in the waste bin, nearly thirty years before.

January, 1960

'HOW WAS IT?' RITA'S eyes are narrowed against the intrusion of sudden sun into the ward. Annie looks at her and a line from the letter returns – *the decent one.* 'I saw you through the window, you know. You really did look super in that hat. Quite the couple.' She laughs gaily. 'Rivalled only by Paul and me, I suppose.' She steps over to Annie, running a finger over her lower lip. 'You wore lipstick too? Gosh, I didn't realise we were supposed to go the whole hog. You've a smudge ... there.' She ran her finger over Annie's lip again, a little harder this time. 'Can't have you giving Matron an embolism, turning up to the ward wearing lipstick. What's that, anyway?'

Annie looked down at the bundle of papers. 'I'm not sure.' She saw Rita's brow furrow slightly and added, 'Something Dr Lewin asked me to pick up.'

A single phrase was still kneading at her. *Brainless little flopsy.*

'Ah well, to hear is to obey, I suppose.' Rita gave a little mock gesture of deference, leaning on her mop like a cane. 'You needn't worry, though. Matron seemed happy enough.'

'Why should I be worried? What do you mean, happy enough?'

'Oh, just that it's all paperwork to her.' Rita resumed mopping. 'She's just going through the motions. In fact, I think she's rather distracted. I suppose Sam told you the same story he told me?'

'What?' Annie is seized by the longing to shake Rita. A conversation with her is like water, always slipping out of grasp.

'How she ended up here.' Rita leans forwards, confidential, eyes shining. 'She was a girl of seventeen, you see, in love. Her sweetheart was wounded at Ypres. When you think of all those young men ...' She trails off. 'Anyway, he wasn't killed, but the horror of losing all his mates had sent him into a deep shell-shock. Never recovered. And Matron – she came to Fairlie Hall to nurse him.'

Annie feels inexplicably ill at the thought. Perhaps it's the idea that Matron was young once, a girl like her. Perhaps it's the thought that any one of those old men were young men before, young and beautiful and desired and loved.

'She's been here ever since,' Rita continues. 'He – Matron's young man – he's still here too. On *our* ward. And, Sam said,' here she takes on a tender look, 'she still loves him. As much as she loves anyone. Anyway, now he's got an infection and Sam says she's very worried. I don't know ... wouldn't part of you be relieved? If he dies then she can remember him as he was, when he was young. Maybe she'll finally get herself out of this dreadful place.'

Annie can see Matron clearly in her mind's eye, as she'd seen her on that first day. Those patent shoes, those childlike skinny calves, the way her face so resembled a bleached bone. Is this what love can do to a person, she wonders? Strip them of everything that makes them human?

'At any rate, she's terribly distracted,' Rita continues. 'Perhaps she wouldn't notice if you did turn up wearing lipstick. Though I must say, I rather prefer the one you wore the other night. This one looked a bit . . .' She pauses, tilting her head to one side. 'Muted.'

'It was supposed to be subtle,' Annie says, to the wet floor. 'Natural.'

Rita laughs. 'It's lipstick.'

'I was just trying . . .'

'But darling, there's no point in trying.' Rita seems to discard the idea of looking busy, and edges between two beds to look out of the window. 'This place . . . It's not here to make anyone better. Surely you've understood that by now? So what's a little fib?'

'What fib?'

'Well, I said to Matron, yes, Paul's as macho as anything. Quite the hunk. Must have just been confused before.' She frowns, looks suddenly a little worried. 'Hope I didn't overdo it. But that's the point . . . I don't think she'd care either way. I told her what she wanted to hear, that's it. He can go home now, and the whole ghastly thing's over.'

'You lied?'

Rita turns away from the window, her silhouette suddenly looming large against the beam of wintery light. 'Annie, you can't change people,' she says softly. 'Surely

285

you've understood that by now. We can't change poor old Bernie, or Ronnie, or anyone else. So it's just a question of being gentle with them.'

She takes a step closer. Her breath brushes at Annie's face. 'And really I'm starting to lose track of who's mad and who's sane.' She laughs a little. 'I'm starting to suspect that the only sane ones are the ones who want to get out. Look at Sam and Anthony and the others. It sounds like all sorts goes on in those tunnels under the Hall.'

'What do you mean?'

Annie can't quite see Rita's face, still darkened by shadow, but she hears her laugh. 'Surely you've . . . do you mean you truly haven't noticed?' Another peal of laughter, and then she seems to catch herself. 'I'm not laughing at you, Annie, you know that, don't you? But I need to get away from this place.' She pauses. 'I think we both do.'

Annie hugs the bundle of papers closer to her.

'It's just . . .' Rita continues. 'I've always felt like the person who didn't notice things properly.' She sounds softer now, kinder. 'But it isn't just me, is it?'

'I focus on my work.' Annie takes a step backwards. 'Perhaps you should too.'

'Oh darling, don't be like that.'

Annie frowns. 'I'd better be getting on.' Her voice is cold now. 'There's work to be done.'

'Well, you know I'm no use at any of that. Not that it matters.'

The peals of Rita's laughter follow Annie as she hurries back off down the ward.

June, 2020

'I WANT TO TALK to you, Paul.'

I managed to keep my voice steady, but there was no hiding the seriousness. And Paul, not being one for confrontation, did his best to head me off at the pass.

'If it's about the wedding, then don't bother.' He spoke very quickly, as if he'd rehearsed it. Paul always had a way of forming his words very carefully, as if he polished them enough then they could slide through the world without catching on anything. But there was a note of force that I'd never heard before.

'The wedding? Why would I want to talk to you about the wedding?'

'You're Rita's oldest friend, aren't you?' Without warning, he suddenly sounded on the verge of tears. That seems to be happening in more and more conversations I'm having these days. With Rosie, with Jim. People have suddenly realised how close they are to breaking. 'Listen Annie, I know it probably seems really soon, but me and Alec . . .'

'Oh, it's nothing to do with Rita,' I said quickly. 'She'd have led the conga line if she'd known.'

It was true. Rita had been thrilled when Paul had met Alec.

'Lizzie's grown up now,' she'd told me. 'He's been as good as his word. Better than I ever expected. He's raised our daughter – my daughter, strictly speaking. Now he ought to be happy.'

'You were the one who insisted that the two of you didn't get a divorce,' I carried on. I had no idea if I was making any impact on Paul, but it occurred to me that there were things that he needed to know, that no one had ever spelled out to him before. 'She told me. She'd have been thrilled to know that you and Alec were going to be happy.'

'I loved her, you know,' Paul said, and his voice had that quality again, like it was going to rupture. 'She was my wife.'

'I know she was, love. I know.'

There was so much about Rita and Paul's marriage that I'd never truly understood. Despite that, I'd never doubted their love for one another, whatever form it took. It fitted the bill of what love was supposed to be. It was patient, it was kind. And – in its own way – it rejoiced with the truth. That was more than a lot of people could say.

'I know lots of people would say it wasn't a real marriage. And I used to worry about how it affected Rita, but she never cared, did she?'

'She didn't.' That was what could always be said for her, and it occurred to me that perhaps this was a power beyond anything else that she'd possessed.

'And she taught me not to care either, and then it all worked. We always talked to each other, right up until the end. We never stopped liking each other.'

'I know you didn't.' I sighed. 'Paul, there's nothing about Rita or Alec that you need to defend to me. None of it. That's not what I wanted to talk about.'

I felt Paul's uncertainty, his deflation, even at the other end of the line. 'What *do* you want to talk about then?'

'Fairlie Hall.'

I blurted the words out quickly, and as I did I felt as though my throat had gone suddenly dry, as if I had a mouthful of dust. I heard a crackle on the line as Paul drew in a deep breath. But his voice when he spoke wasn't the wavering, uncertain one. He was calm.

'I've been back, Annie. I've made my peace. I did the therapy and the EMDR and Alec and I went together and really, it's such a beautiful place. I've decided it's time to show them, time to show them all.'

I didn't bother to ask who 'they' were.

'That's up to you, Paul.'

I don't know how long I've got left on this earth, but I suspect that it's not long enough to ever fathom how Paul could willingly go back to that place – choose it as the venue for his wedding. But that's all right. I suppose there are plenty of things that I do that aren't legible to anyone else.

But there are certain things that need to be understood.

'Paul,' I said. 'I need to tell you about Fairlie Hall. I need to tell you about how it was that Rita came to be sacked.'

'I know why she was sacked,' he said. His voice was as impatient as it was confused. 'She told me, right when it happened. Matron worked it out, about Lizzie, and they used the letter thing as an excuse to get rid of her.'

'No, Paul.' I shook my head, even though there was no one to see me. 'That's what they told her. That was what she always thought. But there are things neither of you knew.'

Love does not delight in evil, I thought, *but rejoices with the truth.*

January, 1960

'MY UNDERSTANDING WAS THAT you'd told Matron that you believed him cured.'

Dr Lewin's face is pink, his expression sulky. How is it, Annie wonders, that a person with so much white hair could remind one so indelibly of a baby?

'I said what I believed to be true at the time.'

Dr Lewin looks up; there's something appraising in his face, something cold. She adds, 'I don't really know what it all means, Doctor. I thought I'd better show it to you.'

Dr Lewin's beard twitches. 'Don't be coy, girl. I daresay you've had enough love letters in your time to know one when you see it.'

Annie suspects that the best response to this is a smile. Dr Lewin appears to soften, and adds, 'Of course, it's not quite what it appears. There's more to it than meets the eye.' He leans back in his chair. 'I know his medical history, some of the stuff was classified. Had to sign the Official Secrets Act.' He smiles up at Annie from behind his desk. 'You didn't hear me say that, of course. But some rather extraordinary stuff happened after the war.' He touches the letter lightly with one fingertip. 'This John chap – if

I'm not mistaken, he's his handler.' He sighs. 'Among other things. There are layers to that letter, I'm sure of it. Nasty stuff. Who knows what they're planning. He's used to writing in code. They all are. They have their own language, you know. Dolly this, vada that.'

Annie nods. She has no idea what Dr Lewin is trying to explain, or even allude to. The door opens behind her and Matron enters.

'You've trained your nurses well, Matron,' Dr Lewin says. His voice is louder now; Annie realises that he was speaking in a special, soft sort of tone, just for her. Then he gives a small, snuffling snort. 'Some of them, at least.' Without speaking further, he hands the letter to Matron. Annie notices how terribly drawn her features are, how her fingers are shaking as she picks up the paper. Yet she still looks entirely herself – the nurse, the woman in control. She reads quickly; her face doesn't change. At length she speaks. 'What does he mean, the same way as last time?'

'Ah well, Matron. This brings me to the point.' Dr Lewin gives a strange smile. 'It seems, based on the search that we conducted of his papers, that our man has been smuggling letters in and out of the hospital.'

I need to post a letter.

Annie remembers it now. After they'd sat in the tea shop in Fairlie talking about ghosts, walking to the pillar box with Rita and watching her post the letters. It was just paper, she thought. Almost as light as air. All that upset over a few bits of paper.

'That's not possible,' says Matron flatly. 'None of our protocols allow that.'

'Ah, Matron.' Dr Lewin leans back in his chair and takes off his spectacles. 'You know as well as I do that there's more to life than protocol.'

Matron's head jerks towards Annie; for a moment it seems that she is indicating that this conversation should not be taking place with a lowly nurse present. But Dr Lewin shakes his head. 'It does her no harm to hear these things, Matron.' He replaces his glasses on his face, and Annie sees that his blue eyes are sparkling. 'Really, it's all a question of gaining experience.'

He turns back to look at Annie. 'I give you one opportunity to respond to this question, Nurse Grye, and I know that you will do so honestly.' He takes a long pause; Annie knows it is merely for effect, but she begins to doubt her answer before he has even said the question. 'Were you the one to smuggle the patient's letters in and out?'

'Smuggle?' The thought of anything so clandestine, so calculated, is so overwhelming that Annie is past speech. She shakes her head. 'I wouldn't know how. I wouldn't know where to begin.'

'Nurse Graie isn't without her weaknesses,' Matron intercedes. 'But I would not count among these a disregard for the rules. However . . .'

She trails off delicately. Dr Lewin seems to catch her drift.

'Perhaps it's time that we spoke to Nurse Blythe.' His voice is soft and fleecy, Annie thinks, like clouds floating away. 'And we'll need to get Donoghue back in the side room for another round of emetics. The conditions haven't been right for successful treatment, it seems.' He sighs. 'I must bear the responsibility for that, I suppose. I let him write. Against your advice, Matron.'

Matron says nothing.

The conditions. Annie tries to think of the little side room, the smell. But it's as if that place has been shut off from the rest of her mind, shut off and locked away.

Then Matron and Dr Lewin are gone. No one has told Annie if she is dismissed. No one has told Annie what to do or the role she should play now. She feels as if the pressure from outside is growing, that she might collapse into nothing.

She looks out of the little mullioned window to the lush greenery of the Fairlie Estate, and thinks again about the Bomb. Better to be in the radius of the first blast, she thinks. Better to be vaporised than to let the fallout infect you, to come apart slowly.

Her eye drops towards the wastepaper bin where Dr Lewin threw the crumpled letter. Stooping, she closes her hand around the balled words. They seem so absurdly light.

John.

All I need to do is write your name, and I know again who I am.

Do you remember, when we were in the camp together, how we'd spend hours sitting around, talking about all that we would do together when we were freed? Those sumptuous meals we used to plan. Or rather, I thought they were sumptuous. You said my imaginary spreads were bog-standard Oxford college fare, and you were quite right; apart from Red Cross parcels and nursery food, that was all I knew. Yet from you, amid the barbed wire, I learned a better definition of luxury. It's a quieter, smaller thing than one realises. You always said you just wanted a good fire, a perfect piece of buttered toast, a proper cup of tea. Sometimes you'd say you wanted a brandy, and we'd pretend to toast each other.

Now, if I could have anything in the world, it would be to sit beside you on a park bench, dressed in my own clothes, wearing my own watch yet perfectly unconcerned with the passage of time. If I could have anything in this world it'd be a cigarette smoked while looking at you, looking at the view. Knowing that, if I wished it, I could take your hand.

The place I'm in – it's a terrible place. I didn't say so in my last letter. Perhaps I thought it hardly needed saying; perhaps I thought I might, in some peculiar way, protect you. You've always been the one to protect me. But now I must tell you that no one, mad or sane, deserves to live this way.

We knew that this would be a trial. Yet this is what we chose. Some of the things they do here are enough to almost make me wish that I had taken the offer of prison. Almost. I have an idea that I might feel more like myself in prison; I find myself thinking back to where we met, and observing that there are worse things in the world than being caged. Where everyone else saw barbed wire and watchtowers, you taught me to trace the distant ridge of mountains with my fingertip. You taught me that if nothing else, I could look up and always see the sky, or that beneath our feet there always carried on a humming world of insects, burrowing animals, growing things. Everyone in the camp knew about you and me, didn't they? But no one cared. We've never talked about that since. What it was like to live without shame, and in the full sight of all our fellows. Yet I do not wish I had chosen prison. I would take three months of torture to then be reunited with you, over years of separation.

I'm writing slower now, not merely to eke out the space on the page, but to savour the knowledge that by some miracle these scratchings permit me to talk to you. With a little luck, this will find you in a few days, assuming that I can get it out the same way as last time. The blonde nurse – the decent one – she says she'll help. If I am fortunate she will put it in this evening's post. Perhaps you will read it in bed tomorrow morning, with your coffee and your cigarette. It'll be like we're lying there together.

They're sending me out on an 'outing' with one of the trainee nurses – some brainless little flopsy. Presumably this is to check that I really am cured. I want to laugh in their faces, but I promise not to break my cover. You have trained me well.

I keep myself so that whatever it is that you see in me remains intact. On the day that I throw this place off and walk outside, a man again, I can give it all to you. I love you. This can never be said enough.
Peter

Walking back to the little cottage that night, the bundle of papers held close to her chest, Annie turns to look at the Hall. The windows are lit, like eyes reflecting firelight; the great dark mass against the blue of twilight. Fairlie Hall has stood for such a long time, Annie thinks. Far longer than the idea that the mad are worth caring for. And when that idea has faded away, she knows that Fairlie Hall will still stand. The floors might sink further and further into their dizzy angles, the beams soften imperceptibly with rot until they bow like suppliants, the glass on the windowpanes distorting until any real daylight is blocked off. But somehow, Annie knows, Fairlie Hall will continue to stand.

October, 1987

'I READ IT TO him,' Annie said, after Peter had finished with the yellowed piece of paper and put it back down on the table. After thirty years it was a miracle that it was still legible; Annie had kept it carefully, away from the sunlight. The pencil scratchings had never faded. 'He was sedated and unconscious. I don't know if he heard. But you'd addressed it to him, so I thought he ought to get it.' The unease sat in her chest like concrete, and she had no idea if speaking would ease it or allow it to grow still further. Yet speak she must.

'That wasn't for you to decide,' he said tonelessly. 'It's been thirty years since John and I were together.'

'Don't you mean it anymore?'

'Of course I still mean it. But that letter . . .' She could tell she'd caught him in such a moment of strange shock that it hadn't yet occurred to him to be angry. 'That letter was for me, as much as for him. I expect it kept me alive. Just having a place to write the truth.'

'You hid it well,' Annie said. She closed her eyes, and she was back in the side room again, approaching the little table with its pile of papers, her heart beating fast at the prospect of finding out what happened next in

Donovan's story. 'I thought it was just part of the book, at first.'

'I suppose it was. It was part of writing things down in a way that made them feel clearer, anyhow. But yes, that was our system.' Peter's voice was thick now. 'I'd write the letters and then I'd leave them out, tucked under the manuscript. Dr Lewin let me write, you remember? And that other girl – the other nurse . . .'

'. . . Rita.'

'The blonde one.'

'The decent one.' She articulated the words clearly, dusting them off after they'd lain at the back of her mind for thirty years, forever untouched in their glass case. He waved a hand, like none of it was important.

'She'd take them for me, and put them in the post. When he wrote back, she'd bring me the reply.'

'I know,' Annie said. 'She was found out. She got the sack.' She paused. It had to be said. 'I showed Dr Lewin the letter. I gave her away.'

For a moment he held her in the vice-like grip of his gaze. Then he said, 'Better for her, to be away from that place.'

'Better for her. Worse for those left behind.' Annie couldn't name anyone else who'd suffered from Rita's departure. The patients on the ward – all those old men – they hadn't had names to her. But Rita had known their names. 'I didn't mean for that part to happen.'

'But you meant to give me away.'

'The treatment hadn't worked.' *Of course it hadn't. It doesn't.* Annie felt something in her caving in as she reached back, thirty years, for the memory, or rather the feeling, and spoke the words she didn't believe. 'I thought I was doing the right thing.'

'I was almost free.' His voice was hard and sharp, jagged glass. 'I was *convalescent*. And they made me do it all again. Because of you.'

'Yes.'

For a long while there is silence.

'You know, I was only at Fairlie Hall two months.' Peter's body seemed to slacken, his eyes unfocused, but his hands were gripping hard onto the arms of his chair. 'How can a life of thirty years be destroyed in sixty days? Yet mine was.' He blinked slowly. 'I was in love, you know. And that went. That's all gone now.' The fire gave a low crackle. 'I couldn't be with him after I got out of that place. Too much had happened, it didn't work between us.' He sighed. 'Or I suppose it's possible that we just weren't as suited to civilian life together as we'd thought.'

He turned very slightly to look at where Annie still stood in the doorway. He seemed to remember that she was there – a physical presence, a real person. He gave a half-smile and continued conversationally, 'Did you know that Dr Lewin became one of the major advocates of changing the law against homosexuality?' He leaned forwards to poke the fire. 'I suppose he thought that if his cure didn't work then the thing couldn't be done. Are you married?'

The question came from nowhere. Annie felt as if she'd been caught without her armour, and when she said, 'I was,' she felt that she'd disclosed to him the essential part of her existence. 'He died,' she added.

'And did you say goodbye?'

'It was an accident. I never had the chance.'

'But then after the accident,' he pushed. 'Did they let you in to see him? Did they lower their voices when they spoke to you? Did they let you choose the flowers for the funeral?'

'Of course they did,' Annie said in a low voice. 'He was my husband.' Then, unexpectedly even to herself, she added, 'I loved him.'

She and George had never much used the word love, except in their wedding service and as a passing endearment, falling from their mouths like scrap paper.

'Nobody told us that we could love.' Peter's voice was soft, so soft that it was almost impossible to hear the bitterness there. 'Nobody told us we could be loved.'

'That's a terrible thing,' Annie said. She thought of Keith, wetting Vic's tongue with a damp sponge on a stick. She thought of Jim.

'It is a terrible thing, I suppose.' Peter's voice had somehow grown lighter, airier. 'But I could never be a victim.' He poked the fire again. 'It simply didn't suit me. Still doesn't.' He glanced down at his walking stick with a look of contempt. 'It was easy to look down on all those people. Paul – his passion for conformity, his Church of England morals. That absurd quack, Lewin. That dried-up battleaxe of a Matron. Most of all,' he flexed his hands harder on the arms of his chair, 'on you.'

This was no surprise to Annie, but still it caught her off-guard. 'What do you mean?'

'Well, you know what you were like.' He was smiling now. 'This ridiculous, defenceless little rabbit. I thought well, there's nothing for it with someone like that, they're just going to do what they're told. It's in their nature, can't expect anything more of them. So I didn't blame you.' He studied her. 'Not until now. Because it turns out, you had it in you. You could have done things differently. You just decided not to.'

'I was . . .'

'You were what? Young?' He took a sharp breath, stood up abruptly and went over to stare out of the French doors. 'Half a dozen of my schoolfriends died at Dunkirk, you know. We were what – twenty? You've seen boys dying, the ones who're dying right now. Making the best of it, laughing, taking care of each other. They were the same age as you. Only they won't get the chance to grow old and nurse their regrets.'

'Maybe they don't have regrets,' Annie said.

'Maybe.' He put out his cigarette. 'Maybe not. Maybe they've had a good time, and they wouldn't want to change things.' He looked at Annie through narrowed eyes. 'But you still think, deep down, that they ought to sit at home and keep their cocks to themselves, don't you?'

'I don't . . .' Annie's response was so automatic that it almost choked her. 'It's up to them. It's their choice.'

'But you still think it's the wrong choice, don't you?' The venom in his voice was unmistakable. 'Is that why

302

you take them? So you can have front-row seats to their despair? I expect they all think you're marvellous, putting up with them.'

Annie gripped the doorframe for support. She could not look at him. 'I'm not like that,' she said. 'Life. It's made me a different person. I'm a mother now, I'm a widow, I'm—'

'As if that does it,' he cut across her, snapping. 'As if people change. As if they get better.'

'Would you rather I didn't do it?' An anger was building up in her now – a light, fizzing sort of anger. It made a change from the terrible weight; she let it grow. 'You'd rather I just left them? They've nowhere else to go.'

'And you can make them better.' His voice dripped with contempt.

'They're not going to get better,' Annie said flatly. 'They're dying.'

'And you put yourself at the centre of it all, like some sort of medieval nun, all redeemed and holy.'

'I'm not a martyr.' The fizzing anger filled her throat, then burst. 'I'm a nurse.'

'Like when they used you to hold people down and force poison down their throats? You used to call that nursing.'

Annie shook her head violently. 'That's not how it happened. I never held anyone down. I ... they all consented.'

To her astonishment, Peter started to laugh at this. His laughter was uncontainable, perhaps unhinged, and she stood there, still, in the half-darkness of the doorway, watching him. After he stopped laughing he gestured her forwards.

'For God's sake, if we're going to have this conversation then you might as well sit down.' His face darkened. 'I've had enough of you hovering over me. Enough for a lifetime.' He slid down in his armchair, leaning his forehead into his hand as Annie sat.

'I suppose it's true,' he said quietly. 'I suppose I did consent to it. It was a public lavatory where they got me, of all places. You know they used to claim that we – that homosexuals – were aroused by the smell of urine?' He gave a bitter laugh. 'They used a police officer. Entrapment. John and I were never . . . it wasn't like we were married, the whole point was to be free. And they gave me the choice – prison or that place. We talked about it, the two of us, and made a decision together. Yes, I suppose I could have gone to prison. I don't know how long I'd have stayed alive there, or what might have happened to me. But I could have done it.' His eyes filled with disgust. 'And instead they made me beg to be sent to a mental hospital. Instead they let me ruin myself and then called it a choice.'

His eyes slid away from Annie and ranged over the bookcases. 'Wilde wrote *De Profundis* in prison, did you know that?'

Annie did know that. In fact, she'd read it. But he seemed to perceive her expression wrongly. 'Why would you know?' He muttered it to himself, seemingly as an afterthought.

'You always did that,' Annie said. The accusation was without anger, but it could not be repressed.

304

'Did what?'

'Made me feel small.' Annie swallowed. 'Made me feel stupid.'

'Perhaps you were.' Said swiftly, a parry.

'Perhaps I was.' Still Annie felt no anger. 'A brainless little flopsy, was it?'

For a second he held her gaze, then looked away. Perhaps he was ashamed, perhaps just uninterested. 'But people can do some dreadful things,' she carried on, 'when they've been made to feel stupid.' She looked down at the handbag by her feet. 'Some unforgivable things.'

She reached down, and pulled the sheaf of yellowed papers from her bag. They were covered in handwritten lines written closely in pencil. She did not need to read any. She'd read the words so many times over the years that she knew them by heart.

'I can't give any of it back,' she said. Her voice started to tremble, but she swallowed so that when she held out the manuscript, her words were strong. 'Except this.'

Peter's face was frozen, even as his hands darted out to take the papers from her.

'You kept it,' he murmured. For the first time since Annie had first seen him, thirty years ago, he seemed lost for control, lost for words.

'I kept it,' Annie said. She could look at him no longer, and stared at the floor. 'They told me to put it in the incinerator. But I kept it. Read it. Read it again.' She looked up at him now. 'That's the thing about a good book, isn't it? You read it at different times in your life, don't you? You find something different each time.'

Peter was still silent. His hands were moving over the manuscript in his lap, feeling over the pages as if he recognised them better by touch than sight. For a long while he said nothing. Then his eyes seemed to come back into focus.

'You know I can no more publish this now than I could back then?' He gave a bitter snort. 'Less. I've something to lose now.'

Annie looked around the house. It was big, bigger even than her own house in Pimlico. She could see through the French doors – open, even in the chill of autumn, to the back garden. A fountain splashed softly.

'You have all this from writing books?'

'Screenplays for Hollywood. Brainless war films, mostly.' He looked around the volume-lined room. 'There isn't money like this in writing books.'

He looked back to Annie. 'And no. I don't think you should stop taking in those boys. I don't care what your reasons are. I care that you're doing it.' He shrugged, his hands grasping again around the manuscript. 'Perhaps if I were a little more admirable then I'd do the same. I've got the space. But I don't need the money and I haven't got much of a capacity to care for people. Anyway, that sort of thing is always better done by . . .'

'. . . Women?'

He looked a little surprised that she'd spoken, but nodded slowly. 'I suppose that is what I mean.'

Annie looked at the old man in the chair. She rose to her feet.

'Well, a woman's work is never done,' she said. He'd probably think that she was stupid, spouting clichés like that. 'I'd better be getting on. Getting back to the boys.'

My boys, she thought, gathering up her bag.

'Be careful about trying to be forgiven.' She did not turn back to look at him. 'Once you start trying to balance the books,' Peter carried on, 'you realise that forgiveness will always jump just out of your reach.' She could almost hear his little twisted smile. 'I did some pretty terrible things during the war. You're in trouble, when you start trying to pick fights with history.'

'That's not what I'm doing,' Annie said. 'I'll let myself out.'

He waited until she was in the hall to call after her. 'The problem isn't just that the past can't grant forgiveness.'

Annie stopped. 'It's that it can't withhold it, either.' A pause, as if he were taking in a great, shaking breath. 'It can never tell you that there's no prospect of you being forgiven, so you always feel that hope. You always think, if I do enough . . .' He broke off. Annie lingered for a moment longer in the hall, but he stayed silent. So she left.

June, 2020

When I'd finished telling Paul about what happened, what I'd done, the phone line was silent. For a mad second I wondered if he'd even heard me. Maybe he'd been cut off halfway through the story. Could I repeat the whole thing again? Could I recover the truth for a second time? Or would it already have changed too much, slipped into set phrases and rehearsed delivery?

But then he spoke.

'I've known you sixty years, Annie.'

'I know.' I looked down at my hands. They were an old woman's hands now, wrinkled and brown-spotted, skin chiffon-thin. I decided that I was old enough to be brave, to let him be angry with me if that was what he needed. To let him dismiss me, crumple the last sixty years and throw them away like rubbish. 'I won't come to the wedding.'

'What?'

I didn't know why he should be surprised, but he was. 'What're you talking about?'

'You didn't know who I was before, Paul. What I did at Fairlie Hall. It was my fault. I gave Rita away. And I never even told her, and now she's dead.'

'She knew, Annie.' He sounds tired. 'We talked about it.'

There was a trembling feeling deep inside me. I swallowed. 'I always wondered if she might have worked it out.'

'Of course she did. She wasn't daft.'

'But I never confessed it. She wanted me to tell the truth and I . . .'

'She forgave you.'

'You don't want me there, Paul. Not back at Fairlie Hall, at your wedding.'

'You said I didn't know who you were before.' Paul's intonation was flat.

'I—'

'I went to the GP, you know,' he interrupted. He sounded half in a dream. 'I told him that I was miserable, and asked him to make me normal. And he sent me to that place. He told me that he didn't think it would work, but it was worth a try.'

I stayed quiet.

'Dr Lewin, he sat me down in that office of his.' I wasn't sure if the line was crackling or if it was Paul's voice shaking. 'He told me that he didn't see me as a criminal. And he gave me this benevolent smile. And you know what, Annie? Do you know how I felt?'

I said nothing, but I breathed in deep. I let Paul know that I was still there.

'Grateful.' The word dropped down the line like a stone. 'I was so bloody grateful. And then they took me off to that horrible little room. Had to be separate, didn't I? So they could keep all that filth in one place, I suppose. Shut the door and forget about it. Maybe they thought

I'd fancy the mental patients. God knows. But they took my clothes, and they took my watch, and my books. They left me for hours, Annie. And that wasn't the worst of it. You know what the worst of it was?'

The line crackled.

'They made me drink stuff. They made me sick. And while I was being sick they made me look at things. Men. Men who were beautiful, to make them ugly.'

He was crying now, but somehow it made his voice stronger.

'They played tapes to me, Dr Lewin, going on and on for hours and hours about how much better my life would be when I was normal. And then they left me lying in my own sick, Annie. They left me there like a dog. It was torture, Annie. There's no other word for it. Torture.'

'I'm sorry, Paul.'

A soft rushing sound on the line, as if my words had disappeared into nothing.

'If I can forgive you for making me sick with that stuff,' Paul said, his voice suddenly controlled, 'I can forgive you a lot of other things.'

'And have you forgiven me?' Perhaps I shouldn't have asked. It wasn't fair, putting a question like that to him. But I couldn't help myself.

For a long time he didn't speak. Then he said, in a cracked voice like an old man, 'I'm a Christian, Annie. You know that.' He sighed. 'Did I ever tell you,' he carried on, after a pause, 'that when AIDS got bad, they wouldn't let me take communion at church?' He laughed bitterly. I'd never heard Paul sound bitter before. 'They knew what

I was and they gave me this love the sinner, hate the sin speech. They didn't mind my fiver on the collection plate. But they wouldn't let me take the blood of Christ.'

I said nothing to that. I still don't quite understand people who believe in God.

'I wasn't even positive, but they told me that God had done this. To people like me.' His voice dripped with rage. 'Blaspheming bastards.'

My hand was shaking as I gripped the phone closer. Outside, I could see a few more people than I was used to in the street. We were starting, gradually, to come back to life.

'All I ever wanted was to be a history teacher,' Paul carried on. 'Talk about the past all day. Learn from it. Tell stories. But they would never have let me do a job like that. Even with a wife and child, even if I was respectable. If I'd ever been found out ... they'd have said I was a threat to the children. Maybe even to my own child, to our Lizzie. A threat.'

I swallowed.

'I'm angry with you, Annie,' he said. 'I'm angry with you for what you did, and I'm angry that I've got to be angry with an old friend when I don't have many of those left. I'm really bloody angry.'

Paul never swore. It almost sounded funny, in his soft, gentle voice.

'So you can bloody well come to mine and Alec's wedding,' he continued. 'You can come, and you can watch us say our vows, and you can toast us. You can dance. You can help us show them that we won.'

311

October, 1987

JIM WAS SITTING AT the kitchen table. Only the orange tip of his cigarette flared in the darkness. He must have heard Annie come in, though he didn't turn around.

'Rosie's gone out to Julie's. Says she'll sleep over. I gave her the bus fare.'

'Thanks.' She sat beside him in the dark. 'All right?'

'I went to the clinic today.'

Annie put down her handbag on the floor beside her. It was very light now, without the manuscript. 'And?'

'And what do you think?' Jim sounded like he'd intended to snap, but there was no force behind it. 'It seems I'm positive.'

Annie had been waiting for this. She'd seen the gauntness in his cheeks, the wine-dark patch behind his ear.

'How're you feeling?'

'How am I feeling?' He snorted. 'Like it *seems* I'm positive. Seems that way, that's what the doctor said.' His voice was shaking. 'Didn't even have the courtesy to say *you are positive*. Just *you seem to be positive*. I suppose it made him feel bad to tell me I was dying.' He laughed, and it turned into a cough. 'Keep a positive mental attitude. That's what the doctor actually said to me.' He took another drag on his cigarette. 'You'd think they'd get some training, wouldn't you? Top five things not to say to someone after you've just told them they've got HIV.'

'Idiot.'

'Not his fault,' Jim said flatly. 'They don't know, do they? They're just doing a job.'

'They're supposed to take care of people. That's what they're trained to do.'

'Can you train a person for this?' He turned to her in the darkness. 'Can you actually sit someone down and give them what they need to handle this?'

'I don't know,' said Annie. She wondered if she ought to call Rita. 'I'm sorry, Jim.'

'It's all right.' His voice lighter now. 'You know, it actually is all right. Ever since Robbie, I've known that he probably gave it to me. Little sod.' Annie thought about reaching out for him. He was overburdened, waterlogged with love.

'He might have done.'

'Might not have been him though. I've had a lot of boys since Robbie. Couldn't let the side down, could I? Even if I did do all that moralising. Safe sex sometimes. But sometimes not. Sorry, Aunty Nan.'

'I've never been a condom-waver, Jim. You don't need telling what to do.'

'Wouldn't have thanked you if you had. Who needs more morals? I just think I thought – well, they just said cut down, didn't they? Like cutting down on fags. And there were boys that I could have had and I didn't. You know. When conscience seized me.' He stubbed out his cigarette. 'Wish I had, now. We'd have had a good time.'

'You seem like you've had a pretty good time anyway.'

'That's true.' She could hear the smile in his voice in the darkness. 'I was a bit boring before I met Robbie. Ashamed, scared, all that stuff. I don't think I'm boring now, do you?'

'I don't.' Annie can feel the tears tugging at the corner of her eyes. 'But I suppose you never seemed boring to me.'

'Honestly, Annie.' He took a drag of his cigarette, the tip burning like hot coals. 'I'm not feeling bad. I've had a goodish life, altruism-wise. And I've had more than my fair share of fun. No more pretending, no more worrying that I *might* have it. No more kidding myself. You'd think I'd have learned about that, wouldn't you? But we don't learn. It's funny how we don't learn. Still.' He put the lid on the ashtray with a soft clunk. 'That's my last cigarette.'

'You're giving up?'

'Oh yes. Got to take care of myself now, haven't I? No more casual sex.' He flicked his lighter on and off. 'It was fun while it lasted. Freedom.'

'There are lots of ways to be free, you know.'

Jim cocked his head. 'Are there?' His voice was very cold. 'Getting the lecture on sexual liberation from Aunty Nan, am I?'

'I'm not your aunty,' Annie muttered, picking up the tray and letting her elbow stick out enough to jab him as she brushed past.

'If there's a better version of liberation then I'm all ears.' Jim picked up his empty cigarette packet and started to fiddle with it. 'I can see them already, the people looking at me and thinking, you've got what's been coming to you, mate.' He put the packet down. 'Maybe part of me thinks that too.'

'What you think is the only thing that actually matters.' Annie hesitated. 'Do you want me to call Rita?'

'Rita?' Jim's voice was incredulous. 'Why would I want you to call Rita?'

'She's better at this stuff. Being with people. I do the practical bits.'

'If I wanted to talk to Rita I'd have called her myself,' said Jim. 'I don't want Rita. I don't want anyone trying to find the beauty or meaning in all this. I don't want anyone telling me that I'm brave. I don't want to die.' His voice cracked a little as he crumpled the cigarette packet between his two hands. 'I want to live.'

He looked at Annie. 'I've decided to pack it in. Hand it over, anyway. The activism stuff. I've sounded the alarm, we bridged the gap, and now there are people pushing it who're better than me. Not as bitter. Princess Di's on the case. Lighthouse is open now. No need for me anymore.'

Or me, she thought. She didn't know if she was glad.

He folded his hands on the table.

'I've decided I'm going to get my old job back, do some extra training. Go for promotion, earn a bit of money. It'd be good to move. I'm too old to be a lodger.'

'You're not too old for anything, Jim.'

'All right then. I'm sick of living in one room. I want a nice new sofa. There, will that do? We can go to Heals together to choose something. I want to make sure I get something you like.'

Annie stayed quiet for a few minutes, and then she said, 'Don't be daft, Jim. It doesn't matter what I think.'

'I'm offering to take you out for tea and shopping, you mad old stick. Don't look a gift horse in the mouth.'

Annie let the silence hang for a minute. Jim was shredding the cigarette packet, staring into space.

'Whatever comes,' she said, 'I'm with you.'

He looked at her from the side of his eyes and gave a little smile. 'I know. No current plans to die. But anyone could, couldn't they? Any time.' Still his fingers worked away, shredding the cigarette packet. 'Mad to pretend otherwise. But it's all right, I'm not going to get obsessed. There's enough time for anything I want to do.'

'And you'll go to all your hospital appointments, won't you?'

'Bloody hell, Aunty Nan. Yes, I will. Your nagging really helps.' He smiled at her again, a small smile. 'It really is all right. We've been at war, haven't we?'

For the second time that day – for the second time in thirty years – Annie thought of Matron's face. Exsanguinated, empty. A face that could witness physical horror and senseless loss.

'I've read my Susan Sontag, I know we're not supposed to use metaphors.' Jim inhaled. 'But I've got HIV and she hasn't, so I'm the one who gets to decide, and I say we've been at war.' His voice was very low now. 'And I'm not sure that there's really anything worth coming home for.'

'I'm glad you're home.' Annie took the shreds of the cigarette packet away and placed her hand lightly on Jim's. She could feel the beat of his heart in his veins. Just be gentle, she thought. How could something so simple be so hard? 'You and Robbie. You saved me from an empty house.'

'You'll learn to cope with that in the end. You'll have to.'

Annie nodded. 'I know.' She placed Jim's hand back on the table. Softly, but not like it was made of glass. Just flesh, she thought, and bone, and blood. 'But not yet, eh?'

He leaned over and put his arm around her, leaning his head into hers. She could feel his dark curls pressing against her cheek. 'Not yet.'

July, 2020

'HAS IT CHANGED MUCH, Mum?'

'Barely at all,' I murmured. Driving up to the hotel didn't feel like some enormous bridge in time. There was no particular moment when I was overwhelmed by the force of memory. But I suppose that's because I've never really left. I see Fairlie Hall wherever I go.

The outline of the Hall was so familiar that it took me a few seconds to notice that the Tudor wing was gone. Or rather, the substance of it was gone. A glass atrium stood in its place, its roof and gables following the original outline of the old house, but with all the sunlight shining into a reception area. I recognised the great leather sofas – someone must have finally got them out of the library and re-upholstered them.

'Gorgeous, isn't it?' Rosie had come in from parking the car. 'The way they've done it.'

'Alec's always had good taste.'

'It's spectacular.' Rosie's face was alight. She's come back to life now that things are opening up. Most people are moving gingerly, feeling their way. When I asked her if she wanted to come to the wedding with me, I wasn't expecting her to say yes, but she'd been delighted. And she'd told me that I had to go for the posh room with the funny bath.

'Treat yourself, Mum. Who knows when you'll next get the chance?'

She's all life now, my girl. I'd forgotten what it was like to be in a room with her, to see her face change from mine to George's to something indefinably her own. We sang in the car.

I'd asked Jim if he'd come with me to the wedding. His answer was swift and unequivocal.

'No.'

'You're worried about safety?'

'I can't stand weddings.' I could hear his shudder down the phone. 'All the flowers and napkins and cufflinks and not getting to talk to the people you actually want to talk to and listening to someone's aunt banging on. Heterosexual nonsense.' Then he laughed, and his tone softened. 'I'll send Paul and Alec a bottle of something. But I think it's probably best if you go without me.'

When Jim got his diagnosis he really did give everything up, apart from our gin and tonics. He'd look both ways when he crossed the road. He took up jogging. For years he was probably the healthiest he'd ever been, but eventually he withered into nothing, lost all his colour. I knew that death was close, or thought I knew.

But then the drug cocktail became available. People talked about the Lazarus effect, and for Jim it really was like that. Paul called it a miracle, I called it science. For a while in the late Nineties he let himself be enfolded by drugs. Not partying, although that would have been easy too. But no. He would take pills alone, codeine and protease inhibitors, Prozac and anti-retrovirals. It was all the same to him. When I rang him he'd often put the phone down on me.

It was only at the turn of the millennium that he seemed to accept he was going to live. He turned up on my doorstep with a bottle of champagne and we walked down to the river and watched the reflections of the fireworks in the dark water.

Meanwhile, Paul went domestic. He retired and got a voluntary thing in the British Museum, telling tourists who asked about Greek statues and Benin bronzes. In the evenings he and Alec – who he'd introduced to Lizzie by that point – stayed in and watched old films, while Rita went out to parties with her art students. She'd sleep with men and women much younger than her, so young that I didn't know whether to scream or laugh when she told me about it.

'They seem to like something about me,' she'd say, shrugging, helpless with laughter. 'Haven't a clue what it is.'

That was the thing about Rita. She never quite learned to harness her own power. It just reared up sometimes, in ways that she couldn't account for. And then sometimes, just as unaccountably, she got it wrong. It happened a few too many times with the boys in my house. She got too far into the woo-woo and she forgot how to listen.

It was me and Jim who stayed in touch, properly in touch. I liked being around Jim, partly because he never tried to get me to date, never told me that I ought to get back out there. We both had relationships of sorts, here and there, but they were always partial, limited. After Rosie decided that she wanted to move away, to be suburban, we still had each other.

They kept us waiting at the reception. I wouldn't have particularly minded if it hadn't been for all the meaningful looks from the other guests, the sofas that had been roped off seemingly at random. There was a couple with two small children queueing ahead of me, although it hardly feels like a queue when you're that distanced from each other. I have never understood people who take their children to expensive hotels.

One of the children – a girl of maybe four or five – was skipping in aimless circles, and veered away from her parents and towards me. Her mother grabbed her arm. If she'd taken a step towards me it wouldn't have been a difficult manoeuvre, but she didn't dare. Instead she stood there, feet tight together, caught off balance by the force of her flailing daughter. The girl wriggled and was free, hurling herself between me and the great oak reception desk. The mother looked at me in a way that I suspected was supposed to be apologetic, but seemed almost murderous. If I hadn't been there then the child being a child wouldn't have mattered. My age and frailty were ruining everything.

'This used to be the main nurses' station,' I told Rosie to distract myself, pointing. 'Look, you can still see the bells on the walls.' The sight of them had made me freeze at first, as if they might any moment go off and send a crack of electricity coursing through my blood. I found that I was struggling to breathe as I stood there. It was as if some heavy, tight arm had been draped over my shoulder, pulling me close.

'Go and sit down, Mum.' Rosie's eyes were on the kids; she looked wary. 'I'll check us in.'

There was a little room off to one side. We used to use it as a kitchenette, for brewing the great urns of tea. That memory reared up as I passed through the door, clinging to the air. The room had been painted a fresh white, a white that you don't realise is expensive until you've worked in greying institutions. There was a single, plush couch against one wall, and it mercifully wasn't roped off. I sat down, because even though I wouldn't have said I was tired, even though I had done quite enough sitting in the car, gravity is just so insistent these days.

There was a series of black and white photographs hanging on the wall, made uniformly elegant by their minimal black frames. I reprimanded myself for sinking too far in the sofa; I had to almost claw my way back out. When I was standing again, I went to read those little blocks of text. Even the font looked expensive.

There were portraits of Fairlie Hall, going back to its beginnings as a Tudor house. Then there were little scraps, pictures of those early patients. The rows of young men, their minds shredded by shrapnel and the screams of their mates. One of them, I thought, would have been Matron's young man.

PTSD, the little card said.

I wanted to curl my mouth around the sounds – pee-tee-ess-dee – but my tongue wanted a thicker, claggier word. Shell-shock, not PTSD. Heavier, less tight and scientific. We did learn about it at nursing college, but we called it a gross stress reaction. Outsize, bloated beyond the proper scale. We didn't understand.

There were other photographs, too. The wards – they all looked the same, yet I somehow knew by the cast of the light that this was not a ward of mine. All those drum-tight bedsheets, the vases of flowers sticking out like periodic watchtowers. A single nurse walking down the middle aisle, eyes downcast. Her uniform made her voluptuous: a sexy, comic distortion of femininity.

I saw a photograph of one of the men's wards. I recognised some of the patients, even with their features blurred by the old camera. Why was I frightened of those old boys? They smiled at the camera with gummy mouths like newborns.

And there was Dr Lewin. He peered down, ever-genial, with his childlike lips – I could see their pink despite the black and white of the photograph – curled into the usual bright, curious smile. The placard said he'd become a pre-eminent sexologist and campaigner, who'd invented several important medical instruments.

Then I saw another photograph, a series of figures grouped around a bed. The occupant of the bed was lost to history, smothered out by a white sheet, their face turned away from the camera. But at the head of the bed stood a doctor, his arms raised mid-explanation, his gaze fixed loftily on the middle-distance.

And then, two nurses to his left, there I was. Eyes down and slightly off to the side. I was smiling in a way that I always used to smile when I was afraid. I looked like a young girl in the Fifties, a stock photograph or, with a few little tweaks, a vintage poster. A sexpot or an ingenue. Barely able to breathe in that cramped little space marked 'woman'.

I looked deeper into that face, into its dark lines and shadows, seeking for them to open up into some greater void, to widen and expose some hidden grotesqueness. Was I more monstrous than any other frightened, under-educated girl?

'Mum?'

I turned around.

'Trip down memory lane?'

'That's me.' I pointed. She leaned forwards, smiling.

'Gorgeous.' Then she paused, squinting to lean closer. 'God, you look so young.' She sounded a little discon-certed, even alarmed.

'I was terribly young,' I agreed. 'Hard to believe now.'

'So how come you left?'

'Hmm?' I was too busy reeling from the price of two gin and tonics to pay much attention. There were a few of the wedding party around – Alec's friends who I didn't know.

'There's a terrace up there,' Rosie said.

'What? No there isn't.'

'I found it earlier. Follow me.' Rosie led me through a corridor, up a couple of floors in the lift, down a few stairs, and then we were out in the fresh air, facing over the green lawn. The terrace was equipped with space heaters, thick wool blankets, lit with lanterns. There was no one there.

'Never been out here before.'

'Maybe it wasn't here last time.'

'It must have been.' I looked at the old brickwork. 'I probably just never found it. It was such a maze in those days.'

'How long were you here again?' Something about the place seemed to have sparked Rosie's intrigue. Her eyes were keen.

'About a year. Year and a half. Rita and I met when we were nursing here together, did you know that?'

Rosie smiled. 'I never think of you and Rita meeting. I suppose you must have done. But it was like you always knew each other.' She took a sip of her gin and tonic. 'So why did you leave?'

'Oh, well. You know.' I fudged it. One of the hidden tricks of being old. No one notices if you're a bit vague on the detail. 'I got married.'

I wish I could say that I left mental nursing after all the stuff with Rita and Paul and Peter, but the truth is that I stuck it out for another year and a half. It was only after they gave Ronnie a leucotomy that I realised I couldn't take it anymore. I made sure he had nil by mouth. I shaved his head for the procedure. They offered to let me assist, and most ambitious nurses would have said yes. I said no, thank you.

It wasn't Dr Lewin – he wasn't interested in performing leucotomies himself. It was never subtle enough for him. Some young guy. Zealous. It took months for Ronnie to be able to go to the toilet by himself, and at that point I decided I'd had enough of cleaning up piss and shit. That's probably why I put off having Rosie until my thirties.

'And it got more and more difficult, over time,' I added. 'If you're not careful you can get very hard. It's tough work, caring for people.'

'I'm amazed it took you so long. I could never have done it.' I wasn't expecting that. I turned my head to look at her. She shrugged. 'There's a reason I don't have kids.'

'I hope I didn't put you off.'

'Not everything's about you, Mum.'

We sat in silence. I looked down at the atrium where the Tudor wing used to be. It was flooded with soft, golden light.

'I expect I owe you an apology,' I said quietly. I could tell by the quality of Rosie's silence that she wasn't expecting that. We're not the apologising sort in our family, I suppose. 'I brought all those chaps into the house. I never really explained to you what was going on.'

'It's OK, Mum. You were right. I did love having them around.'

'But then they died.'

'Yeah.' Rosie's voice was husky. 'They were very ill.'

'I didn't want to be like my mother,' I said. My voice was very tight now. 'After my father was killed in the war, you know.'

'Well, Nana was always a bit of an old stick, wasn't she?'

'Not always. I don't think so. I think I remember . . .' I trailed off, then took a deep breath in. 'I think it was losing my father – it made her afraid of everything. She shut everything out. I didn't want to be like that. I didn't want you to see me being like that.'

'She was depressed?'

'Never thought of it like that.' The ice cubes rattled in my gin and tonic as I lifted it to my mouth. 'I suppose that's what we'd say now. I always just saw it as she just gave up.'

'Well, you never did that.' Rosie's voice was grim.

'And you're still cross with me about it.'

'I probably just wanted you to be a bit more boring, Mum. But you were a good nurse, I know that.'

'Not the best mother.' Now I was fishing. She knew it too. She didn't say anything but put an arm around my shoulders, pulling me close, just for a second. Then she seemed to remember that we'd agreed no hugging, we're being careful – and let go.

As promised, the room had a clawfoot bathtub. After I'd hung up my frock for the wedding I looked at the tub for a long time. It seemed absurdly, almost shamefully, decadent.

Then I remembered how many hours I spent in this place, exhausted and racked with fear, and I turned on the taps. There was a fan of magazines. *Vogue, Tatler, Vanity Fair.* The latter advertised a feature on the posthumous publication of Peter Donoghue's lost work.

After my bath, wrapped in the ridiculous towelling robe, I lay on the bed and read. The article was by Peter's editor, who he'd worked with for decades.

I had lunch with John Handler (or Peter Donoghue as was his real name) some months before he died. We ate at our usual spot in the Wolseley, and over champagne he explained, in his characteristically laconic manner, that his condition was incurable. That he had no interest, he said, in subjecting himself to the miseries of chemotherapy to add a few months on to his life. His longtime partner, Edward Robinson, was taking good care of him, and the two of them intended to spend as much time as possible in their beloved Italy. He said all this rather impatiently, as a precursor to the real purpose of our lunch. And, because it was Peter, and because I never wanted to do much else when I was around him, I listened.

We talked about any number of things. He always maintained a lively interest in contemporary literature, even as many of his peers disappeared into curmudgeonliness. He told me, 'There are certain young writers around these days, they've got the capacity for iconoclasm. And seeing it in others makes one realise that one doesn't have it oneself. It's not just a question of age, I'm afraid. I never had it to begin with.' He looked deeply rueful, and I told him that I felt his work had been transformative, in its way. He dismissed my suggestion – politely, but comprehensively. 'I used old ways of writing and tried to say new things with them. I told myself that was good enough, that I could move the needle that way.' I did not ask what he meant by this. It was very like Peter to drop hints, to only expose his full meaning when it suited him.

For Peter, it was not a question of being seen as a literary radical, but of exploring the novel as a moral project. He was never much interested in how his reading public perceived his work. 'I mean this with the greatest respect, but I don't mind anymore what people say. I gave that up years ago, along with the cigarettes. Taking those up again, incidentally.'

Usually he was reticent to talk about his work. If I pressed him he might brush upon certain details – specifically, the ways in which being captured as a prisoner of war (he was held in Stalag Luft IV, in Poland, for more than two years) and later being recruited as a spy had affected his perspective. 'Of course, I'm good at living a double life,' he'd joke. 'I was brought up Catholic and went to public school.' There were few things that Peter did not view through the lens of a certain black humour. But this once he allowed the conversation to range towards something different, something that might be termed his aesthetic.

'I suppose I have always been inclined to create beauty in places where it did not belong,' he said thoughtfully. 'That came in useful in the camp, I think. If you breathed past all the fumes and smoke, there it was. The scent of pine trees.'

He told me that although this was the end of his life, his career was not quite over, that there was another manuscript forthcoming. He explained that it had been written at a much earlier period and, though he was not sure whether it was his best work, it was certainly his truest. Peter was always rather alarmed by the bald statement of truth, inherently preferring obfuscation and elusion. More cerebral than Fleming and more playful than le Carré, Peter's novels carry a sense of enigma that goes beyond their espionage subject matter.

He made me promise that I would only read the novel after his death. Though I had never been able to exercise patience where reading the new John Handler was concerned, I agreed. Nothing less than a deathbed request could have made me resist the temptation to devour the manuscript, but of course there was a terrible pain in Peter's request. I put the thing in a drawer and wished that somehow the day would never come that I be allowed to read it. Alas, this period consisted only of a month or so.

He left a note on top of the manuscript, asking me to forgive him for not sharing the work sooner and quoting Eliot – 'in short, I was afraid'.

I looked at the photographs. Peter, as a young man, in his army uniform. Peter, older, sitting behind a desk covered in black files. Peter as I'd last seen him, in that book-lined room. And finally, the cover of the new book – *The Love Song of Captain Charles Donovan*. It was being published in a couple of weeks. After thirty years, I was looking forward to reading it again.

January, 1960

RITA IS NOT ON the ward in the afternoon. Annie walks home alone. When she gets into the little shared flat it's dark, apart from the single lamp in the kitchen. She goes in. Will she speak, she wonders? Will she acknowledge what has happened, when it's so much easier to pretend?

Rita is sitting on the kitchen unit next to the sink, smoking, her feet shoved into several pairs of socks. She's reading a newspaper.

'Don't you ever think it's funny,' says Rita, not looking up from her newspaper, 'that we're all tucked away where no one can see us?'

'Everyone knows we're here,' Annie says, lingering in the doorway. In the hours since they spoke on the ward Rita has turned into something else in her mind, something both larger and more diminished than the figure of the girl sitting before her. 'They talk about the nuthouse all the time, don't they?'

'That's different from seeing us.' Rita turns a page. 'For so many people it's just an idea. A thing to fear.' She blows a smoke ring. 'A thing worth keeping yourself in line for your whole life so you can avoid ending up in a place like this. And then,' she takes up her pencil and begins to do the crossword, 'here we are. It's just a building, with walls and chimneys and windows and bedspreads and mops and dirty dishes, and people who are too tired and cross to care about things as much as they ought to.'

'You weren't on the ward this evening,' Annie says. She can't bring herself to ask the question, not when she already knows the answer.

'Oh, they've sacked me,' Rita says. She speaks casually, almost as if she's surprised that Annie has mentioned it. But the way that she looks up from her paper, just for a moment, to hold Annie's gaze, tells more than words could.

'Rita, I'm sorry . . .'

'They didn't give a reason,' Rita interrupts. She's gone back to looking at her paper. 'That surprised me. I know I'm a pretty rotten nurse, but it's not as if people are queueing up to do the job, is it? But they were looking for a reason to get rid of me. Matron's got those eagle eyes. She's worked it out.'

Now Annie is wrongfooted. 'Worked what out?'

'Oh, come on, Annie.' Rita unwinds her legs from the sink and puts down the newspaper. 'You're a nurse. Or close enough, anyway. You *will* be a nurse. You ought to have done enough medical training to be able to see that I've started a baby.'

'A baby?' Annie stares at Rita – not into her eyes, which she knows to be holding tears, but at her body. The vast breasts, which clearly have swollen still further, or the stomach, which has always curved softly.

'No one here,' Rita says hastily. 'A chap at the university. That awful anatomy lecturer – married, luckily, so there's no point in getting him involved. You'd have thought a medical man would have done a better job at taking precautions, but I suppose that didn't matter much to him.' She sniffs angrily. 'I'm pretty far along. No one noticed because I'm so plump anyway. Far too late to do anything about it. Hadn't noticed much about my periods because all the days are the same here – you lose track of everything. I thought you'd realised. You really hadn't?'

'Are you going to tell him?' Annie cannot take her eyes from the front of Rita's dressing gown. 'The father, I mean?'

'Tell him?' The blue of her eyes seems to harden – liquid no longer. 'What possible good would that do me?' She folds her arms across her heavy chest. 'I need a plan. If I'm not careful they'll take the baby away. They could even shove me somewhere like this. Some married man getting notions that I'm a problem to be solved – or, heaven forbid, that he owes me something – is the last thing I need.'

'I'm sorry.' Annie knows that she's very close to crying too. 'I wasn't expecting this. I'm trying to help.'

'I told you because lying is too exhausting,' Rita says. Her voice is very tired. 'That whole wretched building – I walk into that place and I feel like I might choke on all the lies.'

'What lies?'

'Oh, you know full well.' Her eyes narrow almost into nothing, and for a second blind panic slices into Annie's chest.

'I really am better off this way,' Rita carries on. 'I can't stand it here anymore. Just tell the truth, Annie.'

'I don't know what you mean.'

Rita holds her gaze for a hard minute. Despite the softness of her body she is all ice, all steel. Then she says, 'The only honest people here are the ones who we insist on calling lunatics.' She starts to laugh, and for a moment Annie feels slightly frightened of her. Then she gathers herself. 'So what's one more lie?'

'What do you mean?' Annie can't imagine Rita lying. Not because she possesses some sort of saintly honesty, but Rita isn't the calculating sort. Rita hadn't lied about the letters, Annie realises now. She simply hadn't been curious enough to ask.

'Paul's going to help me.' Rita slides off the kitchen counter to stand.

'What do you mean?'

'Well, haven't you noticed?' Annie sees it, a flash of Rita's usual mischief, amid all the steeliness. 'Paul and I. We're in love.'

Annie stares at Rita. Perhaps she really has gone mad. Perhaps they both have – too much time at Fairlie Hall. 'What're you on about?'

'He hasn't got me a ring or anything,' Rita carries on determinedly. 'But we're engaged, actually.' She meets Annie's eyes, defiant. 'Why shouldn't we be? He'll help me, and I'll help him.'

Annie starts to shake her head. 'No one will believe it, Rita.' She looks down at Rita's belly. How could she not have seen it before? The rest of Rita is soft but the curve of her stomach stands out somehow, stronger than everything else. 'The dates don't line up, for starters.'

Rita laughs. 'As if anyone cares about the dates, Annie. As if anyone cares about anything but how the thing looks from the outside.' She brushes past Annie. 'I need to pack.' She pauses in the hallway, standing so close that Annie has to tilt her head to look at her. So close that she can smell the soft scent of Rita's talcum powder and sweat beneath the tang of hospital. 'And if you're able to make it look a certain way from the outside, inside you're free to do whatever you like.' She pauses, and something new enters her voice, something that Annie doesn't recognise. 'You've never understood that, have you?' And she is suddenly sad. She looks as if she might want to reach out to touch Annie's face, but thinks better of it.

'You have no idea how much better it makes you feel, just telling the truth. You just do it, and then you're free.'

July, 2020

GETTING READY FOR WEDDINGS used to be the best part. When everyone I knew was getting married I'd scrape together some new outfit from thin air, finding fabric for nothing or ripping something to pieces, making it up again in a style copied from *Vogue* or a Hitchcock heroine. It baffles me slightly to look at that gorgeous girl in those black and white photographs – her narrow waist and her little row of calligraphed black curls – and remember that she was afraid. What did she have to be afraid of?

But it's not a question of that really. I have so much more to fear these days – every little lump in the pavement or uneven stair is a potential death sentence. Yet I've never been less afraid in my life.

Still though, I wasn't delighted at the sight of myself in my wedding getup. It was too hot to wear sleeves so I'd got on a little lilac sheath dress. It didn't fit the way it ought to; it was a little tight on the hips and then bunched ludicrously at the waist. There was a time when I could have fixed it with half an hour and a needle and thread, but my hands shake too much these days.

Paul and Alec were both just sort of standing about on the lawn, where the stipulated thirty chairs were set up, all at a distance from each other. Usually there would have been a certain amount of milling, but we were all pretty much sticking to our seats. Half of us wouldn't have been able to get up even if we'd wanted to, and the other half were probably so worried about infecting the first half that they barely dared breathe, let alone move around.

I remember, from my own wedding, how grateful I felt to be apart from it all. That I could sit in a little side room and do my face and not worry about whether George's mother was getting along with mine or whether everyone was sitting exactly where they wanted. I could be apart from that and no one minded, it was all anyone expected. Conventions have their uses. I think Paul would have liked to be alone with a stiff drink but instead he was fluttering around anxiously. In his slippery dress shoes I was a little worried about his balance. We can all of us fall at any time.

Eventually someone cleared his throat. A man in his fifties who I'd taken to be a guest was walking to the front, messing around with the buttons of his black shirt. He turned to face us, and I realised that he'd been putting on his dog collar.

'Before we begin,' he said, his voice carrying across the abruptly quiet range of chairs, 'I have to ask a small favour of you all.'

He cleared his throat, and I could see that he was twisting his fingers together reflexively.

'As you all know – ah . . . I'm not supposed to be doing this.'

A softening in the silence.

'And if I get found out then I get found out.' His voice was very quiet, but all the stronger for it. 'That's all right. But with that said,' he grinned, 'no need to broadcast it, eh? So . . .' He looked at an old man, ninety at least, wearing a Liberty-patterned suit in the front row. 'Don't tweet it, all right?'

That made us all laugh.

Paul and Alec came down the aisle together, Lizzie between them. Rita had never lied to Lizzie, she'd always known that Paul wasn't biologically her father. Lizzie said she didn't care, Rita told me. She'd said that if she could choose anyone in the world to be her dad, she'd choose Paul. I've always liked Lizzie.

They got to the front and stood before the priest. They weren't holding hands. People didn't, in our generation. Sometimes you'd walk arm in arm, but holding hands wasn't a thing. Paul was wearing a violet suit that clashed horribly with his pink cheeks. He looked mad – a complete waste of beautiful tailoring. Alec was in his usual charcoal, still as slim as a teenager. They would have been a peculiar-looking couple if there hadn't been some indefinable air that drew them close, that made them make more sense together than apart.

I thought of George, of the way he'd looked at me on our wedding day, and tears swirled through my vision. Nobody could see, I knew. We were spaced too far apart, and the brim of my hat threw my eyes into shade. So I just let the tears fall.

They weren't terribly original in their choice of readings. Lizzie read the lines from Anthony Kennedy's Supreme Court ruling. *A love that may endure even past death.* I thought of Rita. The way she used to dance in the kitchen. I thought of George.

Then the vicar read the standard fare. *Love is patient and kind. It does not rejoice at wrongdoing, but rejoices with the truth.*

There wasn't much of a party because of the restrictions, but I don't think Paul and Alec cared about that. We all ate in a conservatory which used to be where the patients would rest under rugs in wicker chaise longues. There were speeches, and Paul was much more confident and much more funny than I'd ever seen him. There was a toast to Rita, and then, in a quieter voice, 'and to all those we lost along the way.'

We drank champagne. I was at a table with Alec's nephews and their wives and kids, and they didn't bother much about talking to me. I didn't mind. It gave me chance to think about them all. Robbie, Vidur, Mackie, Keith, Graham, Davey, David. Lee, who'd been in my home barely twelve hours. Any number of others. Peter.

And yes, Rita too.

I stayed for what seemed like a decent amount of time. I even danced, because I'd promised Paul I would. I probably looked ridiculous, dancing at a distance from everyone else, but I'm far too old to care about things like that. I don't think Paul and Alec noticed me going. They were together now. They'd be together for however long they had. 'I'm an old lady,' I thought, rather self-righteously. 'If I want to sleep, then I bloody well will.' I gestured to Rosie that I was going to bed, and I think she was relieved. As I left I noticed she was going off herself, with Lizzie and a bottle of Prosecco. They've always got on, those two.

They played songs – silly songs from years ago, but even the young people danced. ABBA and Fleetwood Mac and the Trammps. 'Disco Inferno'. 'Hold Back the Night'. I went to bed with the synths warm in my ears and I thought of the first boy, the boy in the waiting room, and wished again that I'd said something to him, or smiled.

Sleep was hard to come by. Just as I'd taken off my dress and lain down in the dark, a soft fuzz of sound began, thickening the quiet until it turned to velvet, and then a moment later some jazz began to play. A trumpet crying out into the dark.

I crossed to the window and looked out. Beneath me on the lawn, in a pool of light that spilled out of the open doors, stood two men. At first they looked like any other young men, but as I looked closer I saw, from the parting of their Brylcreemed hair, the cut of their suits, the looks on their faces, that they belonged to a different time.

Look, Rita, I thought. *Ghosts.*

One of the men offered his hand to the other, and then they began, very slowly, to dance. It wasn't my business to keep watching them, not when they believed themselves alone. I stepped away from the window, but not before I'd half-seen another figure in the distance, heading off into the trees. A figure dressed in starched white, a tall nurse with golden hair, disappearing into the night. Perhaps I'm not so far behind, I thought. Like I always was with Rita – close, but not touching.

I shut off all the lights and lay there, the notes of the trumpet draping over the darkness, the window open, and the cool, fresh air slipping through into Fairlie Hall.

Author's Note

The idea for this book emerged from reading research undertaken by Tommy Dickinson. I would encourage anyone interested in this subject matter to read his extraordinary and important work of nursing history, *Curing Queers*.

There are too many other works that were important in the making of this book to list them all, but I'd like to pay particular tribute to *Love from the Pink Palace* by Jill Nalder and *All the Young Men* by Ruth Coker Burns.

For anyone interested in learning more on the history of the AIDS crisis, may I recommend the BBC's excellent documentary *AIDS – The Unheard Tapes*.

Acknowledgements

All books take a village, but this one took really more of a midsize town, so a lot of thank yous are in order.

First thanks must go to my incomparable agent Marilia Savvides of The Plot Agency, who saw the potential in this idea when it was nothing more than a twinkle in my eye. Thank you to my editor at Manilla, Sophie Orme, for her thoughtfulness, patience and support. Thank you to the rest of the team at Bonnier, especially Beth Whitelaw for her publicity work.

Thank you to Jeanette Winterson, always, for the wisdom and generosity.

Thank you to all my colleagues and most especially my students at Winchester University, Bath Spa University, Roehampton University, the University of Bristol and the Faber Academy. To my students in particular: I'm so lucky that I get to see you grow into writers.

To the nurses who agreed to be interviewed in the research for this book: my mother-in-law Diane Gwartz, Lee Bateman, Claire Panell and Alie Banner Simpson. Your insight, stories and passion for your vocation were crucial in the early formation of this book. Thank you also to the staff at the Royal College of Nursing, who were so helpful in supporting my research.

A couple of early readers gave vital insight and support, so big thanks to Eleanor Shearer and Ted Levermore.

The usual suspects: Mum and Dad (for the endless support and the careful attention to historical accuracy!), Izzy (for saying this book was a banger), Joe, Angie and our newest addition, the wonderful baby Mimi. All my friends. To Peggy and Mort, I suppose you were also there. You were good for morale, less good at refraining from sitting on the keyboard while I was trying to write.

My husband Jason Gwartz, always.

My most heartfelt thanks go to David Carr, who was so generous in sharing his memories (as well as many crucial documents). Thank you so much for your time, your insight, your openness, as well as for reading the manuscript. It helped this book more than I can express.

And finally I need to thank Mark William Tyack, who I never got to meet, but whose presence was so strong and vivid in the memories that David shared and the words that he left behind. Thank you.